THE QUIET NEIGHBOR

J.D. BARKER
ADAM ROACH

THE QUIET NEIGHBOR

Published by:
Hampton Creek Press
P.O. Box 177
New Castle, NH 03854

Worldwide Print, Sales, and Distribution by Simon & Schuster

For information about special discounts for bulk purchases, please contact Simon & Schuster Special Sales at 1-866-506-1949 or business@simonandschuster.com

Cover Design by Domanza

Book design and formatting by Domanza

Author photograph by Bill Peterson of Peterson Gallery

Manufactured in the United States of America

PART 1

ANGELS

CHAPTER 1

JOURNAL

DEATH. IT'S A fascinating concept. The reality and finality of it have always intrigued me. I'm not sure when I noticed it. It's not like I've had many people in my life die. I guess, for me, the idea of death is one that society has formed. Movies, TV, the news. There's just always been something inside me that's focused on the end. Why do some die so young and others not until they're over a hundred?! The entire belief that one day we simply aren't here is curious to me. I assume this is one reason many people become doctors or nurses—to help people avoid death and live long and prosperous lives.

For me, though, it's a bit on the other side of the spectrum. Even more than just the concept of death, the thought that a person can actually control whether someone lives or dies is mind-bending! I guess if I were a doctor, I could become one of those 'angels of mercy' you hear about. From what I've heard, though, they're mainly about easing someone's pain. I don't think that would scratch the itch I have.

The need I have is to feel that power, that control—I mean, just thinking about it gets me going. It's not about someone who was already in pain. It's more about taking someone who is per-

fectly healthy, living their life, then BAM! Nothing. Gone. The End. And to be the one who controls their destiny? Wow!

Come on, who wouldn't want that? Isn't that what people are looking for when they become police officers, go into politics, or start businesses? Aren't they all looking for the same thing? Control? Power?

I don't know, maybe I'm projecting a bit too much. I've been thinking more and more about this whole ideology of death. You hear it said in movies all the time—that taking someone's life changes you. But they never say if it changes you for the better or the worse.

I think it wouldn't change me for either—better or worse—but rather, I would finally feel, God, what's the word—satisfied. Yes! Satisfied. Like I'm doing what I'm supposed to do. But really, who's to say? I won't truly know until the first time it happens.

On that note, how does it happen? How does one go about killing someone for the first time? The fact I'm even writing that down gives me a thrill. I mean, what if someone found me right now, writing in this journal, and read that sentence? What would they think? Do I even care?

The answer is no.

I guess the first step would be to plan it out. What's the point of killing someone if you don't want to get away with it? It's not just the idea of having control over someone's life or death, but also to have that secret. To know you got away with it. To know you are out there, exacting what you feel is necessary. To know that others are afraid of you, and they don't even know it's you they should be afraid of!

Secrets are exciting, aren't they? Everyone has at least one. I have several, but this is definitely the biggest one. No one, and I mean NO ONE, knows these thoughts. I wish sometimes I could talk to someone about them. Not in a 'fix me' kind of way, but to share these thoughts with someone who understands me, someone who can see where I'm coming from and not try to lock me away.

Are there killer mentors out there? Or would it be mentor killers? No, probably killer mentors. The other sounds like you're hunting mentors. Ha, that would be something.

At this point, I'm way off topic from my original thought, which means I should probably wrap this up for the night. Besides, the pain is back, and it's getting worse. It's like a dull drum beating at the back of my skull. Sleep usually helps, but lately, not as much.

I guess I'll finish with this thought: I know it'll happen soon. I'll have an answer that has been plaguing me for a long time. Someone will be my first. I just wonder who it will be. Do I choose them? Stalk them? Plan it out? Or will I do it in the spur of the moment and figure out the aftermath?

If I had my choice, which I believe I will, it would be a bit of both.

Time will tell. I'll let you know how it goes.

CHAPTER 2

NOW

CYNTHIA CLUTCHES HER coffee, steam rising from the cup of liquid gold, and takes a long sip. Even in San Diego, especially on the lagoon, mornings are brisk. She sits in her favorite chair under the covered patio just outside of the wall of retracted sliding doors. She has had dozens of case-winning breakthroughs sitting in this exact spot, thinking. Taking the last sip, she hears David's alarm beep in the bedroom.

She removes the blanket from her lap, folds it over the back of the oversized patio chair, and stretches. She knows David is doing the same thing—standing up and stretching.

Theirs is a dance between floors.

She makes her way to the kitchen and pulls out the various items for breakfast—eggs, sourdough, bacon.

She knows at this point, Tori is already up and putting on her makeup with one hand, scrolling social media or texting someone with the other.

Cynthia lays the bacon on the hot pan, watching it sizzle.

She knows that David is in the shower, soaping up. Like clockwork.

She turns away from the bacon, cracking the eggs into a bowl, tossing the shells into the trash.

She hears the shower turn off.

As she turns back to the stove and pours the eggs into another pan, she knows he is now dressed and holding up three to four different ties, none of which she would pick.

With breakfast almost ready, Tori ambles down the stairs, grabbing a cup and pouring coffee. She is an absolute blend of the two of them. Tori has the wave of Cynthia's hair, but her father's auburn color. She has Cynthia's full, round face, but the angular features of her father's nose and thin lips. All three have crystal blue eyes.

Cynthia chuckles to herself.

"What?" Tori grunts.

Cynthia shakes her head.

"Nothing. You'll understand once you're a mother. It's just odd to see your child drinking coffee. It feels like just yesterday I was watering down your juice in a sippy cup."

"Ugh, Mom."

Cynthia shrugs and pulls a warm plate from the oven, scooping some eggs onto it and sprinkling it with cheese and a few dabs of hot sauce. She turns to the bacon cooking on the stove, drops a few pieces onto the plate, and slides the plate across the marble island to Tori.

David descends the stairs to Cynthia's left, whistling a tune. Cynthia smiles. If she's being honest, even after twenty years, she never tires of seeing him dressed up. Short-cropped hair, broad shoulders, cut physique—he still looks great in a suit.

"Good morning," David sings.

"Morning," Tori mumbles, slurping coffee.

"Morning sweetie," Cynthia says, handing him his plate.

He takes it with one hand and wraps his other arm around Cynthia's waist, nuzzling his face into the crook of her neck.

"Ew, get a room," Tori says.

"Trust me, we have one," David growls, slapping Cynthia's backside.

Tori makes a gagging sound as he loops around the island and sits next to her.

"So what is on everyone's agenda today?" Cynthia asks.

"Did you forget?" David asks.

"Forget what?"

"I guess that's a yes," David says with his fork in one hand and phone in the other. "Remember? I'm leaving for a few days for those depositions at the Texas office."

Cynthia stares at him, her toast an inch from her mouth. "You never told me about this."

She grabs her phone and taps on the calendar. "It's not here."

"Sorry, I forgot to put it on there. But I know I told you."

"No. You didn't."

"Well, either way, I can't do anything about it now. I'm leaving in a couple of hours from the office and should be back by Wednesday night."

Cynthia takes a breath. It's things like this that get under her skin. More than his groping or leaving toothpaste on the sink, it's when he doesn't communicate.

Cynthia takes a deep breath and turns to Tori. "Well, since Dad will be gone, how about you and I have a girls' night? We can go shopping, go to dinner, maybe see a movie?"

"That sounds like fun!" David tries to pipe in.

Cynthia gives him a look she knows he'll understand.

Tori says, "I'd love to, but I won't be home tonight. I have a date."

"What?!" David says in his most dad-like drawl.

"With who? When did this happen? Where are you going?" Cynthia peppers her. "Is anyone else going with you?"

Most of the time, Cynthia tries not to let her own past overshadow the present. She knows better than most what is out there. And because Tori is so sweet and trusting, sudden developments like this one force her senses on high alert.

Tori shrugs like it's not that big of a deal. "God, Mom, calm down. Can you not with the third degree and a million questions? It's just this guy from the coffee shop. He's worked there for a while and we've been talking. When I was there on Friday, he asked me out. I was busy over the weekend, so we agreed to tonight."

"I wish I was going to be here to grill him. Does he have a name besides Coffee Shop Kid?" David asks.

Tori rolls her eyes. "It wouldn't matter. He's not picking me up. This isn't the nineties. And everyone just calls him Blue Eyes."

"Is that because his eyes are blue?" David asks, deadpan.

Tori smirks. "No, actually they're brown."

David and Cynthia look at each other, thoroughly confused.

Cynthia moves the frying pan to the sink and runs some water in it, thinking about how she wants to handle this. The only other boy Tori ever dated was from school, and the families had known each other for years before.

This isn't your past, this isn't your past.

She wants to be quiet about this and play it off like a cool mom, but she can't.

She won't.

"I don't like knowing you're going out with someone we've

never met and will not meet. I don't care if you just turned eighteen. We want to know you're safe."

"Ugh, Mom. Get a life. It's not that big of a deal. It's just a date. I've been on dates before."

"I know, but just be careful, please. Let me know where you're going and what time you plan on being home. You never know what someone is truly like."

"You never know what someone is truly like!" Tori mimics. "You're so dramatic."

"I just—"

"It's nothing, it's just a date, let it go." Tori shoots out of her seat, dropping her plate in the sink. "I'll be home when I'm home and don't wait up!"

Cynthia grabs her arm and Tori looks down at it, shocked that her mom would grab her.

"Believe me when I say there are some terrible people out there," Cynthia says between clenched teeth, "and I don't care if you're mad at me, but I would never forgive myself if something horrible happened to you."

It's been a long time since they've had a mother daughter fight, but this is one hill Cynthia is willing to die on.

"Please, just be careful and keep your phone on you."

Cynthia lets go and Tori groans, walking away. "I'm gonna be late for school."

Cynthia watches her go, then glares at David. "You could have said something, you know."

She strides up the stairs before he can respond, changing out of her workout gear and into her pantsuit. She gives herself a quick once-over in the mirror, running a brush through her stark blonde hair. Grabbing her powder brush, Cynthia does a quick sweep across her apple cheeks.

She hurries back down the stairs, grabs her bag, and heads for the door.

"Bye. Love you," she calls to David, who is still sitting at the bar top. She doesn't wait for him to answer.

Most days, she follows Tori out. But today, Tori stormed out, and now Cynthia wishes she could tell her what she didn't say at breakfast, that she knows exactly what kind of people are out there, and how she knows it.

It's easier, though, to have her daughter think she's just being an overprotective mother, and not someone who has been hiding secrets her entire life.

CHAPTER 3

NOW

THE LAW OFFICES of Williamson, Monroe, and Hart are on the corner of 5th and A Street in downtown San Diego. Focusing on corporate law, the offices have the top five floors of the building. Cynthia sits in her office, sipping her latte and reviewing one of her latest case files. A soft knock on her door pulls her attention.

"Got a sec?" Olivia's soft voice asks from the door.

"Mm-hmm," Cynthia responds, swallowing her sip. "Of course, come in."

"Thanks again for the drink," Olivia says. "I really needed the pick-me-up."

"Anytime. What can I do for you?"

Olivia is a petite firecracker of a receptionist for the firm. Her angular features and heart-stopping green eyes make every client linger just a bit longer at the front desk. Olivia told Cynthia on her first day that she envied her life. Cynthia had laughed, knowing full well that if Olivia only knew half of her actual life, she would not envy it.

"I just wanted to thank you again for the other day," Olivia starts. "It means so much to me to have you to talk to. I've been seeing a counselor, you know, but they get paid to listen. To know you were willing to take time out of your day— and how much your time is worth . . . well, I just can't thank you enough."

Cynthia waves her off. "I should thank you, Liv. The fact that you trusted me enough to open up about what happened to you means so much. I can only hope as Tori gets into her twenties, she'll open up to me like that. No one should have to go through what you went through."

Olivia nods, her eyes glistening. "I'm taking your advice and taking back what belongs to me. I'm looking into self-defense classes."

Cynthia grins. "That's wonderful!"

"You should join me."

Cynthia's smile lessens. She has taken all of the self-defense classes one can take in a lifetime. She knows she won't be joining Olivia, but doesn't want her to feel bad. "Sure. Maybe. We'll see."

Olivia takes a deep breath and says, "Well, I should let you get back to it. And I need to get back to the phones. The last thing I need is Charles looking for me when I'm not at my desk."

Cynthia laughs. She knows the cranky, gruff demeanor of managing partner Charles Monroe. It is not someone whose anger you want. He always reminds Cynthia of one of the cranky old guys from *The Muppets*.

She stands up and comes around, giving Olivia a quick hug. "Anytime you need to talk or you're having a bad day, I'm here. Never forget that."

Olivia walks out and Cynthia comes back around to her

desk. She glances out her floor to ceiling windows at the other high-rises and out to the ocean beyond. She shakes her head, thinking about Olivia's story. She had gotten into what she thought was her Uber one evening after having a bit too much to drink, then realized after it was too late that it was *not* her Uber. The driver had pulled over in an abandoned business park and jumped into the back, trying to rape Olivia.

Cynthia hopes that if something similar happened to Tori, she would have the presence of mind and quick thinking like Olivia did to defend herself by using her keys against her attacker.

As much as Cynthia loves corporate law, the feeling of being able to help Olivia work through some of her PTSD from that experience made her feel wonderful. She knows now, looking back, that the trauma from her own past was there to help others. She hopes beyond anything that Tori will experience nothing like this, but Cynthia knows what this world is capable of, and the sad fact is, more than likely, Tori will experience something like that at some point.

The ping of her cell phone interrupts her thoughts. She sighs, knowing she needs to focus today. She has to prepare her opening statements for this patent hearing and she is not getting anywhere.

Expecting a call from David to let her know he is taking off, she picks up the phone and is confused by the text that comes in:

Tori Burrows is excused for the day.

No, she's not, Cynthia thinks, dialing Tori's number. Voicemail. She hangs up and quickly sends a text:

Why is school saying you're excused for the day? You better be in class if you expect to go on this date tonight.

She waits but gets no response.

Cynthia is up, pacing around her office, and calls David's phone— no answer. She calls Tori again a few times in a row, all with no answer. She waits for a beat, then calls the school.

The receptionist answers; Cynthia tells her who she is and asks, "Why did I get a text that Tori was excused?"

The receptionist replies, "Let me connect you with attendance. One moment, please."

Before Cynthia can think of anything else, another older lady's raspy voice answers, "Attendance."

"Hi, my name is Cynthia Burrows, and I got a text that my daughter Tori Burrows was excused for the day, but I did not excuse her, and I'm 99 percent sure her father didn't either."

"One moment," the lady says, disinterest in her voice at Cynthia's concern.

"She never showed up for her first period. It says here she was excused via phone. Her student ID was given and they said it was a family matter."

"That's impossible!" Cynthia shouts.

"Ma'am. I'm sorry, that's what it says."

"How do you know it was one of her parents and not a friend of hers she was ditching with?" Cynthia fires back.

There is silence on the other end, then the school receptionist replies, "I'm sorry, I don't have an answer to that."

"Fine, thanks." Cynthia hangs up without another word.

She taps her phone against her open palm, staring out the window.

This isn't like her. Tori has never just ditched before.

Cynthia is getting worked up. Only a parent or guardian can excuse a child. As she is bringing up the Finder app—what they use to keep tabs on each other—David texts her.

David: *Hey, we just cleared ten thousand feet and I saw the missed calls. What's up?*

Cynthia: *Did you excuse Tori from school this morning?*

David: *No, why?*

Cynthia: *Because I just got a text that she'd been excused. Who would do that?*

There is no response.

Cynthia: *Hello?*

David: *I don't know.*

Cynthia: *Thanks. I have to go. I need to figure out where Tori is and why she isn't at school.*

David: *Okay, let me know what you find out. I wish I could help.*

Cynthia: *Okay.*

She goes back to the Finder app and clicks on Tori's bubble. It shows an X, telling her either the app or Tori's phone is turned off. The X is at the coffee shop she's always at.

"If she went to see that boy and ditched school—" Cynthia doesn't finish the sentence because she doesn't know what the consequences will be, except severe.

Cynthia looks up the coffee shop online and presses the call feature. The line rings and rings. She hangs up, realizing her day will not go anywhere until she knows where Tori is. She decides she'll head home and stop by the coffee shop. If Tori's not there, but the boy is, then there is the even bigger problem that Tori is missing. If he's not there either, Tori is in even more trouble.

CHAPTER 4

NOW

CYNTHIA MANEUVERS HER BMW through traffic, frustrated that the freeway is never not congested. She always hates driving I-5, but she has zero patience right now when she's trying to find out what happened to Tori. Cynthia calls out a voice command to her phone, "Call Sofia—Tori."

She has to repeat it three times before her phone gets it right.

The call goes to voicemail with Sofia's quick message, "Hey, it's me. Leave a message. Beep."

"Hey Sofia, it's Mrs. Burrows. Can you please give me a call when you get this? Thanks!" Cynthia presses the end button on her phone, which is attached to the car mount.

"Call Sarah—Tori."

Her phone picks up the name right away and it rings. Cynthia has a feeling she knows what's going to happen and hovers her finger over the end button, pressing it as soon as she can tell that the voicemail is picking up.

She does the same thing with the other various friends she can think of that she knows are in her contact list, but none of them answer. Cynthia knows her next call will probably be premature, but she doesn't care. Better safe than sorry.

"Call the police," she says to her phone. She wonders for only a second about why none of Tori's friends answered her call, besides the fact that no teen answers their phone anymore.

As it's connecting, she realizes all of Tori's friends are probably where they're supposed to be—in class.

The phone pops up with 911 on the display, and it only takes a second for a dispatcher to answer. "911. What's your emergency?"

"My daughter is missing," Cynthia says. Saying the statement out loud makes tears well up behind her eyes.

"How old is the child?"

Cynthia hesitates only a moment. She knows the reaction she'll get. "She's eighteen."

There is a second of silence, then the dispatcher says, "What is your address?"

"3465 Las Palmas Drive, Carlsbad, but I'm not at home."

"Let me connect you with the Carlsbad Police Department. Please hold."

Cynthia shakes her head, already knowing where this is going. There's a tone in the dispatcher's voice.

"Carlsbad Police," the next voice says.

"Yes. Hello. My daughter is missing."

Cynthia flicks on her blinker and maneuvers over three lanes of traffic, knowing her exit is coming up.

"How old is the child?"

Cynthia sighs. "Eighteen."

"When did you notice she was missing?" the officer asks in a flat tone.

Cynthia pulls off the exit ramp for Lomas Santa Fe Avenue.

"I didn't. Well, not really. I got a notice from her school that she never showed up for first period, but she left the house at a normal time like she was going to school."

Cynthia pauses only for a breath and continues, "I know what you're going to say, but it's not like her to ditch. She's not that kind of kid."

"It's okay, ma'am. I understand. But unfortunately, until she's missing for a longer period, there is nothing we can do. And she is eighteen."

"But she's missing. I know she is."

"I understand how you're feeling, but like I said, you need to at least wait until the school day is over before filing a report. We can't do anything until then."

"I don't want to wait—I want to file a report now!" Cynthia can feel her lawyer tone taking over as if she was arguing her case before a judge.

"Ma'am, we can't just file reports at your demand. If you haven't made contact with her when the school day is over, call back and we'll help you. But until then, there is nothing we can do. Have a good day."

Before Cynthia can argue any further, there is a click, and she realizes he hung up on her.

She knew that would be the reaction, but she is still shocked he hung up on her. She wants to call back and berate him, threaten them with a civil suit, but she needs to focus on the coffee shop at the moment. Cynthia makes a couple of quick turns, slowing down as she sees The Joe coffee shop up on her right. She parks in the nearest spot on the one-way street, grabs her phone, gets out of her car, and hurries across.

Yanking open the door, Cynthia takes note of the long line ending just inside. The Joe is an open box of a coffee shop, with tables and chairs positioned all along the walls, and a long conference room-like table in the back section. The coffee station and order counter take up the middle section. Sitting to Cynthia's left are four egg chairs for customers to sit and people watch in while they sip their coffee, which is exactly what two young women are doing.

Cynthia doesn't have time to wait in this line. Skirting around various moms, business people, and twenty-somethings, all staring at her, she sidles up to the side of the counter. Cynthia only waits a beat to get the attention of the portly middle-aged man with a bad comb-over.

When he turns and ignores her to take the order of the next person in line, she leans on the counter and says loudly, "Excuse me."

He glances at her, a scowl spread across his face, and says, "What?"

Cynthia feels silly for even asking, but finding Tori is more important than looking odd.

"Is Blue Eyes working today?"

The man stops what he's doing, turns to her, and says, "No. And if you talk to him, tell him he's fired! Next!"

The man turns back and takes the next order, telling the person where to swipe their card. He pivots away from Cynthia as he makes the next two drinks.

She ignores those in line and glances down behind the counter, seeing a list of names, phone numbers, and addresses.

He probably shouldn't be leaving this out, but works for me.

She pulls out her phone and takes a quick picture. She shoves it back into her purse, puts her head down, and walks out.

CHAPTER 5

THEN

SAMANTHA HOOKED HER thumbs into her backpack straps. It was a beautiful fall day, and she was laughing with Vicky and a handful of other girls as they walked out the front gate of Lincoln Middle School. Samantha knew she had become one of the popular kids more because of Vicky than anything she did herself. But she didn't mind.

Vicky was one of those girls that all the boys wanted to date. It was obvious Vicky was more developed than Samantha, but she wasn't sure if that was the only reason. Vicky said it was, and that was all boys wanted, but Vicky liked the attention, so she didn't care.

A line of cars waited at the front entrance of the school where Ms. Barnard stood filtering children to their appropriate cars.

"See ya, Claire! Ava, call me later and I'll tell you all about you know who," Vicky said to two girls as they split off towards an SUV and a red sports car.

As Vicky and Samantha turned to walk parallel to the cars, Ms. Barnard called to them.

"Girls, don't forget your history project is due by next

Wednesday. That means you have all weekend to work on it. And I'm sure you two will be together, so that's a great way to spend your time!"

"Mm-hmm, definitely, Ms. Barnard," Samantha said playfully over her shoulder.

Ms. Barnard shook her head with a smirk. "Oh, and again, happy birthday, Vicky!"

"Thanks, Ms. B!" Vicky shouted over her shoulder, looping her arm into Samantha's.

The girls turned right and were immediately in a neighborhood of single and two-story homes. Lincoln Middle was in the center of a half dozen different neighborhoods that included varying degrees of wealth.

"Can we stop by my house before we go to yours?" Vicky asked.

"Uhh, sure, I guess," Samantha said, trying not to sound nervous.

Vicky didn't live in any of the nicer neighborhoods, but just past them, across the creek. Samantha had been around enough of the other girls to hear the kinds of things they said about Vicky's neighborhood, but she refused to repeat it to Vicky. When one girl, Emma, started talking about how Vicky's family rifled through her trash to find dinner, Samantha tried standing up for her. She'd mumbled, "That's not nice," but with the looks she got, she backed off and said nothing more.

She felt bad about it, but also knew Vicky said plenty of mean things about Emma and her friends. So in her mind, it seemed even.

"Don't worry, you don't need to come inside. I just need to grab some clothes for tomorrow. I didn't want to bring it all to school, ya know?" Vicky said.

Samantha nodded as she glanced down the street they would have taken if they were going straight to her house. She looked ahead and saw a blue sedan coming their way. It slowed down as it passed them.

"Creep," Vicky grumbled, pulling up her top. Vicky had more than once been dress-coded for wearing the top, but each time she said it was because of her backpack and how it tugged down her shirt. She always said if the teacher had given her one more minute, she'd have adjusted it. Samantha knew the whole spiel was a lie—Vicky loved the stares she got because of her chest.

They walked on for a couple more minutes, Samantha only half listening to Vicky's trash talk about Emma and her friends and the gross things Vicky had heard they did with each other. She hadn't seen it, of course, but she'd heard it from Ava, who'd heard it from Chloe, who had been told by someone what they had done.

Samantha glanced behind them and saw the blue sedan make a U-turn. She turned back around, not wanting the driver to know she saw them and hoping they'd just missed their turn. A few seconds later, Samantha felt like the car was slowly following them, driving much slower than the speed limit.

She glanced back again and her heart stopped. It *was* following them. A million thoughts raced through her mind. She tried to think about what her parents had taught her about if someone tried to take her. She wasn't by herself, so whoever it was couldn't grab both of them, could they?

Before Samantha could remember anything else, the blue sedan came up next to them and stopped. The driver rolled down the passenger side window and leaned across the seat.

"Hey girls," the deep voice said.

Samantha leaned down, staying a few feet away from the car. As soon as she did, she calmed down, but only slightly.

It was her neighbor, Mr. Davies.

He ignored Samantha and focused on Vicky. From Samantha's viewpoint, it looked like he was looking directly at Vicky's chest.

"Where you girls headed? I noticed you didn't turn down towards your house, Sam. You both okay?"

Samantha didn't want to give him too much information. "Yeah, we're fine. We know where we're going."

"Well, hop in. Let me give you a ride."

His attention stayed on Vicky.

"We're good," Vicky said bluntly.

"It's no problem. I won't even expect any kind of payment."

Samantha could have sworn she saw him wink at Vicky. The hairs on her arms stood at attention, and a chill rolled down her spine. Something about this was wrong. The way he was staring at Vicky, the tone of his voice. It all just seemed gross to her.

Even with the situation, Samantha's parents had always taught her to be polite. "Thank you, Mr. Davies, but we're fine. We don't need a ride. We'll see you around."

"Yeah, go creep someone else out," Vicky spat, grabbing Samantha's arm. Samantha could see him put his hands in the air and re-situate himself in the driver's seat. As they continued toward Vicky's house, it sounded like his tires squealed as he made another U-turn and headed back the way he came.

CHAPTER 6

NOW

EVEN IN HER heels, Cynthia dashes across the street to her car. She could swear she heard someone say something about her taking the picture, but that is the least of her concerns right now. This kid Tori calls Blue Eyes isn't at work, and Tori isn't at school or answering her phone.

They must be together.

Cynthia's anger is bubbling up. Tori is being extremely irresponsible, and when she shows up later, she'll either fall in line with a severe punishment or she can move out—she is eighteen, after all. And to think Cynthia was ready to file a missing person report. She is almost glad that the officer hung up on her.

She stops at her car and pulls out her phone to look at the list and see if this Blue Eyes will answer his phone so she can talk to Tori. As she does, her phone vibrates in her hand.

That's probably her with an explanation.

Cynthia is a little surprised and relieved to see it's Sofia calling her back.

Sofia and Tori have been friends since kindergarten. Cynthia would regularly tell the story of little Tori being so excited to start kindergarten and walking in on the first day practically vibrating. There were nervous and scared parents milling about, some kids already crying, others running around the classroom laughing.

Tori had stepped in, surveyed the class, and saw one little girl sitting by herself coloring quietly. With no prompting or encouragement, Tori walked up to the girl, her backpack way too big for her little body, and said in her sweet, high-pitched voice, "Hi, I'm Tori. Want to be my friend?"

Tori and Sofia have been inseparable ever since. Almost every weekend through elementary school and middle school, they would spend the night at each other's homes. Cynthia views Sofia as a second daughter. Especially after Sofia's mom passed away from cancer, Cynthia has felt the need to be there for her. She knows the day will come when the girls will be in each other's weddings, and she hopes that one day, they'll have children of their own who will be best friends.

"Sofia, hi. Thanks for calling me back."

"Um, yeah. Hi, Mrs. Burrows. I was in class. Sorry. Is Tori okay? She texted me earlier saying she wasn't feeling well and was staying home. So when I saw a missed call from you, I got really worried."

Cynthia pauses, not saying anything.

This new information gives even more validation to Tori being in massive trouble for ditching school for a boy.

Sofia interrupts Cynthia's thoughts. "Mrs. Burrows? Is everything okay?"

She doesn't want to worry Sofia. Not until she knows more.

"I'm sure everything is fine. We had a bit of a rough start this morning, so it's probably just some miscommunication. I'm heading home right now, and I'll make sure she texts you."

"Okay, thanks. Bye."

Before Cynthia can say anything else, Sofia hangs up.

She opens the door of her car before remembering her entire purpose of being here. She gets her phone back out of her purse and opens her photo app.

Using two fingers, she zooms in, starts at the top, and begins reading the names:

Sarah Williams

Brenda Samuels

Cynthia scans the list and wonders if Tori was even telling the truth about this Blue Eyes kid working there. Every name is female. She's about to give up completely when she gets to the end of the list and freezes. Her hand hovers just above the screen, and her entire body locks up.

Even though the image is blurry, there is no mistaking the name. It's the only male name on the list, but it's impossible. There is no way. He would be around sixty at this point.

This can't be right.

It has to be a mistake.

Can there actually be two people with that exact name?

She guesses there could be, but what are the chances? This can't be a coincidence.

She dials Tori again with shaking hands. Nothing.

She climbs into the car and dials again. Nothing.

She looks at the address next to Blue Eyes' name, quickly goes to her maps app on her phone, and types it in. The directions routing from where she is show it'll take about twelve minutes to get there. Much closer than her own house. If the boy is there, she can get some answers. And if Tori is there, well . . . she'll get some answers. She sincerely hopes Tori is not there, but home in bed, too sick to answer the phone.

But the name . . . it can't be. It can't. She's certain that it can't be the same. Or at least she's trying hard to convince herself of it.

She starts her car and peels out away from her parking spot, not even thinking to look if anyone is coming. She makes two quick lefts to loop around the one-way streets, back to Lomas Santa Fe, and back onto the freeway.

As soon as she merges onto I-5, she grips the wheel a bit tighter and cuts across two lanes of traffic, honking at an idiot who almost cut her off.

It can't be him. It won't be him. Tori would already be dead if it was. *Why didn't he just take* me*?*

While avoiding side-swiping a slow-moving Toyota Corolla, Cynthia slams on her horn, only to swerve past a landscape truck plodding along. With her other hand, she grabs her phone and flips back to the picture of the employee list.

She looks at the name one last time. There, staring back at her like a ghost returning from the dead, is the name Alexander Beaufort.

CHAPTER 7

JOURNAL

I WANT TO talk about control. I've been thinking a lot about it lately. There are so many aspects to it. Some people love it and some people, surprisingly, hate it. I think by that last statement, you can guess which side I fall on. To me, there is nothing more important in life than control. If you don't have it, what are you even doing—really?

I think there are different levels of desiring control. And some think they have control, when in fact it's all a mirage. Like my dad, for example. He thinks he has control over what he watches at night, but it's really up to my mom.

Then there are those who can't function without it. They need to know they control every aspect of their lives, and whenever the slightest scenario deviates from what they wanted, they lose it. They can't function, can't sleep, can't think.

I fall more to this side of the equation. My personal philosophy is we can have all the fun in the world as long as we're doing what I want.

Is that selfish? Maybe.

Do I care? Not in the slightest.

It didn't take me long to realize that I have always been this way. I can't remember a time in my life where I did not feel the absolute need for control over everything.

I remember this one time I was playing with a couple of other neighbor kids, and this one girl didn't want to do what I wanted. I remember seeing red. I know people say that as an idiom for being angry, but literally, I saw red. Everything had a red hue to it. I couldn't think or speak or feel—really.

So I grabbed her arm and slammed it against a tree trunk. The sound her arm made when it snapped in two—I'll never forget it, like snapping a large twig. It would make most people feel ill, but even today, when I think about that sound . . . the only word I can think of is exhilaration. As soon as I did it, everything calmed down. I was in control once more. I knew from then on, the other kids would do exactly as I said.

And trust me, they did.

Going back to my last entry and the thought of death, I think these two concepts go hand in hand very well.

Is there anything more empowering or thrilling than being in control of whether someone lives or dies?

I think that is the ultimate statement of control. Just the thought of it gets me going. The time is coming when I will be in control of someone's lifeline, when I will decide if they live or die.

That is thrilling. And if I decide they get to live and they never even know it, oh wow. Even better!

I think the closest I've ever gotten to this was a party I went to. There was this group of girls who were always hanging around my friends. They drove us crazy—and not in a good way. They were trying so hard to be liked by us and it literally made me sick to my stomach, so I took matters into my own hands.

One of the super popular kids was throwing a "no parents"

party, and I made sure to invite these girls. We all got there, and I told my group of friends to follow my lead.

I know I sound redundant, but I just love being in control.

So anyway, we fed them drink after drink, until they literally couldn't stand by themselves. We took them upstairs and, like a band conductor, I instructed my friends on exactly what I wanted them to do and how to position the girls. I had another friend take a bunch of pictures and then I just left.

Why did I leave? Because I was in control, and I had decided I was done.

At school, I made sure those photos made their way around.

Oh man, the look of horror on the girls' faces. They couldn't leave school fast enough, tears streaming down. No one got in trouble because I had been in control and had set up several layers of so and so told so and so to do so and so.

Also, all my friends knew by this point not to cross me. Even if one did, I didn't actually do *anything. I told other people to do everything, but my hands didn't do anything wrong. That's the trick and benefit of control.*

When you have others do everything for you, then no one can convict you of actual wrongdoing.

So no one actually knew who had orchestrated the whole thing.

Once I decide and commit and choose who I will kill, no one will know. It will be perfect.

I tell you, I will get away with it. Nothing is going to stop me.

Except maybe this damn pulsing drum in the back of my skull. It has to be a brain tumor or something.

It almost feels like I'm losing control. And we can't have that.

CHAPTER 8

NOW

"TURN LEFT AND merge onto I-5 for three miles."

Cynthia knows this is probably not a good idea.

She has no clue what she's walking into and no one knows where she is.

"Call Gabby," she commands to her phone.

It rings twice and a soft voice answers, "Hey you. I was gonna surprise you. I'm in town for a conference!"

Cynthia and Gabby have been friends since the first day of law school. When Cynthia had arrived in Legal Skills, there were only two open seats in the lecture hall. One was next to a large, sweaty guy who looked at Cynthia and was very eager for her to take the open seat next to him. The only other option was on the aisle of the first row. All Cynthia could tell from the top of the steps was that there was a girl sitting next to the empty seat.

She took her chances and was taken aback by the beautiful girl next to her. She stuck out her hand and with a firm, soft voice said, "Hi, I'm Gabriella, but everyone calls me Gabby."

Cynthia stuttered for a moment, completely lost in Gabby's sparkling emerald eyes. They absolutely popped against her soft milk chocolate skin.

If I wasn't completely straight, she might turn me, Cynthia had thought.

She shook her hand and said, "I'm Cynthia. Nice to meet you. I'm sorry, but you are gorgeous."

This got a laugh out of Gabby, and the two quickly became friends.

"What's up?" Gabby asks now.

"Tori is missing."

"What do you mean, missing?" Gabby asks, her sweet voice turning to a strong, questioning tone.

Cynthia takes the next several minutes walking her through the morning, the date with the coffee shop boy Tori was supposed to go on, and finishes with where she is going.

"I don't think that's a good idea. Call the police and have them meet you there."

"I tried that already and they hung up on me."

Gabby sighs. About halfway through law school, Gabby had decided being a lawyer was not her calling and pivoted to law enforcement. Rather than making tons of money in corporate law, she decided her time would be better spent working for the FBI, helping to find lost children and putting away the horrible pieces of trash that abused them.

"Listen, unfortunately they are right. Before they can file a report, you at least need to wait until the school day is over and see if she shows up."

"You don't understand," Cynthia says, getting ready to drop the bomb on Gabby. Gabby is the only one who actually knows of Cynthia's past. She had never even shared it with her own husband. Cynthia kept meaning to, but as time went on, it just got harder and harder. She never thought this day would come, when her past would catch up to her.

"The boy's name is listed as Alexander Beaufort."

"Shit."

"Exactly." Cynthia sees the directions change on the heads-up routing on her phone and turns left. "I mean, how? How did he find us?"

"I think we're getting ahead of ourselves," Gabby says calmly. "I learned long ago that I can't convince you once you've made up your mind, so be careful, please. And if you see anything or feel like anything is off, call the police. And if they won't help you, I'll bring the full force of the FBI."

"Thanks Gabs. I don't know what I'd do without you. I'll let you know what I find out."

Cynthia hits the end call button and turns right as the directions let her know she's arrived at her destination. She looks around and then at the address, grabs her phone off the dock, and quickly brings up the employee list again, verifying that she has the correct street and house number.

"This can't be right," she mutters to herself. She gets out of her car and walks up to the gate of the home this supposed Alexander lives at. She had expected to come up to some apartment complex or some run-down home that was obviously rented by a bunch of single guys. But rather, she finds herself standing in front of a gated home that rivals her own.

She knows what she and David pull in annually, and there is no way a kid working at a coffee shop can have the same kind of money. Even if he was a drug kingpin, she wasn't sure he'd pull in the same kind of cash.

There are three cars parked at the top of the roundabout right next to the front door.

Someone must be home. Cynthia presses the intercom button but gets no response. She looks for some other way in. There is a row of hedges on a planter wall lining the fence. She does a quick glance at the street, but everything is quiet. In this kind of neighborhood, she assumes the only people around during the day are landscapers and housekeepers.

She takes off her heels, climbs up on the wall, and grabs the crossbar at the top of the metal fence. Jumping up, she is able to get her foot on the bar and hops down onto the other side.

She takes another quick glance back at the street.

Who have I become?

Cynthia walks up the stone-paved drive to the front steps. The home itself looks like a miniature version of the White House, with the white marble pillars in the front holding up a black and white porte-cochère. The front door has to be at least ten feet tall, and wide enough for two and half of her to fit through.

Maybe they're all out back and didn't hear the intercom.

How am I going to explain I hopped over their fence to see if my daughter is here?

Cynthia throws the questions out of her mind and pounds on the oversized mahogany door. She waits, and hearing nothing, she hesitates for only a moment before grabbing the door handle. She squeezes the latch and pushes, expecting to meet resistance.

Her heart thumps in her chest as the door glides smoothly open.

Cynthia calls out, "Hello?" but the word stops in her throat. An overwhelming stench of rotting meat mixed with a sweet, sickly smell slams into her, shoving her backwards.

She gags and turns to the bushes that line the side of the

house. She vomits into one of them; eggs, bacon and sourdough toast.

Cynthia stumbles forward, away from the house, grabbing her phone in her back pocket. She presses Gabby's name, and before Gabby can say anything, Cynthia yells, "Dead! There's—dead—body!"

"Cynth, what are you saying? Are you okay?"

Cynthia dry heaves right next to the tire of the Aston Martin parked in the driveway. "There's a body. The door, it just opened. Before I could—I could smell it. Saw it."

"Okay, calm down. Do nothing. Do not, I repeat, DO NOT go inside. Do you understand me?"

"But—"

"No!" Gabby yells at her. "No but. You hang up and call the police. Now!"

"Tori" is all Cynthia can say.

"We'll find her, I promise. Right now, you need to call the police. Don't move until they get there. Do you understand me? Tell me you understand."

"I—I understand," Cynthia stammers.

"Good. Now hang up. Call the police and get as far away from that door as you can."

Cynthia nods as if Gabby is there with her and hangs up. She brings up the keypad and presses 911.

CHAPTER 9

NOW

CYNTHIA IS SITTING on the far side of the fountain, as far away from the front door as she can get. Part of her wanted to run to the fence, scramble over it, get in her car, and drive as far away as possible, but she knew she had to stay. If she ran, it would look even worse.

With her elbows on her knees and her fingers interlaced in her hair, she focuses on her breathing. It's a practice she learned years ago when she first started in yoga.

What was it that got her started in yoga? Was it a case she was working on? Was it because of Alexander? She can't remember.

Her thoughts are scattered, but she welcomes the distraction from her key question. *Whose body is that in there? Where is Tori? Where is my little girl?*

She knows Tori is certainly no longer her little girl. She's hoping that later tonight, they'll look back on this, shake their heads at the craziness of it all, and laugh.

But there's that one gnawing name. As much as she wishes, wants, and hopes this is all some massive misunderstanding, there is no way it is a coincidence that the name Alexander Beaufort popped back up in Cynthia's life the same day that Tori went missing.

Before she can think much more about it, a sedan pulls up with two police cruisers right behind it. An arm reaches out the window, punches in a code, and the gate swings inward.

Cynthia tries to push herself up, but her legs buckle and she collapses back down to where she is sitting. She waits while the three vehicles drive up and park twenty yards from her. The man in the sedan gets out first and Cynthia knows it must be an unmarked car. He has detective written all over him.

Cynthia pushes herself up again, taking time and care to make sure her legs are steady. The last thing she needs is to fall down in front of these officers.

"Were you the one who called 911?" the man asks.

Cynthia nods.

He looks young to be the one in charge, especially as the officers who walk up behind him are grayer and more weathered, but his firm jaw and high and tight haircut suggest time spent in the military. As if the officers and police cruisers behind him aren't intimidating enough, his piercing, deep brown eyes give the impression he could get whatever answers he needed.

She isn't sure what she expected a detective to wear, but his wardrobe isn't it. He is wearing black pants with cargo pockets, and a tight t-shirt with the Carlsbad PD logo on it, which his biceps are pushing against the sleeves. A gun is holstered on the right side of his hip and a badge is clipped to the front of his pants.

"What's your name, ma'am? Do you live here?"

Cynthia shakes her head and sighs. How is she going to explain this situation?

"Cynthia. Cynthia Burrows."

"Okay, Cynthia Burrows. I'm Detective Miguel Harrison. So, if you don't live here, how did you get in? Dispatch said something about a dead body?"

Cynthia takes a deep breath and explains as much as she can.

"My daughter is missing. She never showed up at school today, but the school said someone called in and excused her. She was supposed to go on a date tonight with this boy from The Joe coffee shop. So when she wouldn't answer her phone, I left work and went to the coffee shop to see if he was there, but the manager said he never showed up for work. I saw an employee list and the only male name on it was this address. I figured maybe she was with him at his house, so I came here. When I saw the cars, but no one answered the gate, I hopped over the fence. I knocked, no one answered, and when I tried the door, it creaked open. I smelled something rotting, saw what I thought was a dead body, and called 911."

Cynthia stops talking and breathes. She studies the detective's face, trying to see if he believes her or not.

His gaze is boring into her.

He scratches at the back of his head, looks at the two officers, and nudges his head toward the front door. The officers unclip the snaps for their service weapons and move toward the front door.

"We'll stay out here while they search the house," Detective Harrison says, more a command than a suggestion.

"So if your daughter is missing, why didn't you call us?"

Cynthia whips her head back to him and snaps, "I did. You hung up on me!"

Detective Harrison lifts his head slightly and takes a step back, like moving away from a cornered animal.

"I'm sorry they did that. If you know who you spoke with, I'll make sure their superior officer has a conversation with them. Usually, we need to at least wait until the end of a school day to see if the child shows back up."

Cynthia nods her head. "I know, I know, it's just—"

Before she can say anything more, he follows up with, "Why did you feel the need to try the door?"

"I'm sorry?" Cynthia asks, taken off guard by the question.

"The door. Most people don't try to open a front door that isn't their house. If no one answers, you usually just leave."

"I—well, I—I'm not sure." Cynthia stammers.

Before he can pepper her with any more questions, the two officers come out and call, "All clear, sir."

"What do we have?"

"Two bodies, looks like a husband and wife. Mid to late sixties. Someone slashed both of their throats. Looks like the wife answered the door and they surprised the husband coming out of the kitchen."

Detective Harrison nods, pulling out his phone and taking notes.

Cynthia pushes down her gag reflex, refusing to throw up on the detective's shoes. "Was there anyone else? A teenage girl? Blonde hair, blue eyes?"

One of the officers shakes his head.

"Are you certain?!" Cynthia says, lunging toward the officer, who takes a step back and instinctively reaches for his gun.

She stops herself and steps back.

In a calmer tone, she asks again, "Are you sure?"

The two officers look at Detective Harrison and back at Cynthia. "Yeah, we're sure."

"The man, you said mid-sixties? Did he have brown hair and green eyes?" Cynthia asks.

The older of the two officers, with a bushy mustache, looks at her quizzically and says, "No, blond, going gray hair with blue eyes. Why?"

Cynthia shrugs, realizing she is saying too much.

"Thank you, officers," Detective Harrison says. "Can you call it in, get the medical examiner and coroner over here?"

He turns to Cynthia and says, "Would you like to explain that? Who did you expect to be in there? And for that matter, when our crime scene unit gets here, are they going to find your prints in the house? It's best if you let me know that now."

Cynthia shakes her head. "No, I did not go in."

"Okay, who did you think was in there?"

"I—I—I can't tell you that," she stammers.

"I think you're going to have to," he says, taking a step towards her.

Cynthia can feel her stress intensifying. She doesn't know what to do. A wave of nausea and lightheadedness overwhelms her. If he keeps pushing, she's going to tell him everything. She has never felt this out of control before. She has cross-examined some of the strongest CEO minds in the nation and has never stuttered before. But Tori missing, Alexander's name popping up, the dead bodies . . .

It's too much.

She runs her hand through her hair and looks away from the detective. Then, she can't believe what she sees.

Another car is pulling in and stops just inside the gate.

A beautiful woman jumps out of the car as it's still coming to a stop. Cynthia can see the sharp emerald eyes from where she is, and the woman's milk chocolate skin radiates against the blue windbreaker and light denim jeans.

A wide smile spreads across Cynthia's face and she breathes a sigh of relief.

"Gabby!"

CHAPTER 10

THEN

"THAT WAS WEIRD, right?" Vicky asked as they crossed over the bridge.

Samantha looked down at the tiny stream and wondered if the water used to be higher. It felt extreme to build this entire bridge just for that bit of water.

"Hello?" Vicky sang.

"Sorry, yeah. Yeah, it was strange, but that's kind of him. He's always been a little off. My parents just told me to not go too close to his place. I don't really know why. He seems harmless, just odd."

Vicky scoffed. "You're so naïve. Didn't you see the way he was looking at me? Well, part of me?"

Samantha wasn't sure what she was implying. She noticed Mr. Davies' focus was towards Vicky's chest, but in his defense, they were practically hanging out. She knew better than to say that to her, though.

"Can we talk about something else?" Samantha asked, trying to change the subject. "There are a million other things to talk about. Like your birthday!"

Vicky looped her arm into Samantha's and said, "You're right! Let's not let creepy pervs get us down. So what did you get me for my birthday?"

Samantha laughed. "Nope. You aren't getting it out of me that easy. You gotta wait 'til tonight. You know the drill. Same as every year. Right before we go to bed, that's when we get our gifts."

Vicky leaned her head on Samantha's arm as they crossed over the bridge, half skipping, their backpacks knocking against their backs as they went.

"I don't know what I would ever do without you, Sammy."

"Samesies," Samantha said, squeezing Vicky's hand.

"So what should we do first? Scary movie? Makeover? Boy talk?"

"Yes to all the above! But you know we have to wait 'til my parents go to bed," Samantha responded excitedly. And then, a little self-consciously, "Well, at least my dad."

"Yeah, what's his deal anyway?" Vicky asked, letting go of Samantha's arm. Once across the bridge, the environment felt different. All the full, vibrant trees and green grass were gone.

The main street was littered with potholes and cracks in the road. Every car parked on the two-way street looked like it might not even run. Several of the cars had huge rust spots on them, and Samantha saw at least two that didn't have tires.

Any trees on this side of the road were wilted and cracked. A limb hung off one tree as if it had given up.

The yards were brown with dried leaves and other debris in them. As they continued on, they walked past a flat soccer ball resting against the gutter, the black hexagons faded out to a light gray.

Samantha ignored all of this and shrugged her shoulders at Vicky's question. "He's a dad, I guess."

Vicky shook her head. "I wouldn't know what that's like."

The two stopped at the end of a driveway. The front yard had an overgrowth of weeds and brown grass. There was a rusted, broken down truck on cinder blocks. A tarp covered half the garage, and as the two walked up the drive, Samantha could see that the paint was peeling on the front of the house.

She knew Vicky didn't have a good home life. In fourth grade, some boys and girls would make fun of Vicky for "living on the other side of the bridge." Some of the really mean kids would say she lived *under* the bridge.

Samantha never cared about the difference between where she and Vicky lived. Her parents, on the other hand, certainly did. Samantha could never spend the night at Vicky's house. She wasn't sure if it was because of the location of Vicky's home or because of Vicky's parents—well, her mom and her mom's latest boyfriend. Samantha assumed it was more of where she lived because she wasn't sure her parents had ever met Vicky's mom.

"Wait here. I'll get my stuff and we can go," Vicky said.

Samantha nodded and stood at the edge of the cracked and crumbling walkway that led to the front door from the side of the driveway. She glanced toward the garage and the tarp, only being able to see a little way inside. She wasn't sure what the tarp was protecting from the weather, but it looked like the garage was full of boxes.

She looked around the neighborhood. How did it get like this? It couldn't have always been this run-down, could it?

Before she could think more about it, there was yelling and screaming coming from inside.

"Shut the hell up!" a male voice yelled.

"No! Make me! You're worthless. Do something with your life!" a female voice snapped back.

"I could say the same to you, but you already do something with yours, you fucking whore!"

Samantha couldn't move. She didn't know if she should go see if Vicky needed help or if she should run down the driveway to the street.

"No wonder your daughter looks like that. She'll end up just like you!" the male voice continued.

Samantha jumped back as she heard glass shatter inside.

Vicky ran outside, the screen door slamming against the house, tears coming down her cheeks. She grabbed Samantha's hand and ran down the driveway, not stopping or saying a word until they got back to the bridge.

Once there, Vicky slowed to a walk and Samantha looked ahead, but she could hear the sniffles and Vicky's breath catching as she tried to steady her breathing.

"It's okay," Samantha tried to reassure her.

Vicky just shook her head, wiping at her eyes.

"No, it's not. He's an ass. One of the worst. I don't know why she lets him stay."

Samantha was at a loss for words. She put her arm around Vicky and squeezed her.

"If it ever gets so bad you need somewhere else to live, my home is your home. I'd love for you to be my sister."

Samantha glanced at her and saw a small smile peek at the corners of Vicky's lips.

"Thank you. I don't know what I'd do without you," Vicky responded, laying her head on Samantha's shoulder.

CHAPTER 11

NOW

AFTER THEY'D FIRST met in Legal Skills, Cynthia and Gabby were inseparable. Even though Cynthia had met no one she trusted more, she still had not planned on telling Gabby about her past. That was until Gabby brought it up herself.

They had been in the law library studying when Gabby leaned across the table and whispered, "Hey, listen to this."

At that time of night, the library was sparse, but she wanted to be sure she didn't get whisper-yelled at by one of the many librarians patrolling the floor.

"So I'm putting together all this data for this forensic psychology class. I wanted to focus on serial killers and the reasons they kill. But my slant is on lesser-known killers. Everyone knows about the Dahmers and the Bundys, but there are so many regional killers that maybe only killed three or four people, so they barely classify as serial killers, but technically they still do."

"Okay," Cynthia had said, feeling nervous about where this was going. She knew her name wasn't in any papers or anything, but still she found herself wondering, *what if?*

"My goal is to see if I can pinpoint some kind of traumatic event in their past that sent them down this path. And I think I found my anchor data. I'm gonna build the entire argument around this guy."

Gabby had stabbed her finger at a law book and spun it around for Cynthia to see. Cynthia hadn't needed to hear any more as soon as she saw the name Alexander Beaufort. She gulped as Gabby continued.

"There was this killer named Alexander Beaufort, and he supposedly murdered ten to fourteen-year-old girls. He never raped them or sexually abused them. He crushed their skulls in with a hammer from behind and would remove their right index fingers. They found a shoebox of fingers in his bedroom. They were hidden in the closet behind a fake panel in the drywall. During his trial, a psychologist uncovered Alexander Beaufort's brutal past and how a female cousin his parents brought into their home, in a live-in type situation, tortured him."

Cynthia's vision was getting blurry while Gabby was talking.

Gabby continued to explain, "From what the psychologist could gather for the defense, who it looks like were going for an insanity plea, the torture began when he was four and the girl was ten. It continued for the next four years until Alexander was around eight.

"Local police came to the house and determined the girl 'accidentally' slipped and hit her head on a rock. I think—as do others from the looks of the court transcripts—that this was Alexander's first kill, and it sparked something in him he's been chasing ever since. How great is that for a foundation for my paper?"

Cynthia felt her stomach churning as she asked something she'd wondered about for so long. "Why the fingers?"

Gabby's smile spread wider. She pointed her finger at Cynthia. “That’s the kicker. The psychologist was able to put him in a state of hypnosis and get him to go back to that time. The girl would jab at him in spots all over his body until he would start to bleed. She would then swipe a bit of the blood and make him lick it.”

All these years later, Cynthia can still recall the queasy feeling in her stomach that day.

Detective Harrison marches toward Gabby, yelling, “Who the hell are you and why are you at my crime scene?”

Gabby’s hands go up. One flashes her FBI badge while the other makes a calming motion.

“No way in hell I’m letting feds take this over,” Detective Harrison yells. “There is no jurisdiction here for the FBI, so you can turn around and go back to where you came from.”

Gabby’s calm tone works to diffuse the situation. “I have no interest in taking over your investigation. I’m simply here as her best friend, but I’m not leaving without her.”

Detective Harrison stopped, pushing his hands into his pockets. “Well, at the moment, she is a witness to a murder, so she isn’t going anywhere.”

“Then we seem to be at an impasse. Because I’m not leaving without her, and you say she isn’t leaving.”

The detective looks at Cynthia and then back to Gabby.

“I can’t let her go,” he says, a little calmer.

“Well, unless you want me to make this a federal case and call in the US Marshals while I’m at it, you’ll let her go.”

The detective takes a step back and says, surprised, “The Marshals? What the hell do they have to do with this? What is going on here?”

Turning to Cynthia, he jabs a finger toward her. “You said you didn’t know the people in there. Were you lying to me?”

Cynthia shakes her head profusely as Gabby touches the detective's arm.

He whirls around as she says in a calm, even tone, "There is much more at stake here than you could know. If you need her, here's my card. Call me and I'll bring her to you."

"Give me your badge number and let me make a couple of quick calls," the detective says.

While he walks away, Gabby comes up to Cynthia and gives her a big hug.

"Are you okay?"

Cynthia ignores the questions and says, "How did you know where I was? How did you get here so fast?"

"The app we've used before," Gabby says, rubbing Cynthia's arms.

The warmth of her hands is welcoming. Cynthia didn't realize she was as cold as she is, probably from shock.

Detective Harrison comes back and says reluctantly, "Okay. You can take her with you, but I will need her to come to the station in the next day or so to give an official statement."

Cynthia nods and Gabby pulls her away.

"I hope you find your girl," the detective calls after her.

They walk away from him and Gabby says, "I'm worried about you. You're hopping fences, finding dead bodies? I know Tori is not answering her phone right now, but do you really think Alexander took her?"

Cynthia runs a hand through her hair. "I don't know what to think, Gabby. It can't be a coincidence."

Gabby nods. "I'm sure this is all some crazy case of mistaken identity. There has to be more than one person in the world with the name of Alexander Beaufort."

Cynthia nods.

"You're obviously not buying those theories," Gabby says, knowing her friend. "Do you want me to come home with you?"

"No, that's not necessary. I'll be fine. I'm going to head back to the coffee shop and see if I can learn more about this boy Tori was supposed to go out with. Maybe this was his grandparents' home or something. I need to get back to the office. There is nothing more I can do at the moment, and I can't just pace my house until the school day is over."

Gabby nods, studying Cynthia. "Okay, I have some things to take care of, but I'm going to stay around until we know what's going on, alright?"

"That would be great, thank you."

Cynthia gives her a big hug and turns to leave, but Gabby grabs her arm. "Don't do anything rash. She'll turn up, I promise."

Cynthia gives her a half-hearted smile, heads to her car, and gets in as quickly as she can. Images of Alexander and his victims are flashing through her mind, and her emotions over take her. Sitting alone in her car, fear, anxiety, and worry collide inside her, unleashing a torrent of hysterical sobs.

A flurry of questions floods her system.

There is no way he could have found her, is there?

If so, did he take Tori? What would he want with her?

Is this his way of finally getting back at Cynthia? After all these years, why now?

Why not just kill Cynthia and be done with it?

Cynthia knows the answer, but she pushes the thought out of her mind.

She calms herself down and checks her makeup. She takes a couple of deep breaths, grabs a Kleenex out of the glove box, and dabs her eyes and nose with it. Grabbing her compact, she tries to make herself look more presentable. She decides it'll have to do and tosses it on the passenger seat.

She presses the start button of her BMW and makes a quick U-turn, heading back to the coffee shop.

CHAPTER 12

NOW

CYNTHIA PULLS UP to The Joe and parks in the same spot as earlier. How was that only an hour or so ago? She gets out of her car and takes a moment to look around. Directly across the street from the coffee shop where she is standing, there's a grocery store and a couple of fast-food restaurants. Just to the left of The Joe is a small alley which has a parking lot for the coffee shop and a yoga studio.

Knowing it's a one-way street, she still takes a quick look in each direction and hurries across. Opening the door, the line is gone, most of the seats are full, and the portly man who was working furiously behind the counter is at the back cleaning tables.

Standing at the coffee station, wiping down the espresso machine, is a young woman. She looks to be about Cynthia's height—around five feet eight—and has the look of someone who would work in an indie coffee shop. She has short-cropped hair, a tattoo sleeve on her left arm, and a variety of rings and studs in her ears and nose.

Cynthia can only imagine the attitude this girl is going to

give when she asks questions about Tori, Blue Eyes, and anything else.

The girl looks up from the counter and gives Cynthia a warm, broad smile, all of her white teeth gleaming. There is a sparkle in the girl's big brown eyes, and Cynthia is ashamed at her snap judgment.

"Hey there," the young woman says with a slight twang. "How can I help ya?"

Cynthia stands there stunned and actually says, "I was not expecting that voice."

The young woman laughs, her southern accent coming through even more. "Yeah, I get that a lot." She motions down her body and says, "This look certainly don't scream Texas. But here I am, as southern as a belle. That's b-e-l-l-e, not b-e-l-l."

Cynthia smiles.

"I'm hoping you might help me," she says, making her way to the counter.

She pulls out her phone and brings up a picture of Tori. "Do you know her?"

The young woman brightens and says, "Tori?! Of course! Everyone loves Tori. She's in here jus' 'bout every day. She's always buyin' multiple drinks for her friends 'n stuff."

This is why Cynthia is so worried. This sounds like the Tori she knows. Not one who would ditch school to hang out with a boy.

"That's great to hear. I understand there is a guy who works here named—" Cynthia pauses, forcing herself to say the name, "—Alexander. Can you tell me anything about him? Why is he called Blue Eyes?"

The two stare at each other for a moment. The girl glances behind her toward her boss.

"Did you want to order something?"

It only takes Cynthia a minute to understand what the young woman is doing.

"Sure, can I get a cafe americano? What was your name?"

The girl taps on the screen and flips it around for Cynthia to pay. She moves to her left to the espresso machine and makes Cynthia's drink.

"It's Annabelle. What do you want to know?"

Cynthia nods and asks, "Do you know how long he's worked here?"

Annabelle shrugs. "Four, five months, maybe."

"What kind of person is he? Is he nice? Does he have a temper?" She knows she is pushing her luck, but hopes, with the drink, Annabelle will talk.

"I'm sorry, I definitely have the southern hospitality built in, but can I ask why all the questions?"

"Of course," Cynthia says. "Tori's not at school, which isn't like her, and she was supposed to go on a date with him tonight."

Before Cynthia can say anything else, the girl laughs.

"I'm sorry. Did I say something funny?"

Annabelle looks back at Cynthia while pouring the espresso into a cup. "No, I'm sorry. But Blue Eyes don't date girls. He bangs 'em, ya know? As to why his name is Blue Eyes, I have no idea. He came in with that nickname, prolly about four, five months ago now."

That statement is bouncing around in Cynthia's mind: *He doesn't date girls, he bangs them.*

What kind of guy was Tori going out with? Did she know this about him? Has she been with other guys? Cynthia stops herself from that line of thinking. There isn't time right now to worry about that.

"When was the last time you saw Tori?"

"This morning, course. Ya know, there was something a lil' bit off. I'd asked her if she wanted her regular group of drinks and she said, no, just hers today. I thought that was odd because she always gets her group drinks on Monday."

"Anything else out of the ordinary?" Cynthia asks, the first hopeful thing she'd heard.

Annabelle scrunches her nose and looks towards the open ceiling with the white painted air ducts.

"Actually yeah. As soon as Tori had paid, she turned around and there was this older dude. Had to be, I dunno, fifties, sixties maybe? She seemed to know him and looked around real quick, and the two of them left together. It was odd, 'cause he came in, didn' order nothin', and then just left."

Cynthia's heart is pounding in her chest. She looks towards the exit and sees something she hopes can help. Wheeling back around to Annabelle, Cynthia asks, "Can I look at your security footage?"

Annabelle purses her lips and looks behind her. Cynthia knows she's glancing back at the manager.

She waves Cynthia closer and whispers to her. "Come back just before close. We close at six. I'll help you out then."

Cynthia grabs her hands and profusely thanks her.

As she heads out, the intrusive thought rams back into her mind: *He doesn't date girls, he bangs them.*

She can't believe Tori would date someone like that. She wishes she could ask someone and then has an idea. She pulls out her phone and sends a text to Sofia.

Cynthia: *Can we meet? Today?*

She doesn't have to wait for a reply. It's almost instantaneous. It amazes her how quick kids are on their phones these days.

Sofia: *Is Tori okay?*

Cynthia: *It'd be better to explain in person.*

Sofia: *I have a half day today and have water polo practice right after school. If you want, you can meet me at the pool around 1:00?*

Cynthia: *Perfect, I'll be there. Thank you.*

CHAPTER 13

NOW

CYNTHIA PULLS UP to her house. She had every intention of going back to the office, but decided she would come home before meeting with Sofia. After everything she learned at the coffee shop, she is determined to tear apart Tori's room to search for clues.

Maybe she didn't know her daughter as well as she thought she did.

She carefully guides her BMW over the driveway dip so as not to scratch the front end and leaves it parked out front. Heading toward the front door, as if preparing for court, she goes over what she knows so far.

Tori never showed up for school and someone claiming to be family excused her, knowing her school ID.

She went to the coffee shop like normal, but didn't order for her friends and then left with an older gentleman she seemed to know.

She was supposed to go out with a boy named Blue Eyes whose actual name is Alexander Beaufort.

Cynthia rifles through her purse, looking for her house key.

The front of their home is usually a tranquil spot. The sloped green grass, disappearing toward the lagoon, always provided fantastic sunset pictures. She and David love to sit out here in their Adirondack chairs and watch the sun disappear beyond the lagoon, with oranges and purples reflecting off of it.

There is nothing tranquil about standing in this yard right now.

As Cynthia finds her keys, the thought of the bodies floats to the front of her mind and she pushes down her gag reflex.

The boy's address, the dead bodies—Tori was supposed to go out with him?

What is she caught up in?

Cynthia fumbles with the keys and they fall into the tall grass. She rummages around for them, trying to reason with herself.

No matter what, there is no way he could have found her. Is there?

She had never even told her husband about her past. Only Gabby, Marshal Wright, and a few others in the US Marshals service truly knew who she was.

She grabs the keys and steps up to the front door. Putting the key into the slot, her phone begins to vibrate in her purse. Cynthia leaves her keys dangling from the lock and pulls out her phone, looking at the caller ID.

Blocked.

She hesitates for only a moment. She doesn't want to answer it, but knows she has to. Somehow, she knows who is going to be on the other end. She still can't fathom hearing his voice after all these years, but it has to be him, doesn't it? She waits one more second and presses the green answer circle on the screen.

She puts the phone up to her ear and waits. She's too afraid to say hello.

As the voice on the other end speaks, a chilling dread washes over Cynthia, starting at her head and cascading through every inch of her, down to her toes.

"Glad to see you made it home safe."

The voice sounds familiar, yet different. The years on the run have not been kind to him, she can tell. The voice she remembered was youthful, vibrant, playful.

This voice is deep, tired, and has an edge to it, but there's no denying it's him—Alexander Beaufort.

Cynthia is unable to speak. She spins in place, trying to grab any of the thousands of thoughts spinning through her mind.

"Hey, you there? I know it's probably quite the shock to hear from me, but trust me when I say I have been searching for you for a very, very long time. In fact, if it wasn't for Tori, I'd still be looking for you. You can thank her for that—well, that is, if you find her in time."

Cynthia wants to yell and scream. Demand he give Tori back. Curse him for still being alive.

But nothing comes. Hearing his voice silences her.

"I'm going to give you the chance to save her though," Alexander continues, "Just like old times, right? It took you, what, about three days to find—"

Knowing the name that was about to touch his lips was all that Cynthia needed to find her voice, her courage, her burning anger.

"Don't you dare speak her name!"

"Ah, so you are there. Good to see that fire is still there, too."

Alexander pauses and Cynthia can feel the pressure of the silence closing in around her. Before she can say anything, the voice continues, "Well, anyway, I'm giving you 'til Thursday to find Tori. If not, I'll make sure her body is easy to recover. Possibly a shallow grave? At the edge of the yard?"

Cynthia hears him chuckle and the line goes dead.

She grips her hair, pulling at it, and screams at the top of her lungs. She doesn't care who hears. She can't believe he found her. Cynthia drops to her knees and tears pour from her eyes. How is this happening? How did he find her?

It takes her a moment to gain her composure and she looks up, wondering if anyone in the neighborhood heard her or had any concern for her well-being. No one is there. No one is looking out a window or came out front to see what was going on.

Directly across the street, at the Harris home, she notices a curtain billowing in one of the upstairs bedrooms. The sound of a jet ski taking off on the lagoon causes her to jump.

She takes a couple of deep breaths, smooths out her pant legs, and finds the will to stand. She knows for certain now that Tori didn't just skip school. She has no idea how, but Alexander Beaufort is back in her life and is playing his sick games again. Cynthia turns to the front door and unlocks it, heading straight to Tori's room.

She has three days to find her daughter.

CHAPTER 14

THEN

"CAN YOU IMAGINE if we were actually sisters?" Vicky asked as they crossed over the bridge. "Do you think we would get along as well as we do?"

Samantha paused and glanced at Vicky. There were black lines running down her face. She reached up to Vicky's bubbly cheeks and tried wiping it off, but it just smeared across her face.

"You have black lines," Samantha stated, showing Vicky the black on her finger.

"Ugh, that's my mascara," Vicky groaned. She wiped her face with the back of her hands and rubbed at her eyes with her knuckles. She wiped under her eyes and looked back at Samantha.

"How's that? Better?"

Samantha choked down a laugh.

"What?" Vicky asked.

"I love you, but you look like—like, a raccoon," Samantha said, not being able to contain her laughter.

"What?!" Vicky moaned, stopping at the edge of the bridge and taking off her backpack. She rummaged around for a second until she found her compact and pulled it out, looking at herself.

"Oh my god!" Vicky exclaimed. "Should I start rummaging through the garbage now?"

Vicky made a motion toward Samantha like she was going to bite her and squealed. "Maybe I'll bite you and give you rabies!"

The two girls fell to the ground laughing. They landed on the edge of a small grassy hill on someone's front yard and laid there for a moment, watching the puffy clouds above.

"You—you do look a lot like a raccoon," Samantha said between giggles.

"Yeah, well," Vicky retorted, but had nothing to say.

Samantha got up and helped Vicky to her feet. The two walked on, enjoying the sunshine. Samantha took a deep breath, thankful for the chance to help Vicky laugh. She would have sworn it smelled fresher over on this side of the bridge, but she'd never say that to Vicky.

They walked on, and as they came to the corner of Samantha's street, Vicky broke the silence. "So what do you think, would we?"

"Would we what?" Samantha asked, trying to remember what they'd been talking about.

"Would we get along if we were actual sisters?" Vicky reminded her.

Samantha wanted to say yes, of course, but she wasn't sure. She didn't know if she could handle Vicky all the time. She loved her, no doubt, but to have her actually around twenty-four hours a day—that would be a lot. Samantha pushed the thoughts aside and said what she felt. "Of course! We may fight like sisters sometimes, though."

Vicky shrugged. "That's fine. That's what sisters are supposed to do, right?"

Samantha smiled. The sun was shining, the birds were singing, and the two of them were heading back to her house for a weekend sleepover. She was going to give Vicky her birthday present—nothing could ruin their day.

Glancing at Vicky again, Samantha wondered when her own parents would let her wear makeup. She was a teenager now and all the other girls were doing it. She was fairly certain her mom wouldn't care; it was her dad. He was weird about the things he was strict about.

Almost any kind of music, sure. Makeup, no way. Going out with a boy, absolutely not. Eating sweets in the middle of the day, no problem.

The two turned down Samantha's street, and she could see her house several homes up. They walked past Ms. Sarah's home with the extra tall bushes. She had one of those arched hedge entrances that made it seem magical. As they passed, Samantha could see Ms. Sarah sunbathing like she did most afternoons, on the grass just to the right of her stone walkway.

She was always sunbathing on that side, and Samantha wasn't sure if it was because she wanted people to see her or not. If they walked the way Samantha and Vicky were and looked beyond the wooden gate, they would have a full view of her, but if they walked the other way, they wouldn't see her at all.

It's probably because she doesn't want Mr. Davies to see her, Samantha thought as they reached the edge of her hedges.

The next house belonged to Mr. Davies. As soon as his home was in view, Samantha saw his blue car sitting in the driveway and her stomach dropped a bit. She was wary of having him stop them and talk to them some more. Vicky wasn't super nice when he'd offered the ride, even if it was odd.

They reached the end of his fence and Samantha breathed a sigh of relief. He wasn't there.

But then his front door opened and his deep voice bellowed to them, "Hey girls! Hey, wait up a sec."

He hurried down his steps and across his well-manicured lawn, his stomach bouncing as he jogged towards them. Mr. Davies had a bushy mustache and thinning brown hair on the top of his head, with thick brown eyebrows hiding his sunken eyes.

"I hope I didn't weird you out earlier when I offered the ride," he said, trying to act casual.

Samantha noticed he focused one hundred percent of his attention on Vicky and her mascara-streaked face as he spoke.

"Hey, you okay there, sweetheart? Did someone hurt you? I'll take care of them for you if you need me to."

"Uhh, no. I'm fine," Vicky said flatly, pulling at Samantha's arm.

Mr. Davies reached across the fence and grabbed Samantha's other arm as they both pulled her, making her feel like a wishbone about to be snapped.

"Hey, I'm trying to apologize here. Can you please wait a minute?" Mr. Davies grumbled, letting go of Samantha's arm. "I realize I may have come across as creepy and I didn't mean to at all. I was really just trying to be neighborly. Any time either of you needs a lift, I'm here for you."

He focused his attention on Vicky again. "I mean it. If you ever stay late at Sam's and you need a ride home, I'd gladly give you a lift. It's no problem at all. You sure you're okay, sweetheart? Do you need a hug?"

“Definitely not,” Vicky said, yanking Samantha’s arm and turning her back on him.

“Sorry, Mr. Davies, we have to go,” Samantha said, trying to be polite.

The two moved quickly past his driveway and broke into a run across the street. Samantha focused on her house, which was two doors down, and made sure to not turn around to see if Mr. Davies was still there watching them.

CHAPTER 15

NOW

CYNTHIA HAS HER phone clutched in a death grip with one hand and is tearing off the sheets of Tori's bed with the other. She has no idea what she's looking for. She knows instinctively that there won't be anything here to give her any clues about Alexander or where Tori may be, but it's the only thing she can control right now.

She is listening to a male voice asking her to leave a message because he is currently away from his desk. At the beep, Cynthia says, "Marshal Dudeck. I need you to get back to me as soon as you get this. My name is Cynthia Burrows. I can explain everything as soon as you call me back. I'm sure Marshal Wright left notes for you explaining my file before she retired. Please call me. Please."

Why didn't Marshal Wright let her know she was retiring? She assumed after all those years together, she would have given her a heads up, right?

As Cynthia makes her way around to the other side of Tori's room, she dials David's number. As expected, she gets his voicemail.

"Hey, can you please come home? Tori is still missing. I can't get into it on voicemail, but I really need you here. I know it's asking a lot, but can you fly back please? Our girl is—"

Cynthia's voice cracks. She takes a moment, breathes deep, and finishes, "—our girl is missing. Call me. I love you."

She hangs up, setting the phone on the desk. Wiping the tears from her eyes, she takes a look around.

Tori's room looks like a normal teen's bedroom. Her dresser is next to the door. Set up against the other wall, across from her bed, is a floor to ceiling bookcase filled with colorful spines of various books. One thing Cynthia has always prided herself on was instilling a love of reading in her daughter.

A pile of clothes sits at the base of the bookcase, spilling out of the closet. Cynthia shakes her head and wishes she had instilled her love of a clean home in Tori. She opens the closet doors and stares at the clothes, glancing up at the boxes on the shelf above. Cynthia pulls one down and rummages through it but finds nothing of value. She leaves the box on the bed and flops into Tori's desk chair, staring out the window, realizing she can see directly into Jacob Harris' room. With the current glare and position of the sun, she isn't sure if he's there or not.

She wonders if Jacob knows anything. Talk about him being creepy, always staring. Cynthia decides as soon as she's done here, she's going to find out. Glancing down, she sees the laptop and admonishes herself for not starting here. She quickly opens the computer and waits for it to boot up. A password screen greets her and she pauses, her fingers hovering over the keyboard, wondering what she should try.

As her fingers come down ready to type, her phone vibrates on the edge of the desk. Cynthia jumps, the rattle startling her. As she reaches for her phone, she knocks it to the ground and it tumbles underneath Tori's bed. She gets on her knees quickly, searching for the device, when she feels another box. Cynthia pulls out a shoe box along with her phone. She answers the call without looking at the caller ID.

Assuming it's Mark calling her back, she snaps, "Mark, what the hell? How did Alexander find me?"

There is quiet for a moment on the other end, then a soft female voice responds, "Cynthia? It's Olivia from the office. I was calling to give you a heads up that Charles is on the rampage looking for you. Do you know when you'll be back? Where did you go?"

"Shit," Cynthia mutters. "I am so sorry, Liv. I will take care of it, I promise. You should not have to deal with that. If he comes at you, tell him to call me right away."

"Oh, it's okay. I can handle him. I was more looking out for you. Is there anything I can do?"

"No, it's fine. It's just a family situation. I'm sure I'll be back in the office in the next hour or two. Thanks."

Before Olivia can ask anything more, Cynthia hangs up, dropping the phone on the bed. She sits next to it with the shoebox in her lap. She has no idea what she's about to see and hesitates to open it for a moment.

What if whatever is in here is something she doesn't want to deal with on top of everything else? What if this explains where Tori is? What if Tori doesn't want to be found?

Cynthia realizes she has no reason to think this and flips the box open, expecting to see love notes or something like she used to keep under her bed. But it's nothing like that. She is shocked and confused.

There are dozens of detention slips for various infractions: cheating, showing up late, bullying. She can't believe what she is looking at. Every piece of paper has Tori's name on it, and many have Cynthia's signature. She looks at the dates, which range from as recently as last week to over two years ago.

How has Tori kept this from her for so long? What happened to her sweet girl?

And what about the phone call from Alexander? Now she has to wonder, was it actually him? It *was* his voice, wasn't it?

It's been such a long time since she actually spoke to him, and she had been thinking about him because of the name on the coffee shop list. Maybe it wasn't him. Maybe this was some elaborate prank by Tori, but how would she have found out about her past? He said her name, didn't he?

Cynthia is reaching for an explanation, for anything that would make some semblance of sense, rather than accepting that Alexander Beaufort has actually found her—and worse, kidnapped her daughter.

Cynthia throws the papers into the box, tucks it under her arm, and grabbing her phone, she marches out of Tori's room. As she is walking down the stairs, the family pictures adorning the wall stream by her like cars on the freeway. Like a truck barreling down the wrong way, the dead bodies from this morning smack into her mind.

Did she have the right address? Maybe she inverted some numbers from the employee list and she stumbled onto some gruesome murder-suicide with some random husband and wife.

Standing in her living room, Cynthia has a thought. She sets the box down and pulls out her phone. She quickly Googles:

"Instances of teens faking a kidnapping to get away from their parents."

There are dozens of results, all across the US. She clicks two links and briefly reads the first few lines of each article.

"Candy thought her parents were being completely unfair because they wouldn't let her go out with a twenty year old . . ."

"Joseph had been angry because his mother wouldn't loan him the car she needed to go to work . . ."

"Danny and Matthew were twin brothers living with their grandmother. When she put her foot down finally, telling them they needed to get a job, they thought they'd get even and make her think they'd been kidnapped . . ."

Cynthia can feel her world beginning to crumble around her. She remembers the last time her world fell out from under her. It was a lifetime ago, and in someone else's body, and she refuses to allow it to happen again.

She realizes this research would be a lot easier on her computer, but it's at the office.

Every time in her life when things feel like they are slipping through her grasp, she focuses on what she can control. Right now, the only thing she can control is where she goes and what she does.

Quickly glancing at the box under her arm, a plan forms in her mind.

Looking at the time on her phone, 12:30, she knows Sofia will be done with practice shortly. She can go meet with her, head back to the office, get her laptop, tell Charles to cut the shit, and stop by the Marshals building, as it isn't far from her office downtown.

With a plan in place, Cynthia nods at herself, pockets her phone, grabs her purse by the door, and brings the shoebox of detention slips with her. She needs to figure out exactly who Tori is and if Alexander is actually responsible.

CHAPTER 16

NOW

CYNTHIA STARES AT the dashboard clock of her car, sitting in the parking lot of Shoreline High School. A newer addition to San Diego built five years ago, it looks more like a college campus than a high school. The buildings are modular in design, with enough space in between them for large, shaded trees, various seating areas, and grass patches where students hang out between classes or study halls.

Cynthia parked her car between the edge of the school and the beginning of the sports complex. From where she is, she can see the edge of the pool along with the tennis courts and a bit of the grass from the softball field. Most of the parking lot is already empty as the half day cleared out the majority of the student population. She assumes the cars that are still here belong to teachers and those students who are at their various practices.

When the clock turns to 12:55, Cynthia grabs a handful of the papers from the shoebox and gets out of her car. She is rushing towards the pool but then realizes she still has a few minutes. She slows down, thinking about how she wants to play this.

Cynthia doesn't want to spook Sofia and cause her to shut down, or just say what she thinks Cynthia wants to hear. She turns on her defense attorney's mind and thinks about this like a case.

She needs to find out what Sofia knows about Tori, and the truth about what Tori's been up to. She decides she'll save the detention slips for the very end, only if Sofia paints some kind of rosy picture of Tori.

Arriving at the edge of the fence, Cynthia peers in. The girls from the swim team are doing various exercises. There is a big dry erase board at the edge of the pool with a combination of numbers and words written on it. The only words Cynthia understands are the words "push-ups" and "frogs," but she has no idea what they mean as they relate to swimming.

She scans the pool for Sofia, but doesn't see her. There are a few girls that could be Sofia on the far end, but they're all wearing swimming caps. She watches one girl she thinks is Sofia doing what looks like part of a burpee, jumping up, then squatting down. Cynthia counts her doing this five times and then watches as she dives into the pool, swimming toward the side where Cynthia is standing.

The coach blows the whistle and the girls finish whatever exercise they were currently working on.

"Great practice, ladies! Get some rest and eat right tonight. We win our meet tomorrow and we go to CIF!"

All the girls cheer. Cynthia isn't sure what CIF is, but she assumes it has to do with playoffs or something.

A few of the girls near Cynthia are already out of the pool with towels wrapped around them. They grab their bags and head toward her. A couple of them smile while a few others stare at her, confused. She knows she looks out of place in her pantsuit and heels.

She waits for them to pass and steps into the pool area. Cynthia keeps her eye on the girl she thinks is Sofia until she takes off the swimming cap and a head of blond hair tumbles out.

Definitely not Sofia. The coach makes eye contact with Cynthia and moves towards her, taking care to avoid the wet spots of the pool.

"Can I help you?" he asks, not in a rude manner, but a helpful tone.

"Is Sofia here? She said she had practice. She and my daughter are friends."

"Wish I could help. She didn't show up for practice, which is weird because I know she was at school today and it's not like her to miss practice."

Cynthia swallows hard. A knot is forming in her gut, but she doesn't want the coach to see her worry.

"Okay, thanks anyway."

"Maybe your daughter can reach out, make sure she's okay?"

Cynthia nods and walks away, waving at him without turning around. She picks up her pace and heads toward the front doors of the school. Her heels click and clack on the tile floor as she marches down to the front office. The receptionist is hunched over, her cat-eye glasses perched at the end of her nose. A scowl is spread across her face as she hunts and pecks at the keys of her keyboard.

"Excuse me," Cynthia says, a little too harshly.

The older lady jumps back in her chair and puts her hand to her heart over her gray cardigan. Cynthia can see the overtly bright colors of a yellow floral top underneath.

"Oh my dear. You startled me. I'm sorry, but all the students are gone."

"I know. I'm actually hoping to talk to my daughter's teachers. Are they still here?"

The older lady reaches up and twirls the ends of her straight gray hair, which is parted in the middle and hangs loosely at her shoulders.

"Yes, but they had a staff development day and aren't really available to speak right now."

Cynthia slams the stack of detention slips on the counter and says, "Look, I know none of this is on you, but my daughter is missing. I just found these and I need to speak with her teachers about them. Please."

From behind the receptionist desk, a door opens and a younger woman, who looks to be about Cynthia's age, steps out.

"Hello, may I help you? I'm Principal Andrews."

"Yes, you may. My name is Cynthia Burrows. Tori Burrows is my daughter. Someone told me she never showed up for school today and was excused. But her father and I had not excused her. Now we believe she's missing and I found these under her bed. I need to speak with her teachers to see if they know where she might be or who she might be with."

Principal Andrews goes rigid. "Oh yes. Burrows. Well, are you sure? Many times, these teens think they're in control and act out to prove it."

Cynthia sighs and rubs her temples. "Honestly, I'm not sure of anything anymore. But I need to find out what I can. It's urgent. Please. I can't get into everything, but I need to know if my daughter is truly just acting out or if something bad has actually happened."

There is a moment of silence between the three, with the receptionist's eyes bouncing between the two women. Principal

Andrews then asks the receptionist, "Can you please look up Tori Burrows' teachers and send them all a message to meet me in the library as soon as possible? Let them know her mother is here."

CHAPTER 17

NOW

CYNTHIA FEELS LIKE she is being cross-examined. It is just her on one side of a table in the library with all the teachers and Principal Andrews seated opposite her. The size of the library is impressive for a high school. It reminds her how much of their taxes go to this school. Did they know about Tori's behavior? The detention slips indicate they did. Did they think she, as a parent, would just simply sign her name to all of those without follow-up?

As soon as the teachers are focused on her, Cynthia asks her first question: "Can any of you help me understand the kind of student Tori is?"

Or was?

The errant thought flows through her. She knows if Alexander has taken her, she will still be alive. He said he'd give her three days, because that's how long it took her to find—

She can't.

She won't allow herself to dredge up her past right now, not in front of all these teachers.

The last thing she needs is to break down in front of them all.

All the teachers look at each other and one of the male teachers clears his throat. "Here's what I'll say," he starts.

"I'm sorry. Can you please introduce yourself? I don't know who you all are," Cynthia asks.

"Of course," he says, nodding. He can't be over thirty years old, and Cynthia imagines many of the female and maybe some of the male students have a crush on him. He looks like he stepped right out of a *GQ* magazine with his broad shoulders, thick chestnut brown hair, chiseled features, and piercing blue eyes.

"I'm Mr. Montgomery. I teach English. As a student, Tori is basically straight A's. I think she has been bored with school for some time. But she doesn't cause noticeable trouble in my class."

Before he can continue, one of the older women chirps, "Yeah, because they're all in love with you."

Principal Andrews chides her, "Rebecca, please."

The woman puts her hands up and Principal Andrews says, "Robert, please continue."

Mr. Montgomery nods and says, "As I was saying, she doesn't cause noticeable trouble in my class. I know from observing her and the other students that Tori is definitely within the inner circle of the A-Crew."

"What is that?" Cynthia asks.

"The A-Crew is what the popular kids have dubbed themselves. They are the class president, the captains of the sports teams, etcetera. As they walk around campus, students will literally move out of their way, like Moses parting the Red Sea," Mr. Montgomery says, making motions with his arms.

For a moment, Cynthia's pride envelops her, hearing that her daughter is held in such high regard. But Mr. Montgomery continues, quickly deflating any feelings Cynthia has.

"The reason all the students move out of the way when A-Crew is walking through is because they don't want to get any retribution from them. The student body has learned that if you stay out of A-Crew's way, they'll leave you alone and won't humiliate you. We have had problems with A-Crew for the last few years.

"They're almost like a gang with their initiations. It's not like it's one group of kids and when they graduate, it'll go away. They recruit new members, many of whom are freshmen, and that's who they get to do their dirty work. We know this because we typically see an influx of freshman violations at the end of the first quarter, which tapers off as the year goes on. This cycle repeats each year."

"Why don't you put a stop to it?"

Principal Andrews smiles as if Cynthia just asked the funniest question. "We have tried and tried. Trust me. But A-Crew gets wiser and wiser as the years go on. We've started to talk with the local seventh and eighth grade classes around town, trying to instill doing the right thing. But only time will tell if that will work."

There is quiet among the teachers for a moment. Cynthia is confounded at what she is hearing and wonders how Tori is involved.

Almost as if reading her mind, Mr. Montgomery continues, but pauses just as fast. "Tori is—"

Cynthia leans forward, waiting for him to continue. She makes a motion with her hand, trying to get him to continue. "She's what?"

"I don't know exactly. At times, it seems like she knows what she is doing is wrong, but then other times, it's like she is pushed, convinced, then follows the others into trouble. It's been this way since freshman year."

"I'm sorry, freshman year?!" Cynthia says, shocked. This is way worse than she could have imagined. What is Tori caught up in? What does any of this have to do with Alexander and him taking her?

Cynthia is rubbing her temples, trying to digest this information.

"What about boys and Tori? Did she have a boyfriend here? Were there a lot of guys who hung around her?"

The older teacher bobs her head up and down. "Ms. Beauregard, Math Three. I wouldn't say there was any one guy. Guys and girls in A-Crew flow between each other and no one is really committed. I do recall recently, when I was on lunch duty, there was some kind of dust-up between one boy and Tori. I remember her talking loudly to him that he didn't know who it was and to drop it. He walked off and that seemed to be it."

Cynthia doesn't know if this means anything. She's finding it difficult to know how any of this could have led to Tori's disappearance.

"Is there anything else I need to know?"

Cynthia isn't sure she can handle anything else. She thinks the teachers see that in her eyes, and all of them shake their heads and give her looks of sorrow. She nods, puts her palms flat on the table, and pushes up.

"Okay, well, thank you, I think. Can I call if I have any other questions?"

Cynthia looks to the principal as she asks this and Ms. Andrews nods. "Of course, of course. You can always reach out and check in. We know she'll turn up, and please let us know if you need anything more from us."

Cynthia finds enough resolve to get her feet moving and focuses on walking out of the library without wobbling. As soon as she's out of the room and down the hall, she stops, placing her hand on the wall to steady herself.

"Excuse me, Mrs. Burrows?" a soft voice calls behind her.

Cynthia tries to compose herself and not look like she was about to faint. She turns and runs her fingers through her hair.

"Yes?"

It's one of the teachers that was in the library, but she hadn't said anything. She is young, similar to Mr. Montgomery, and pretty. She can't be more than twenty-six or twenty-seven, and just as the one teacher talked about the girls being in love with Mr. Montgomery, Cynthia is certain the boys have some thoughts about this teacher.

"I'm Ms. Samuels. I teach life skills."

"Yes. Hello," Cynthia says, reaching out her hand, hoping it isn't too clammy. "Was there something you thought of?"

"Well, actually," Ms. Samuels starts, glancing behind her. "I—I'm not sure. I teach life skills, so I learn a bit more about what kids do these days, so I can try and relate to them with what will be waiting for them after high school."

"Okay?" Cynthia responds, completely unsure where this is going.

"I know you learned about a new side to Tori today. And I have no idea if she has one of these or not, but I felt you should know about it, just in case. There's this thing called finsta. It's like Instagram—well, it is Instagram. It's just a different Instagram account some kids have. You might want to look into it and see if Tori has one."

Cynthia is confused. She obviously knows what Instagram is, but Ms. Samuels isn't making much sense.

Other voices fill the hall and Ms. Samuels glances behind her as the other teachers are making their way towards the two of them.

"Feel free to give me a call if you need help or anything, if she has one," Ms. Samuels says. "I hope she doesn't."

The other teachers reach them and Mr. Montgomery asks, "Hey Beth, you joining us for lunch?"

"Of course," Ms. Samuels says, her voice a bit higher and more flirtatious.

As she walks off with the other teachers, she touches Cynthia's arm. "Let me know if I can help. Please."

The teachers walk off, leaving Cynthia alone in the hallway. She reaches into her purse, grabs her phone, and searches, "What is finsta?"

CHAPTER 18

NOW

THE WORD BOUNCES around in Cynthia's mind as she gets back to her car. Finsta. Finsta. What is finsta?

It is the first thing she Googles as she reaches her car door. She reads the first result:

"Finsta is an abbreviated slang term for fake Instagram. It refers to a private account teens can create and keep secret from their parents. The account their parents see is the Instagram account the teen wants them to see, but usually, their finsta account is their real one, under a different name."

Cynthia rereads the breakdown several times, trying to grasp the notion that her daughter would have one of these finsta accounts. She brings up Instagram, finds Tori's profile, and looks through the pictures and reels.

They all look wholesome—pictures of Tori and Sofia at different school events, funny reels of Tori and her friends doing the latest dance trends, sunset snaps from the beach, and even a couple of Cynthia and David.

She goes back to Google and searches: "How to find a finsta account."

Most of the results reference having a conversation with your child and searching their phone while they're logged in.

"Easier said than done," Cynthia mutters to her phone.

She finds another blog that gives her more of what she's looking for:

"If you're attempting to uncover a finsta account without your child knowing you're looking for it, here are a few tips:

If you can get into your child's phone, look for another account they have access to from the app.

Place a tracking software on your child's phone and record when they go into the app you want to know information about.

This one is a bit tricky, but if for whatever reason you can't get your child's phone, you can look through all of those they follow and see if any account stands out. Is there a follower with the name of their childhood imaginary friend? The name of one of their childhood stuffed animals? Kids typically name these accounts something that means something to them. They typically follow this account from their main one—it's easier for them to access it that way."

Cynthia looks up from her phone. It's worth a shot. She can think of a couple of names of imaginary friends Tori had growing up, but she isn't sure Tori remembers those. The name of Tori's favorite stuffy comes slamming into her mind: Fluffernutter. It was her favorite oversized, extra soft teddy bear. David's mom had given it to her when she turned one.

She starts scrolling faster through all of Tori's followers, unsure if Tori would name it exactly the same way. She is getting to the bottom of the list and losing heart. But when she gets there, she stops, her heart rate picking up, just as it did when she saw Alexander's name on the employee list.

Staring back at her was a follower that started with an underscore: _fluff_ER_NUTter.

Cynthia gulps and taps on the name of the account. She can't believe what comes up. Images and videos of Tori and several others in all kinds of scenarios, positions, and situations fill the account. Cynthia can't believe it's public.

What the actual hell is she looking at?

She starts doomscrolling through all the images, not wanting to focus too hard on any one picture. They are all drinking, smoking, making out, doing other obscene things with each other.

Where were these taken? When did this happen? Where were *we*? Where are the parents of these other kids?

How could she not have known about this entire other side of her daughter?

Was she right? Is this whole thing some elaborate prank by Tori?

She leans heavily against the side of the car.

No, it can't be. I spoke to him.

She evidently did not truly know her own flesh and blood. There had been a stranger living under her roof.

Cynthia thought she and David—well, more her than him—had done a good job teaching Tori about the dangers of the world. Evidently, they hadn't done so well. She thinks about all the times she taught her about the kind of people that are out there. How you could think you know someone your whole life and they end up being completely different.

Tears well up as she thinks, *how ironic.*

The one thing I knew so much about was the same thing that was happening right under my roof.

Cynthia stops scrolling at a specific video. It's a clip of Tori making out with a boy and imitating some very graphic acts. Beyond that, it's the boy she is making out with that gives Cynthia chills.

The one boy Tori swore she wanted nothing to do with, the boy who was always cold to her throughout entire life, is the one with whom she is imitating some very disturbing things.

Jacob Harris from across the street.

She filters through Sofia not being at practice, what she saw on the finsta account, what the teachers said, and she knows exactly where she has to go next. The office and the Marshals are going to have to wait.

She needs to talk to Jacob, and she needs to talk to him now.

CHAPTER 19

NOW

THERE WAS NO child creepier than Jacob Harris.

Cynthia doesn't even slow down as she screeches into her driveway, the front end of her BMW scraping on the dip. The car rolls back slightly as she forgets to engage the parking brake.

Cynthia and Mrs. Harris have a tumultuous neighborhood friendship. Mrs. Harris has always thought her son to be the perfect young man, but Cynthia had not only heard stories of him growing up, but had witnessed some fairly concerning behavior from him in the early stages of puberty.

As she marches toward the Harris home, she recalls one instance when Tori had a thirteenth birthday party and Mrs. Harris all but forced an invitation for her son. Even though it was a bunch of tweens, Tori had wanted a bounce house. She and her friends thought it'd be funny. A bunch of them were in there when a couple of the girls came out screaming and saying that Jacob had touched them inappropriately. He claimed he'd been bouncing and fell over. Mrs. Harris swore he would never do such a thing.

Cynthia walks up the staggered stone steps and pounds

on the thick blue door with rectangular inlays. The more she thinks about what she saw from Tori's finsta account and the other rumored stories of Jacob watching the girls play and touching himself, the more infuriated she becomes.

She isn't sure if her anger is toward Tori, Mrs. Harris, or Jacob himself. All she knows is she has to talk to him and learn what she can about his and Tori's . . . whatever it was. All she knows is she refuses to call it a relationship.

She doesn't stop pounding until a heavier-set woman, who is much shorter than Cynthia, throws the door open. Looking down at the top of her head, Cynthia can see the woman's thinning hair, showing the various freckles and marks on the top of her head.

With her glasses perched on the edge of her nose, she looks up at Cynthia and snarls, "What the actual hell?"

"Where is he?" Cynthia demands.

"Where is who?"

"Don't play with me, Margaret. Jacob, where is he? I know he's here. What did he do with Tori?"

Mrs. Harris steps forward over the threshold of her home and down onto the front porch. Cynthia never realized just how short she was, but even with their height difference now more extreme, the woman still forces Cynthia to take a step back.

"He isn't here. And you can show me some respect and call me Mrs. Harris. And don't you ever come over here accusing my son of anything. He's a sweet boy. He's just misunderstood."

Cynthia moves toward her, using every inch of her height, and demands, "Let me in. I need to speak to him."

Cynthia is pushing her way into the Harris home while Mrs. Harris is grabbing her to keep her out when she hears a rattling engine coming up behind her. The wheels give a *thunk,* and Cynthia turns to see Mr. Harris and Jacob pulling up in a classic gold Mercedes.

The two in the car look confused at the sight of Cynthia and Mrs. Harris in a half hold. Cynthia lets go and steps back, almost stumbling backward off the top step.

She stands there and waits for Mr. Harris and Jacob to exit the car. Cynthia finds Jacob's frailness surprising. If he had anything to do with Tori's disappearance, he certainly didn't overpower her. Maybe he and this Blue Eyes kid conspired on this together. Who knows, with today's technology and AI, they probably created some voice saying it was Alexander.

But how would they have even known about him?

As the two approach the front door, Jacob's shoulders sag and he looks as thin as a rail. His greasy black hair is parted in the middle and the sides stick to his head. His beady eyes add to the overall look of creep. Cynthia wonders what ever could have gotten into Tori's head to get anywhere near him, let alone make out with him and do God knows what else.

As he gets to the front door, Mr. Harris goes inside, looking about as small as Jacob does right now. His bald head nods towards Cynthia, and his wire-framed glasses make him look twenty years older than he actually is. It's obvious to Cynthia that Mrs. Harris runs this house, and Mr. Harris can probably only speak when told to.

Jacob stands behind his mother and mutters to Cynthia, "Hello."

"Do not speak to her," Mrs. Harris growls, pushing him behind her, all the while staring at Cynthia.

"Just get inside," she tells him. Jacob obeys and takes a few steps inside, but stays put in the entryway.

Cynthia wonders again if this kid could have actually done

something to Tori. He looks like he's scared of his own shadow. She recalls a time when the kids were around seven or eight and she had offered to take them all to the park. She had been talking to another mom with her back to the children when suddenly, she heard a horrific scream.

She had whirled around, and not seeing the children, she panicked. She had screamed, "Tori!"

A small voice yelled for her, "Mom! Hurry!"

Cynthia realized that the kids had gone down to the lower playground. She sprinted down there, the other mom she'd been with on her heels.

Tori and Jacob stood at the top of the play structure, staring down. Tori had tears streaming down her face, her whole body convulsing in hysterics. Cynthia ran to them and saw the other neighbor girl, Sandy, lying there like a corpse outline, screaming in pain.

"What happened?!" Cynthia yelled.

"He—he—he pushed her," Tori stuttered between sobs.

Cynthia couldn't believe what she was hearing. "Tori! What did you say?"

"He pushed her!" she screamed, moving away from Jacob.

Jacob just stood there, staring down at Sandy.

"Jacob! Is this true?" Cynthia asked while helping Sandy sit up, cradling her head. She felt something wet on her palm. Pulling her hand away, she saw red. Sandy had calmed down, but it didn't take a genius for Cynthia to realize she needed a doctor, quick.

Cynthia looked to the other mom and said, "Call 911, please."

Turning back to the two at the top of the structure, Cynthia asked again, "Jacob! Is this true?"

He rounded his shoulders as if he was trying to turn in on

himself. He glanced at Tori and back at Sandy. A single tear rolled down his cheek, and he subtly nodded his head.

"What do you want with him?!" Mrs. Harris snaps, bringing Cynthia back to the present.

"Tori is missing, and I'm sure he had something to do with it. I've seen obscene pictures of the two of them and he has a history of violence against girls."

Cynthia tries pushing past Mrs. Harris and into the home, shouting at him, "What did you do with her?! What do you know?"

He stands a few feet away from his mom, near a hutch by the middle of the stairs, and rubs his arm. "I wish I could help you, I really do. But—but, I—I don't know where she went."

Cynthia picks up on this strange verbiage. "What do you mean, *where she went*?"

He looks at his mom and back at Cynthia, then shrugs his shoulders.

"Jacob!" Cynthia snaps, but Mrs. Harris is a lot stronger than she appears and pushes Cynthia back.

She takes a deep breath and tries a different approach, softening her tone. "Please, Jacob, if you have any idea where she is or went, please tell me."

"I—I'm sorry, I really am. I really, really wish I could help you. She broke up with me like over a week ago."

Mrs. Harris spins on this and snaps at him, "You were seeing that slut?!"

Cynthia lunges at Mrs. Harris and growls, "Don't you dare speak about my daughter like that."

"All I know is there was some new kid she wanted to hook up with and I was no good to her anymore. That's all I know. I promise."

Mrs. Harris steps inside, grabs the front door, and, closing it, says, "That's enough. He needs to go rest. When he gets riled up, he gets migraines. He was at his therapist and doctor's all morning, so he'll be no more help to you."

CHAPTER 20

NOW

JACOB STANDS FROZEN in his spot, rubbing his forearm. He has several sores from his habit of rubbing the same spot when he's nervous. He knows he shouldn't move until his mother tells him to. She is busy staring out the peephole, most likely making sure Mrs. Burrows is leaving.

Their home looks like a 1980s replica. The couch is a bright orange color and sits against the wall nearest the door. An oversized Zenith TV sits exactly opposite the couch. In between the two, against the far wall, a large hutch displays dozens of Precious Moments figurines. A white linoleum laminate floor paves the way to the kitchen and butts up against the blue shag carpet covering the living room.

Mrs. Harris spins around and snarls at him, "I do not want to hear you speak any of their names ever again. If you do, I will kick you out. Do you understand?"

Jacob nods.

"You're dismissed. You stay in your room until we call you down for dinner. No computer, no TV, no video games."

Jacob doesn't wait around for any more of a lecture. He

only hopes Mrs. Burrows hasn't found out what he did. He knew if she had, it would be more than just her at his front door.

As he pounds up the beige carpeted stairs, his mom yells at him, "I don't want you going anywhere near that woman or her daughter! Do you hear me?"

As he gets to the top, he can still hear her talking to his dad. "She is just a horrible, horrible woman. She has no care or concern for anyone but herself and her family. Didn't you see her try to push me over to enter our home? Did you see that?"

Jacob can't hear what his father is saying in reply as he closes his bedroom door, shutting them out.

His room faces the street, and so many times, with his binoculars or telescope, he would look directly into Tori's window. One day, working on his math homework, he had looked out and saw Tori facing her window, blinds completely open, changing her shirt and taking off her bra. When she'd taken an extra minute to stretch, completely topless, he knew what he needed. That Christmas, he had asked for a telescope, and he'd kept it right next to his desk ever since. His parents never asked him about it, which surprised him, but it worked to his advantage.

Tori never closed her blinds to change, and he swore she would do this on purpose, as if she wanted him to see her. He knew it was what he was supposed to do. It was his right to watch her.

He walks over to the window and stands just out of sight, behind his curtain, so anyone looking up won't notice him.

Mrs. Burrows is standing in the middle of the street, pacing back and forth and turning in circles. She is brushing her hand through her hair and talking animatedly to someone.

Jacob takes the risk while she faces away from their house and slides open his window.

"Gabby, thanks for getting back to me. Yes, I spoke with him. He called me!"

Mrs. Burrows turns back toward their house and Jacob moves quickly to hide behind the curtain. He accidentally moves it and hopes she doesn't notice from down below. He waits to see if she will say anything else to this Gabby person.

He hears her say, "Yes, I'd recognize that voice anywhere. I think. It had to be. But how could it?"

He wonders who this Gabby person is, and who Mrs. Burrows is talking about. He is wondering now if it actually has anything to do with him. Maybe not exactly what he thought she wanted, but he knows he could be of some help to her. He knows Tori isn't at school and wonders if Mrs. Burrows knows that or not. He decides he'll keep an eye on that situation, and if it comes to it, he can always talk to her later, once his parents go to Bible study.

If his mom catches him going across the street, it's uncertain what punishment she will impose on him. He's done a lot of terrible things, but nothing compared to his mother's hatred of Mrs. Burrows.

He can hear her sigh in the street and say, "Yes, I'm sure of it. There is so much more to tell you."

There is another pause. "Okay, thanks. Yes, I'll talk to you soon. Thanks again."

Jacob waits a few more seconds, and when he thinks the coast is clear, he peeks his head around the curtain and looks down. Mrs. Burrows is walking back to her house, and he recognizes the errant thought trying to take over his focus. Like his therapist had taught him, he stops it before it gets too far.

He knows that thinking about where Tori got her figure from would lead him down a path from which he would struggle to recover.

Jacob's room isn't large and has just enough space for his desk, his bed directly behind him, and a closet on the right-hand side. He moves over to it and opens the sliding door nearest his bed.

He moves a couple of boxes of comic books and pulls out his switchblade. Flicking it open, he uses it to pry open a small piece of drywall he had cut out a while ago. He knew he needed a place to hide things from his parents when they did random room searches, which had become more infrequent as he put on the front of "doing the right thing."

Jacob reaches inside the dark gap, gropes around, and quickly finds what he is looking for. He pulls out the old bed sheet and makes himself comfortable on his bed. He waits for a beat, listening for any footsteps coming up the stairs. Confident that he hears nothing, he unwraps the bed sheet, slowly and carefully revealing a worn journal.

Staring at it for a minute and admiring the worn leather, he runs his hand across the cover, caressing it in his own way. He takes a deep breath and opens it.

CHAPTER 21

JOURNAL

YOU KNOW, I'VE been trying and trying to pinpoint the single time that did it for me. I've been wanting to know what the turning point was. I've studied some of the greats: Dahmer, Bundy, Gacy, but it's always hindsight. None of them have any interviews where they talk about knowing the point where they first started thinking about taking someone's life.

I'm sure for myself, they'll know once they look back and outline my whole life, childhood and all. At that point, I'm sure they'll be able to say, "Oh it was here." Or "Oh, this is what started it all."

I don't think, for where I'm at and where I know I'm going, it matters all that much. Whether I can pinpoint the exact moment I began thinking about killing someone doesn't matter as much as knowing it's going to happen. It's simply a matter of when.

There are many times that blur together to form a sort of tapestry, if you will. Like that one time with the girl. I regularly think of that as possibly one of the first times. Even though all I'd done was push her off the play structure, I had wished we were much higher up. I had wanted to see her land on her head. To hear her neck snap. To watch the life leave her eyes.

Unfortunately, none of that happened. She landed on her side and her arm. I definitely saw her head hit hard, and that was something, but nothing like what I'd hoped for.

I think, for the first time, I don't want it to be something extreme or elaborate. I don't want anyone to find the body until I'm ready for them to, and I don't want to be featured on the news. At least, not at first. I want to be able to hone my craft, to get good at death. I want to look back once the world knows about me and realize I have this little secret. So many more kills than anyone actually knows about.

Then, maybe right before my time is up, I'll drop that bomb on the world. Oh man, to see their faces, to hear the commentary of the destruction I will have caused. How sweet that would be.

If you haven't been able to tell by now, I have come to embrace the thoughts and wonders and feelings I've been having. I know this is who I am and I'm okay with it. I refuse to apologize for how I have been made. I won't hold back on the desires I have.

The only thing to focus on now is two things: one, the who, and two, the when.

CHAPTER 22
THEN

VICKY SAT ON Samantha's bed while Samantha brushed Vicky's hair. Like she did every time she came over, the first thing Vicky said was, "Your room is like the size of my living room."

Samantha secretly hated it when Vicky would say this, because she never knew how to respond. To her, her room was her room. She knew it was big, but not compared to anything else. It had space for her four-poster bed, a desk and mirror combo to the right, and on the left, an oversize bean bag chair and a small bookcase with a reading lamp. Sure, she had her own bathroom, but her closet was like any other—it wasn't a walk-in or anything.

"He gives me the willies," Vicky said, shuddering.

"Yeah, I know. I really think he's harmless, though."

"Ugh, you're so trusting. That's gonna get you in trouble," Vicky chided. "You have to watch out for yourself. No one else will."

Samantha looked at her in the mirror they were both staring at. She ran the brush down Vicky's hair and followed it with her hand. She didn't respond right away because she wasn't sure how to. On the one hand, she thought if anyone knew people, it was Vicky. She had been through so much in her life. But Samantha knew she had a good home life with a mom and dad who loved her, and they had taught her differently.

"Yeah," was all Samantha could come up with.

"I'm telling you, if he hasn't taken some girl before, he'll do it soon enough," Vicky said with a hard tone.

Samantha really wanted to be done with this conversation. "Hey! Let's focus on what's important!" She put down the hairbrush and bounced on the bed, getting Vicky to look at her. "It's your birthday!"

The girls squealed and laughed, falling on the bed with their heads opposite each other. After a moment, Samantha reached under her pillow, pulled out a small box, and sat up.

"Here, happy birthday."

"Awww, thanks bestie," Vicky crooned.

She ripped off the paper, opened the lid, and looked confused. She pulled out a multicolored butterfly clip and turned it around in her hand.

Samantha showed her the *S & V* on the back side of it. "I made it and put our initials on it. Do you like it?"

"You made this?" Vicky asked, astounded.

Samantha shrugged. "Put it on, see how it looks."

Vicky took the clip and placed it on the side of her head, getting off the bed and moving closer to the mirror.

"I love it, thank you," she said, hugging Samantha.

The two moved back to the bed and Vicky said, "God, I'm so excited for this weekend!"

"What do you have planned?"

Vicky played with the clip on her hair for a minute, a smirk on her face. "My mom and her boyfriend are going to be gone, and he's coming over!"

Samantha was uneasy about this. She knew Vicky had way more experience with boys than she had. Samantha's dad had told her she was nowhere near old enough to date, and he'd also told her some scary things about boys and what they want.

"Be careful, okay?" Samantha asked, looking at her butterfly bedspread.

"God, you're so boring," Vicky chided, bumping her shoulder into Samantha. "Nothing exciting has ever happened to you. You need to get out there, experience the world." Vicky lowered her voice. "Experience boys."

The two girls giggled and pushed into each other until quiet settled over them. Samantha knew Vicky was the only one she could ask about these things. Any other girl at school would make fun of her and shout her questions to everyone else, just to embarrass her.

"I mean, what are you even going to do with him?"

Vicky's laugh echoed around Samantha's room.

"Shhh," Samantha whispered. "My parents will wonder what we're talking about."

"Well, you see, when he first comes over, we won't do much. Probably just talk on the couch, and little by little, I'll inch closer to him until our knees are touching. I'll let him make the first move, but if he doesn't get the hint, I'll lean my head on his shoulder. At that point, he'll most likely slide his hand into mine."

"Well, that doesn't sound too bad," Samantha interrupted. "It actually sounds pretty nice."

"Ha!" Vicky laughed loudly again. "You're so gullible. As soon as he gets there, I'm gonna jump on him and straddle him and start making out. I'll be lucky if my shirt stays on for more than two minutes."

Samantha's mouth hung open. She couldn't believe what she heard. Before Vicky could say anything more, there was a knock on the half-open door and Samantha's dad poked his head in.

"Hey, you girls want ice cream sundaes? I hear it's someone's birthday."

Samantha and Vicky looked at each other with enormous eyes and both shouted, "Yes!"

They shimmied off the bed and Samantha asked, "Extra nuts and whipped cream?"

"Sure!" he replied.

Vicky mumbled under her breath so that only Samantha could hear, "Sounds like you're describing my weekend."

Samantha had no idea what she meant, so she acted like she never heard it.

Her dad stepped inside the room, fully opening the door, and Samantha passed him first. She turned once she was in the hallway and saw him grab Vicky's arm and look down at her. She wasn't sure if she was supposed to see this or hear him, but she could.

"Be careful," he whispered to Vicky. "Boys want more than you think."

CHAPTER 23

NOW

CYNTHIA MANEUVERS OUT of her driveway and guns it down the street, knowing a handful of the stay-at-home moms are scowling at her through their windows.

Hold your babies tight. You have no idea the kind of people that are out there.

Traffic is flowing smoothly as Cynthia makes her way south to her office. Now that she is still, the stress from the day radiates throughout her back.

How was it only this morning that Tori didn't show up for school?

Where are you? What has he done to you?

That thought sparks a world of ideas that Cynthia wants nothing to do with. She knows the heinous killer Alexander was and most likely still is. The last thing she needs to think about is him touching her daughter.

She can't. She refuses. She won't allow herself to go there.

Just as she is spiraling down a dark path, one she swore to herself she would never go down again, her phone rings.

Glancing at it on the dock, she sees Gabby's smiling contact picture and presses the answer circle.

"Hey," is all she can say.

"You doing okay?" Gabby's sweet voice asks.

Cynthia cries. She's been holding it together well, but with everything, she just can't contain it anymore.

"I don't know, Gabs. Where is my little girl? Why is all this happening? Who even is she?"

"Hey, hey. Calm down, okay? Take a deep breath, in through your nose. I told you I'd call you back as soon as I was out of that meeting. So talk to me. You said you spoke to him? You're sure it was Alexander? What did he say? What do you mean 'who is she?'"

Cynthia breathes deep like Gabby instructed her and finds her center. She needs to stay focused on the road and refuses to break down emotionally while going eighty miles an hour down the freeway.

"He said he'd been looking for me for a long time. I think it was him, but seeing the people Tori was actually hanging out with, I don't know. I don't know if she was involved in this, if the creepy kid next door and the guy she was supposed to go out with took her and made some AI voice—"

"Whoa, whoa. Let me stop you there," Gabby says firmly. "You know, as a lawyer, the simplest answer is usually the right one. Don't start concocting these crazy, elaborate scenarios. I know you are looking for some other option, rather than the obvious one. But if you say he said he's been looking for you for a long time, it has to be him.

"You always said I was the only one to truly know who you were. So the obvious solution is Alexander took Tori. And we can work with that. We'll find him, find her, get her back, and lock him away for good. Okay?"

Cynthia is nodding even though she knows Gabby can't see her.

"What about the couple? What about the kid's name from the coffee shop?"

Gabby is quiet on the other end of the phone.

"Gabby?"

"Yeah, those are mysteries we're going to have to figure out. But if he has been looking for you for a long time, he probably had quite the plan in place, right? That's where the Marshals and the full force of the FBI come in. We have your back. That's what we do. We put the bad guys away. Okay?"

"Okay," Cynthia says, taking another deep breath. "I'm pulling into the parking garage now. I needed to come to the office and then I'm stopping by the Marshals' office. Thanks Gabs. I don't know what I'd do without you right now."

"You're welcome. Don't worry. I'm on it."

CHAPTER 24

NOW

CYNTHIA LISTENS TO the elevator music as she travels up to the twenty-fourth floor. She stares at her reflection in the doors, brushing down her hair and smoothing out her pantsuit. When the doors open, Cynthia is greeted with the law office title in large gold letters against the mahogany paneling. The paneling continues down the hall, but only on the lower half, with the upper half being a semi-frosted glass. Beyond it, there are associates milling about, talking across cubicles and reviewing case files.

Olivia can barely be seen over the oversized receptionist desk. As soon as she spots Cynthia, she brightens up and indicates she should stay there while she's on the phone. Cynthia waits a moment at the desk as Olivia wraps up her call. "Yes, I will let him know. Thank you. Have a great day."

Olivia presses a button on her headset and pulls it off her head. "Hey! How are you?! Is everything okay?"

Cynthia knows she's just being kind, but there is no way she's going to get into everything that has happened.

"Honestly, everything is not okay, but I'm working on it."

Olivia looks shocked that Cynthia didn't say everything was fine. "Is there anything I can do?"

Cynthia shakes her head and offers the best smile she can.

"I appreciate it, but no. I'm sorry, but I have to go," Cynthia says as she walks away.

She regrets leaving Olivia in the dark, but Tori is her priority right now. She doesn't look back to see if Olivia is looking at her, but focuses solely on her office, ignoring the first and second years at their cubicles.

Once inside her office, she shuts the door and sits down, her fingers flying on the keys of her laptop. She is about to Google "instances of teens faking their own kidnapping," but what Gabby said distracts her. Instead, she looks up anything she can find about the escape of Alexander Beaufort. It takes her a few different articles, but she finds what she is looking for from the time he was on trial:

"Alexander Beaufort had been on trial for the murder of at least a dozen girls between the ages of ten to fourteen across four different states. The prosecution supposedly has a star witness with a firsthand account of his crimes. Because of the nature of the trial and the situation, the name of the witness is not being released. Beaufort was expected in court first thing this morning, but sometime last night, he escaped. Local authorities, in coordination with the FBI, are currently searching for him.

Below is a current picture of Beaufort. If you should have any information about his whereabouts, call the tip line at 800-555-3431, or if you see him, please call 911 right away.

As an accused serial killer, he is considered armed and dangerous."

Cynthia sits back in her chair and looks out the window. She doesn't know what she was looking for exactly, but this isn't it. She supposes it's not like there's going to be some article explaining how he escaped.

He was in federal custody. It wasn't some simple little misdemeanor he was on trial for. It was interstate murder, so the FBI, the US Marshals, basically everyone was involved. They had him under lock and key 24-7.

Cynthia shoots up in her chair. "He had help!"

It had to be someone high up. Someone with power had to help him escape, but who? And why? Is that how he stayed hidden for all these years?

Cynthia is pacing now, her mind spinning up every thought and angle. How does Blue Eyes fit into this? That's the biggest piece of the puzzle. It would be one thing if Tori went missing and Alexander popped up, but that kid, using his name. It adds a layer of complexity, and Cynthia knows she is missing too many pieces to figure out. If she could just figure that out, she might figure out where Tori is.

She sits back down at her desk, grabs a pen, and scribbles on a Post-It note:

"Alexander—Blue Eyes connection. How did Alexander find him?"

The bodies come back to Cynthia.

"Couple's murder connected? Did Blue Eyes kill them? Alexander only kills girls.

Had Blue Eyes killed before? Did Alexander somehow find him because of this?

Is Alexander teaching him how to kill?

Blue Eyes would have to have some kind of record. Juvie? Sealed records?

How would Alexander get those? Did he have help? Same help that helped him escape?"

Cynthia thinks about her own life in WITSEC and the level of protections which were put in place to keep her safe. She drops her pen on the desk as a horrendous thought washes over her, ice running through her veins.

She shudders as she writes, "Did someone in the Marshals service help him?"

Before she can follow that line of thinking any further, her office door swings open and Charles Monroe barges in.

"I heard you were back. What the hell? Just because you're a senior partner does not give you the right to come and go as you please without informing me or one of the other managing partners. Especially when we have a case this big on the horizon. Do you understand? What could be so important that you drop everything in the middle of the day?"

Cynthia stares at him for a moment, noticing how much he looks like a bull ready to charge. She wants to keep her cool and get him to calm down, but then she thinks, *Screw him. My daughter's life is on the line.*

"You know what, asshole?" Cynthia says, shooting up out of her chair. She isn't even sure how she got around her desk as quickly as she did, but she's in his face and doesn't care if this is her last day after this. "My daughter is missing. Someone kidnapped her and called me, threatening to kill her in the next three days if I don't find her. So I'd appreciate it if you turned around and marched your sorry-ass excuse of a human being out of my office and back to whatever godforsaken hole you crawled out of."

The look on Charles' face is astonishment, anger, fear, and embarrassment all rolled into one. Cynthia takes a step back and crosses her arms. She glares at him and nods towards the door. Charles opens his mouth but thinks better of it, then turns around and walks to the door. She thinks he mumbles something about an apology, but she doesn't care to know exactly what he said.

As soon as he walks past her wall of glass and out of her sight, she grabs her purse and storms out herself, down the hall to the office of the senior managing partner, Richard Williamson. She calms herself at his door, separating him from Charles. Richard has always been a mentor to her and helped build her career. She lightly taps on his door and hears a deep, elderly voice say, "Come in."

She opens it and only stands in the doorway.

His soft British accent comes through his words. "Cynthia. Is everything alright?"

"Actually no, Richard. It's not. I have a family emergency and I'm going to be out of the office for the next few days. Please keep Charles at bay and as soon as I can get back, I will. I'll be available by phone if absolutely necessary. Thank you."

She doesn't wait for a response, but turns and leaves. She regrets not giving him any more details or the opportunity to offer condolences, but her priority right now is the Marshals and finding Tori. She will do whatever it takes to find her and end Alexander once and for all.

CHAPTER 25

NOW

AT THE DOOR to the Marshals building, Cynthia takes a deep breath and heads inside. She finds herself in a small lobby with a handful of chairs circled around a small coffee table. Beyond this is a wall of bulletproof glass, she assumes. The Marshals logo is prominent on one pane, taking up almost the entire piece of glass. Sitting in the middle are double doors. Cynthia tries pulling on one, but it doesn't move. She looks beyond and sees a heavyset middle-aged receptionist behind what looks like another bulletproof enclosure.

There is a crackle, and a voice echoes from a small speaker to the right of the double doors.

"Yes? How can we help you? Do you have an appointment?" The gruff static voice asks.

Cynthia sees a small button at the bottom with a label instructing the user to press it to speak. She does so and says, "No, but my name is Cynthia Burrows. I'm hoping to speak with Marshal Dudeck."

The receptionist looks at her computer screen for a moment. Cynthia can only see her from the chest up, but she can see her arms making slight movements. She assumes the woman is looking for her file.

A second later, there is a loud buzz and a click, and Cynthia instinctively pulls on the door. It glides open and a faint musty smell wafts out. She steps into a larger room, completely empty aside from the bulletproof receptionist box in the left-hand corner and a couch sitting against the far wall to her right.

Cynthia isn't sure where she should go, but the receptionist squawks through her box in the glass and says, "Have a seat. He'll be with you shortly."

As soon as she sits down, her phone buzzes in her purse. Everything inside her freezes as she pulls it out, uncertain of who is calling. She wonders if Alexander knows where she is right now. But when she looks at the caller ID, she breathes a sigh of relief.

"Hey," is all she can say.

"Hey sweetheart. I just landed."

"What do you mean, you just landed?"

"Remember? You called me earlier and left me a voicemail? I had no problem telling them I had to leave. That I had a family emergency. Have you heard from Tori?"

She doesn't even know how to answer that. It baffles her to think that in the time it took him to fly to Texas and back home, her entire world has unraveled.

"No, I haven't." As she is formulating how to answer him, the door at the far end by the receptionist opens and a man who looks to be in his early thirties stands there and nods to her.

"Cynthia?" he asks, his voice a higher pitch than she would have expected.

"I can't talk right now. I'll explain everything at home, okay? I promise."

Before he can say anything else, she hangs up, feeling a pang of guilt for keeping him in the dark. Not only right now, but throughout their entire relationship.

"Yes. Hello. Marshal Dudeck?" she asks, striding toward him, holding out her hand.

He takes it and offers her a warm smile. "Yes. Please call me Mark. Come on back, let's talk."

He steps aside for her to enter, but before she does, the thought she's had about Alexander having help floats to the surface. "I'm sorry, but before I come back there, do you mind me asking, how long have you been with the Marshals?"

He nods. "I get that a lot. I'm older than I look. I've been with the Marshals for ten years now and spent fifteen before that in the Marines."

Cynthia gives him a curt nod, surprised to hear he spent time in the Marines. Living in San Diego, she has known several retired Marines, and he doesn't fit the description. She would have guessed Air Force or Border Patrol. He looked like your average neighborhood dad—beer belly, graying at the temples. and a floppy haircut that reminds her of Hugh Grant in *Notting Hill.*

He hasn't been a Marshal long enough to possibly be involved with Alexander Beaufort.

She steps inside the door and waits for him to lead her. The two walk down a hallway and into another open area where there are dozens of cubicles scattered, with rows of offices lining the wall to her right. There are two doors in the far left corner, which have no glass to see into. She assumes these are some type of interrogation rooms. Before she can think any more about it, Mark stops at one of the office doors and waves an arm for her to go in.

She steps in and takes a quick look around. The office has sparse furnishings, including two chairs facing the desk and a tall filing cabinet to the left. Cynthia takes a seat in one chair as Mark closes the door and sits himself behind the desk. Behind him are a few awards for various commendations not only from the Marshals, but from the Marines as well. There are two pictures with the same woman, one at the Grand Canyon and another in front of the Empire State Building. She looks like he married up, with her golden brown hair, deep brown eyes, tanned skin, and pearly white teeth in a large smile.

"First off, my sincerest apologies that you were not aware of Marshal Wright's retirement. I'm not sure what happened there, but I promise I'll investigate why you were not informed. I assumed if you needed something, you would reach out. Then I got your voicemail and was getting ready to call you back when Gladys said you were out front. I was surprised, to say the least. What's up? What can I do for you?"

Cynthia nods and says, "Thank you for the explanation, but we have bigger issues at hand. My daughter is missing, and it looks like Alexander has taken her. I don't know how he found me, but he has, and I need your help to get her back."

The look of shock on Mark's face says it all. "What do you mean he took her? Did you see him?"

"No, but he called me," Cynthia says.

"And you're sure it was him?"

"Well, he was going to say—" Cynthia pauses, not able to say the name that was on the tip of her tongue, "—her name, but I cut him off and it sounded like him."

Cynthia is already feeling like Mark may not believe her.

Mark leans back and nods. "Did he identify himself as Alexander Beaufort?"

"Well, no, but he didn't have to. The way he was talking to me, I knew it was him. There is this coffee shop kid who goes by Blue Eyes who's also missing. When I went to confront him at work, I saw the employee list and Alexander's name was on it."

Mark leans forward, his brow furrowed. "I'm sorry. Can you walk me through that?"

Cynthia takes the next few minutes and backs up, giving Mark all the details up to the dead bodies at the house. She decides not to include the details around Tori hiding who she really was.

He stays leaned forward, his arms resting on the desk, his fingers intertwined with one another. Once she finishes, he purses his lips and nods.

"We want to help. We do," he starts.

Here comes the but, Cynthia thinks.

"But unless we have verifiable proof it was Alexander, there is only so much I can do right now. We are already spread thin due to these budget cuts. If you can get me any kind of proof he has popped up and is in town, I promise you we will rain down hellfire. He is one we have been after for a very long time."

Cynthia stopped listening as soon as he said "but." She stands up and tries to maintain her composure, putting her purse over her arm.

"Fine, if you can't help me, I'll have the FBI help. I have a good friend who actually cares about my family, and she is ready and willing to do anything necessary to bring my daughter back. If you want to sit on your hands while one of your witnesses' daughters may be killed, so be it."

He shoots to his feet. "Hey, I didn't say that. I want to help you. Your family's safety is our utmost priority. I just need proof it is actually him."

Cynthia nods, holding back the tears, and walks to the door. Opening it, she turns and says, "Fine, I'll get you your proof. I just hope it's before he kills my daughter."

CHAPTER 26

THEN

SAMANTHA SHUFFLED HER feet and ignored the goodbyes and friends telling her to have a good day. She was beyond concerned for Vicky. Why hadn't she heard from her? She thought through the events from the little birthday celebration she had for Vicky on Friday and tried to think if she said or did anything to upset her.

Late Friday night, Samantha came down with the flu. When she woke up midday on Saturday, Vicky was gone. Her parents said Vicky went home early because of how sick Samantha was. She had stayed in bed all weekend, hardly able to move. She assumed when she got to school on Monday, she would connect with Vicky and see how her weekend with whatever-his-name-was went.

But she hadn't been at school. Samantha tried calling her, but Vicky never answered. So when she still wasn't at school, Samantha got worried. She knew how sick she had been—did she give it to Vicky? At least for her, it was over the weekend, so she didn't miss any school, but if Vicky was sick for much longer, she was going to have a hard time making up all those assignments.

"Hey Samantha," Ms. Barnard called to her. "Let us know if you hear from Vicky!"

Samantha nodded and went on her way toward her house. She thought that was even stranger. The school hadn't even heard from her? Didn't Vicky's mom call the school and let them know she was sick?

Vicky would usually call her and ask for the homework, especially because Samantha was a much better student than Vicky.

She thought about that and realized she wouldn't put it past Vicky's mom to not even think about calling the school. In fact, she probably hadn't even noticed Vicky was sick.

I need to go check on her, Samantha thought. She knew, though, if she didn't come home first, her mom would call the police and be worried sick about her.

She hurried home, ran inside, and yelled, "Mom!"

Samantha's mom came out of the kitchen, a concerned look on her face. "Is everything okay?"

"I—I'm not sure. I need to go see Vicky. I just wanted to check in. No one has heard from her since she was here Friday."

Samantha's mom gave her a look only a mom can give. "I'm sure she's fine. I don't know if I like the idea of you walking over there by yourself."

Samantha dropped her backpack and held her ground. "Well, I'm going. I need to make sure she's okay. You know what her life is like."

The two stared at each other and Samantha's mom flopped the dish towel she was holding over her shoulder. "Okay, but don't you dare go inside, and come straight back here. Do you understand? You should be home in no more than forty minutes."

Samantha ran over and gave her mom a quick hug, saying, "Thank you!"

She hurried out and down her street before her mom could change her mind.

Mr. Davies was out front, but Samantha ignored him and ran down and around the corner.

She made it to Vicky's street in record time and stopped to catch her breath just before turning the corner. Once she'd had a moment, she rounded the corner, but stopped cold. Sitting out front of Vicky's house was a police car.

Samantha walked slowly toward the house and saw two officers, one male, one female, walk to the front door. She didn't want them to see her, but there wasn't really anywhere to hide. She stood at the edge of the neighbor's house with her back to Vicky's, hoping Vicky's mom didn't see her.

She could hear the two officers knock on the door and a gruff voice shout from inside, "What the hell do you want?"

"It's the police, ma'am. Can you open the door please?"

Samantha snuck a peek behind her and saw the screen door swing out. A woman stood there, swaying back and forth with a bathrobe on, her hair matted, and a cigarette hanging loosely out of the side of her mouth.

"I ain't done nothin'," she slurred.

Samantha was not surprised by this. The couple of times she had actually seen Vicky's mom, this is exactly how she had been. Nothing had changed.

Samantha turned back around and knelt down, acting like she was tying her shoes. She was fairly certain that Vicky's mom was in no state to even notice her this far off, but just in case . . .

"We know that, ma'am. We're simply here to do a wellness check. Is your daughter Vicky Smith?"

"Aww hell, what'd she do this time?"

"Nothing, ma'am," Samantha could hear the female officer say. "Her school called and asked us to do a wellness check since she hasn't been in school for two days and—"

"And what?" Vicky's mom snarled. "And we live over the bridge?"

"No ma'am. And she is flagged as a truant risk."

"I dunno what that means, but she's fine."

"May we speak with her?" the female officer asked.

"No, you may not. She's not home."

"Where is she?"

Samantha couldn't take it anymore. She stood up and turned around. She didn't care if Vicky's mom saw her or not.

Vicky's mom shrugged, pulled the cigarette out of her mouth, and flicked it toward the ground. "Probably with some friends. I'm sure she'll be home soon."

"Was she home this weekend? Because the school said she hasn't been there yet this week and they didn't hear from you."

"Yes, she was here. I was with her all weekend."

The two officers were quiet and taking notes. They glanced at each other, and the female one said, "Well, okay. Thank you. Please give the school a call and let—"

Samantha couldn't believe what she just heard. She knew that was a flat out lie. Vicky was at her house on Friday, and she'd said her mom and boyfriend were going to be gone all weekend.

"That's a lie!" Samantha yelled, running up the cracked driveway.

The two officers turned around and Vicky's mom cursed.

"I'm sorry?" the female officer said. "Who are you?"

Samantha stopped short, giving the officers space. "I—I'm Samantha, Vicky's best friend. She spent the night at my house on Friday, but that was the last time I spoke to her. She said that her mom was going to be gone all weekend."

"You know nothing, you little shit," Vicky's mom spat.

The female officer whirled and stepped close to her. "Ma'am, you need to calm down right now or we'll take you in. Where is your daughter?"

"Like I said, I don't know where she is right now. But I saw her all weekend. When she gets home later, you can ask her yourself. Now unless y'all have a search warrant, you need to step off and leave me alone!"

Vicky's mom stepped back inside and slammed the door. Samantha could hear several locks click into place. The tears were welling up in her eyes, her heart pounded, and her palms were getting sweaty. She felt like something bad had happened to Vicky.

The female officer came near her and put a gentle hand on her shoulder. "Do you live nearby? Would you like us to give you a ride home? You can tell us more about Vicky. Would that be okay?"

Samantha nodded and followed the officers toward their car.

PART 2

LIES

CHAPTER 27

NOW

CYNTHIA SITS AND watches the coffee shop. When the clock in her car reads 5:56, she gets out and walks briskly over to the front door. Annabelle sees her and waves her in.

Cynthia isn't in the mood for small talk and says, "Thanks again. Where's the video feed?"

"'Course. Follow me," Annabelle says.

Cynthia follows her to the small corridor at the back of the store, and Annabelle says, "Ya know, I was thinkin' more about what you were askin' earlier. About Blue Eyes and all."

Cynthia is worried for a moment that she isn't going to let her see the footage.

"And I recollected, a while back, I remember Tori actually coming in one day asking about work. I thought she was looking for a job for herself, but she just laughed and said it was for a friend. I remember shortly after, Blue Eyes started workin' here. I dunno if the two things are related, but after you asked about him, it came back to me."

Cynthia doesn't know what to do with this information. Nothing that has happened today makes any sense. It's hard for her to even imagine it was only this morning that she, David, and Tori were having breakfast together. Tori said she'd just met him, right? So those two things have to be a coincidence.

Don't they?

Annabelle stops at a door opposite the bathrooms and pulls out a key. She opens the door and steps in. There is hardly enough room for two people, but Cynthia slides in.

A desk with several monitors spans one entire wall. Cynthia thinks this is overkill for a coffee shop, but she is glad for it. To the left of the bank of monitors and nearest the door is a three drawer filing cabinet with some kind of keycard device on top.

"So you just need to click here," Annabelle says, showing Cynthia the folder for the previous days. "Once you find the day you want, it'll pop up in this middle screen with a play-pause type situation. You can fast-forward or rewind and find exactly what you're looking for. But you need to be quick. I have to be setting the alarm by no later than six fifteen. My boss checks to make sure we aren't just hangin' out in the shop after close. Not that we would."

Cynthia shoves her hand into her purse, knowing she only has hundreds. She grabs one and puts it in Annabelle's palm. She pushes it back at Cynthia and says sweetly, "Naw, I can't take this. It's my pleasure."

Leaning closer as if someone might hear, Annabelle whispers, "I never really liked that Blue Eyes to begin with."

She gives Cynthia a wink and walks out and shuts the door.

Cynthia sits down and gets to work. She clicks the folder for the recordings and double clicks on the file for today.

Black and white videos appear across all six monitors. Two of the monitors display the back portion of the store, while another captures the coffee station with the camera positioned above the front door. One is showing the outside and one is in the alleyway parking lot. The other monitor looks to be showing a live feed from the camera above the front door, as Cynthia can see Annabelle doing her closing duties.

Cynthia presses play and watches as the manager comes lumbering in. He cleans the coffee station and picks his nose. Cynthia fast-forwards the replay and sees people come in and leave. She monitors the timestamp and presses the fast-forward button again until right before she thinks Tori would enter.

She lets the video play at normal speed and watches the various people come and go. The manager gets angrier as he keeps looking at his watch and glancing at the front.

He must be waiting and looking for Blue Eyes.

Cynthia is watching the backs of patrons from the video angle at the front of the store when she spots the back of Tori step up to the register and her heart stops.

Tears burst from her eyes. Where is she now?

Before she can pause the video or do anything, she sees Tori turn toward the front door and smile. Whoever she is looking at doesn't come into the camera view. Cynthia glances at the other two monitors showing the back of the store, but she can't see anything from there either.

Tori moves toward the bottom of the screen and then out of sight. Cynthia waits a moment, but Tori never comes back. She glances at the outside camera and watches Tori and a man walk away, their backs to the camera, and her heart drops.

She had always thought about how she'd feel when she saw Alexander again, but nothing could prepare her for seeing Alexander and her daughter together. She rewinds the file until just before Tori turns around and she focuses on the outside camera, watching as Alexander turns toward the coffee shop from the alley.

She glances at the live feed and sees the manager talking to Annabelle. Cynthia gulps and pulls out her phone. She takes a picture of the frozen image of Alexander facing the screen. She then stands up and quickly fast-forwards the file to when Tori turns around. She takes a picture of that too, and one more when the backs of the two of them are leaving.

Closing the file, she pushes in the chair and cracks the door open, glancing at the live feed. The manager is walking toward her and she panics for a moment when Annabelle calls back to him.

He turns around, his back now to the corridor where Cynthia is, and she uses this moment to exit the office and pretend that she is just coming out of the bathroom. She walks towards the main area of the coffee shop as he turns back around.

"Excuse me, but we're closed."

"Yeah, I know. I'm sorry," Cynthia says as she walks past him, keeping her head down. She doesn't want him to remember her from earlier in the day.

She gives Annabelle a quick glance and mouths, "Thank you," as she heads out.

Cynthia gets to her car and freezes. Her phone buzzes in her purse, but what she's looking at has her undivided attention. Sitting on the passenger seat is a small rectangular box.

She looks up and spins around, searching wildly for anyone walking away. Cynthia glances back at the coffee shop, wondering if their outside camera caught anyone. She knows she can't go back there. Refocusing, she opens the car door slowly, as if it's wired to blow. When nothing happens, Cynthia settles into the driver's seat and stares at the box.

Deep breath, she tells herself. Take a deep breath.

She takes several, and then reaches over and picks it up, her hand trembling. It feels heavier than any jewelry David would give her. She's not thinking straight. Swallowing her fear, Cynthia holds her breath and pulls at the top of the box.

Cynthia screams, slamming the lid back down and flinging the box onto the passenger seat. It tumbles onto the floor. Cynthia's right hand clamps over her mouth, covering it, while her left grapples for the door handle. Getting it open, she bends over and dry heaves into the gutter.

Once she's finished, she sits up, stares at the box, and reaches for a napkin in her glove compartment. Wiping her mouth, her eyes don't leave the box sitting on the floor of the passenger side. She doesn't want to, but knows she has to open it again. She needs to get a closer look.

She reaches for it slowly as if it contains a rattlesnake, coiled and ready to strike. She grabs it and sits back in the driver's seat, taking a deep breath. She closes her eyes for a moment, trying to center herself, and then opens the box just enough to peek inside. Sitting in the box is a human finger.

She quickly closes the box again, not able to force herself to look at it any longer, and places it back on the passenger side. The image of the finger, with its light blue painted nail, is seared into her mind.

Her phone vibrates again in her purse. She searches for it and, seeing David's name, she presses the answer icon. She can only squeak out Tori's name.

She knows light blue was the color of Tori's nails when she left that morning.

"Cynth?"

"It's Tori," is all she can say before she breaks down. Tears pour down her face. Seeing Alexander on camera was one thing, but seeing the finger is destroying her.

"Cynth! Are you there?!"

"I know. I'll be home shortly and—"

"What the hell is going on?!" he snaps at her.

She is stunned. What? Why? Before she can respond, David plows on.

"Why the hell are there FBI agents all over our house? What is going on?!"

"I'm coming," she manages. "I'll—I'll explain."

She hangs up on him again and starts her BMW, gunning it toward home.

CHAPTER 28

NOW

DRIVING DOWN THE hill toward her house, Cynthia quickly understands the reason behind David's phone call. Her street is filled with unmarked cars parked in front of her house, agents moving in and out. She hits the brakes hard when pulling into her driveway to avoid hitting an agent coming outside.

Cynthia fixes her eyes on the frosted glass garage door in front of her. She wants none of this to be real.

How did this happen? How did everything change so fast? Why is there a finger in her car?

Cynthia's fear and trepidation ignite into a scorching anger, because she knows the answer to that last question. Alexander Beaufort. She saw him. Never in a million years did she think she would ever utter his name again, never mind actually see him in the flesh.

She realizes that everything will speed up from this point forward, including sharing her past with David. Cynthia reaches across the seat for her purse, but freezes, fixated on the box. The thought of bringing the box inside is too much for her. The mere idea of what's inside triggers her gag reflex.

Extending her arm over the box, she takes hold of her purse and opens the door of her car.

Let Gabby and the agents deal with it.

Stepping into her home, she is shocked. At least seven agents can be seen bustling about in the great room, with a few seated on couches, focused on different equipment, and several others engaged in a discussion by a whiteboard.

What do they need a whiteboard for?

She needs to find Gabby, tell her about the box, and try to find time to explain to David why she has lied to him throughout their entire marriage. She makes her way to the kitchen and finds them both sitting at the table.

Gabby looks like she is trying to reassure him, and Cynthia knows the look he has. It is one she's seen only a handful of times. One of those times was because of work, when a first-year associate didn't copy and send over discovery documents, which completely blew up their timeline for the biggest case of his career.

Gabby looks over at Cynthia, and all Cynthia can think to say as she breaks into tears is, "There's a finger in my car."

Gabby shoots up and shouts, "What?!"

"A box. On my passenger seat. A finger."

Cynthia can't focus on what is being said except that Gabby is yelling at agents and there is a commotion as she points toward the front door. Gabby is holding out her hand to Cynthia, and she isn't sure what Gabby wants until the word "key" materializes on Gabby's lips.

Cynthia rummages in her purse, pulls out her key fob, and drops it into Gabby's hand. She turns, handing it to an agent, and pivots back to Cynthia, taking her hands. Cynthia didn't realize how cold she is until now.

Gabby's calm voice amidst the chaos settles her. "Come here, sweetie. Sit down. Tell me."

Cynthia sits at the table between the two of them, and for a moment, she completely ignores David. She doesn't mean to, but Gabby has that way of enveloping whoever she's talking to.

"I saw him. I left the coffee shop. There was a box in my car. When I opened it, there was—was a finger inside. Is it, is it—"

Cynthia can't finish the question. She can't say Tori's name.

"We'll figure that out. What do you mean you saw him?" Gabby asks.

"I mean, I saw him. I went to the coffee shop. I was able to look at their security footage from earlier today. And I saw him. I have him on camera."

As Cynthia is rummaging through her purse, David speaks up, his voice strained. "Hello? Remember me? What the hell are you talking about? Where is Tori? Somebody needs to tell me what is happening. Now!" he shouts, slamming his palm on the kitchen table.

"David, remember what I said?" Gabby says softly.

"Yeah, but I'm sorry. I need to talk to my wife. What is going on, Cynth?"

He reaches for her arm as she's pulling her phone out of her purse, knocking it onto the table. The phone tumbles against a glass of water, spilling it across the table.

Gabby jumps up, scoops Cynthia's phone before the water gets to it, and grabs a roll of paper towels.

While she is soaking up the water, Gabby says, "Let's get you a glass of wine and you can start from the top, yes?"

Cynthia nods and takes a deep breath. She watches as Gabby grabs two wine glasses, then opens their subzero fridge and pulls out a bottle of white. She places one in front of Cynthia and the other in front of David, and gives a generous pour.

"I don't—" David begins, but Gabby's eyes throw daggers and he cuts himself off.

Cynthia takes a long sip, feeling the chill of the wine go all the way down.

She walks the two of them through her last forty minutes, when she went back to The Joe after leaving the Marshals building. When she stops to take another sip, Gabby looks at the images of Alexander on Cynthia's phone and says, "Seeing him in person and knowing he was the last one to see Tori gives us what we need, especially with the box. I will coordinate with the Marshals and we will throw this into a full-blown manhunt, starting now. We will get her back, I promise you."

David shoots up out of his chair, grabbing at his hair and pacing. "I'm sorry, but what the hell is going on? Who is this Alexander? Why does he have Tori? Why are all these people just sitting around?! My daughter has been kidnapped. She has been butchered—"

He stops himself and holds back a sob.

"We don't know that," Gabby interjects.

Cynthia has never seen him this worked up before.

"I can explain everything," she says.

David spins on her and continues, "Is he some kind of pedophile or something? Did he abuse you? Why are they tearing apart Tori's room? Why haven't they found her?"

He moves back and forth, looking out toward their backyard and the setting sun beyond the lagoon. He stops and turns around.

His tone quiet and dejected, he asks, "Who is Alexander?"

Cynthia reaches toward him. He's far enough away that he

would have to reciprocate the arm extension to reach, and he doesn't. Rather, he shoves his hands in his pockets and looks at her, his face a mixture of anger and terror.

"Please. David. Sit. Let me explain," Cynthia says, dropping her arm and nodding toward the seat.

Like trying to get a pet in for the night standing at the back door, she waits. After a moment, he moves to the chair and sits down.

She spins her glass, trying to figure out where to start or how to explain everything.

Start with the basics.

"The police won't be much help. It doesn't matter now that Gabby and the Marshals are involved. I've learned quite a bit about our daughter today. Things I never thought possible. I'll go over all that with you, I promise. I called Gabby because she is the one person who knows everything. Trust me, I always wanted to tell you, I just—I just could never find the right time. As time went on, it just got more awkward and complicated."

She pauses a beat, and he says, "Now seems like the right time."

Cynthia nods. She can't take anything he says right now personally. She has hurt him in the worst way possible.

She can feel the knot in her throat. She swallows, hoping it will go away. The noise is getting louder in the house as most of the agents are now inside. She imagines all of them standing around the box, examining the finger. Gabby reaches over and touches her arm again. Her touch always manages to calm Cynthia.

"Why don't you two go out back where it's quiet? I'll get them finished in here."

Cynthia nods and stands up, holding out her hand for David. He stands up as well, but ignores her hand and heads out back.

Gabby gives her a considerate smile and says, "Don't worry. It'll be okay. Just tell him the truth. I'll be here when you're done."

Cynthia nods and follows David out back, trying to figure out exactly how to tell him all about her past.

CHAPTER 29

NOW

DAVID SITS FIRST while Cynthia is hesitant. She figures if she doesn't sit right away, maybe she can delay explaining why she's been lying to her husband for the last fifteen years.

Where do I even begin?

"Well?" he says, his tone harsh. There have been a handful of times David has been angry with her beyond words in their marriage. She hated how he acted in those times. She wished he'd yell, scream, get it out, but he turned inward and shut down. That's why inside was so surprising to her. She'd never seen him get that angry before.

As a lawyer, she knows how to handle words, how to handle anger. But how do you argue, learn, talk through things with someone who just won't talk?

Cynthia takes a deep breath, pulls out one of the metal patio chairs, and sits. She runs her finger over the glass inlay of the table, trying to figure out how to start.

She says just that. "I really don't even know where to start."

"How about the beginning?" he responds, his voice flat.

She isn't ready to start there.

Answer the simplest question.

"The reason the FBI is here and the US Marshals are going to be involved is because I'm in witness protection."

The stunned expression on David's face reminds Cynthia of a frozen Zoom meeting. He blinks twice, his mouth agape. He stands up and starts pacing across the brick patio all the way to the border of their grass and back toward her several times.

"Please," Cynthia pleads. "Say something. Anything. Yell, scream, shout at me. Just say something. Don't shut down. Let me explain everything."

He pivots on the spot as if he is stuck to that one brick and snarls at her, "How will I be able to trust anything you say? Has our entire marriage been a lie? How could you not tell me something like this?"

Cynthia jumps up and shouts at him, "Hell no! My love has never wavered. Our marriage is no different from the day I married you."

"Except the fact that the woman I married isn't even real. Is she?" Cynthia doesn't know at first what he means by this. "Is Cynthia even your real name?"

She doesn't respond, but pauses. She hesitates just too long and he scoffs at her. A snarl creeps at the edge of his lip.

"How can I trust anything you say? Your name isn't even Cynthia."

The two stare at each other. Cynthia can't get herself to say anything else right now. She wonders if it would even help. He's already shut down and won't hear anything she says.

"David," is all she can say.

A sound escapes his throat as he shakes his head. He looks up at the darkening sky as she steps toward him. He keeps the distance between them and shakes his head.

He points a finger and jabs it at her. "No, don't. I can't be here right now. I can't be here with you. You better find Tori, or whatever happens is one hundred percent on you."

Before she can say anything, he turns and walks the length of the house toward the fence separating the yards. Cynthia doesn't follow, but calls after him, "David! Please! Come back. Let me explain!"

She waits, but there is nothing. She can only hear the hum from inside with the agents. Cynthia hangs her head, tears welling up in her eyes and falling to the ground, leaving small, round dark spots on the brick patio.

She crumples onto the chair, staring at the ground. A soft hand settles on her shoulder and Gabby's calm voice asks, "Hey. What happened?"

"He left. It didn't go well."

The hand moves to her back and gingerly rubs it. "He'll come around, I promise. I'll talk to him if it comes to that. I know you and I know him. You two have a love that not even this can break."

Gabby is quiet for a moment, then she continues, "On a positive note, if it can be considered that, the finger doesn't belong to Tori. We aren't sure whose it is yet, but we know for certain it isn't hers."

Cynthia shoots up and hugs Gabby, the tears flowing freely.

"How?" Cynthia ekes out.

"I'm sorry?" Gabby asks.

"How do you know it isn't hers?"

"We grabbed a print from her room and compared it to the finger. They don't match."

Cynthia hugs her again as Gabby runs her hand down the back of Cynthia's hair and says, "Let's head inside. We need to get a tracer installed on your phone for when he calls again."

Gabby grabs Cynthia by the shoulders and pushes her away so she can look at her. They lock eyes and Gabby says, "The most important thing right now is to be as prepared as we can be so that when he calls, it will help us find Tori that much faster. Okay?"

Cynthia nods. Gabby's arms are open wide and Cynthia falls into them again, welcoming the warmth of her embrace.

CHAPTER 30

THEN

EVEN THOUGH SHE knew she wasn't in trouble, Samantha felt odd getting into the back of the police car. She wanted to turn around and see if Vicky's mom was watching, but she didn't want to look at the woman again. How could she not care about her daughter? Where was Vicky?

The female officer opened the back door for her, and with a smile, she said, "I'm Officer Reynolds. It's nice to meet you, Samantha. Have you ever had the chance to ride in a police car before?"

Samantha could only shake her head. The officer reassured her, "I promise you aren't in trouble. We just want to make sure you get home safe. Just so you know, the doors can't open from the inside in the back. Did you know that?"

Samantha nodded. She wasn't sure if she knew that or not, but didn't want to say no.

As she climbed in, Officer Reynolds asked, "What's your address?"

"4533 Blue Sky Lane," Samantha responded.

As the officer closed the door, she remarked, "That's a nice area. We'll get you home in just a few."

Once she climbed in and the door shut, Samantha noticed it smelled weird. Kind of like her grandma's house. Stale and like cigarettes. She breathed through her mouth as much as possible while the two officers climbed in up front and started the car. As they drove down the street to make a U-turn back toward the bridge, Officer Reynolds asked, "So you said Vicky was with you on Friday?"

Samantha nodded, but then realized she might not have seen her nod. "Yes ma'am, but she left early Saturday morning because I was sick."

"You have great manners. Your parents have taught you well. So what did Vicky say to you when you saw her last?"

Samantha chewed on her bottom lip as they drove over the bridge and noticed that the colors of the homes and even the sky seemed brighter on this side.

She didn't know if she should tell the officers everything about the boy. She didn't want Vicky getting in more trouble. As if she could read Samantha's mind, Officer Reynolds said, "I promise, whatever she told you won't get her in trouble. We are simply concerned about where she is and want to make sure she's safe."

Samantha nodded again and regurgitated what Vicky had said. "She said she was excited for the weekend because her mom and her mom's boyfriend were going to be out of town, and she was going to have a boy come over. She said they were going to do stuff, but I'm not sure exactly what stuff. Kissing and stuff. That's all I know."

The officers were quiet and glanced at each other. Neither of them said anything more until they pulled up to Samantha's house. Officer Reynolds got out first and opened the door for

Samantha. "Here we are. We'd like to come in and talk with your parents for a minute. Again, you're not in trouble at all."

Samantha gulped. She wasn't sure what her parents were going to say or do. Before she could even think any more about it, her parents burst out the front door.

"Samantha! What's wrong? Are you okay?"

"She's fine," Officer Reynolds said. "If we can stay calm and head inside for just a moment."

Samantha followed her parents in with the officers right behind her. They headed into the living room and her parents sat on one couch. Her mom waved her over to sit between them while the officers took the chairs opposite them.

"Your daughter is not in trouble at all. The school contacted us and asked us to do a wellness check on Vicky Smith. They consider her a truant risk. When we went over there to talk to her mother, Samantha came up to the front door. From what we understand, she had come over to check on her friend and disagreed with what Vicky's mom was saying about the events from the weekend."

Officer Reynolds looked at Samantha and asked, "Am I right so far?"

Samantha nodded, feeling suffocated sitting between her parents.

"What she told us in the car ride over—" Officer Reynolds continued, but Samantha's father interrupted her.

"I'm sorry, you questioned my daughter without a parent or a lawyer present?"

The officer smiled and said, "No, we were having a conversation. There was no need to even think about the need of a parent or lawyer present, as she was not in trouble, like I mentioned before."

Officer Reynolds waited a moment to see if either of Samantha's parents would respond. When they didn't, she continued, "What she told us was that Vicky was here Friday night and was excited for the weekend because she was going to have a boy come over to her house. Samantha wasn't sure exactly what they planned to do, but Vicky was really excited about it."

She could have sworn that the officers and her parents exchanged some kind of look that grown-ups do from time to time, as if they know something the kids don't.

"We will absolutely look into this situation and find out if Vicky's mom was not home and is lying to us. Our priority and concern is Vicky and making sure she is safe. We understand from Samantha that Vicky had spent the night here and went home early Saturday morning? Is that right?"

"Yes, yes it is," Samantha's mom said, her voice quiet and strained.

Officer Reynolds nodded and took notes. Her partner sat still, his hands resting on his knees the entire time.

"Docs he speak?" Samantha's father asked.

"Yes, I do," the male officer said. "But seeing as Samantha is a young lady, we like to let our female officers take the lead in these situations."

"And what situation is that?" Samantha's mom asked.

"One where a child is missing," he responded.

This news shocked Samantha. She hadn't considered Vicky missing. She assumed she was just ditching or hanging out with that boy. Had something bad happened to her? She could feel her emotions welling up at the thought.

"Hey, hey, it's okay. We're going to find her," Officer Reynolds said, reaching toward Samantha. "Do you know anything about this boy? His name? Where he lives?"

Samantha shook her head. "I'm sorry, I'm not sure. I—I don't want to get anyone in trouble."

Officer Reynolds nodded and said, "I understand. Well, if you can think of anything, please let us know. We'll look into everything else, and if you remember anything about this boy, please let us know."

The two officers stood, and Officer Reynolds handed a business card to Samantha's mom.

She took it and said, "I'm sorry we can't be of much help. We don't know a lot about Vicky's home life. Just that she's always—"

Her mom paused, looking for the right words. "She's always been a little rough around the edges. Her mom may have been home and not even realized Vicky wasn't there."

Officer Reynolds nodded in agreement, as if she knew what she was talking about. Samantha looked from the officers to her parents and felt anger welling up inside her. They weren't taking this seriously enough. If Vicky was missing, they needed to start a search party; they needed to get more police involved.

They needed to be doing more.

Tears cascaded down her cheeks. Her breath hitched, and she sprinted from the room and up the stairs to her bedroom. She couldn't believe what she heard. Her parents weren't even taking her side. How could they say such a thing? Why weren't they starting up search parties if Vicky was actually missing?

Where did her best friend go?

CHAPTER 31

NOW

CYNTHIA STANDS OVER the technician, watching him tap on her phone and open up areas of the software she never knew existed.

"What are you doing? Is that going to mess it all up? Are my contacts going to still be there? Will Alexander know you're going to trace his call?" She peppers him.

"No, you see—" the agent begins.

Gabby cuts him off and replies, "No works just fine. We don't need the explanation."

Turning to Cynthia, Gabby places her hand on her back and nudges her toward the kitchen. "Let's give them some space to work."

Cynthia sits at her marble bar top and Gabby grabs the wine glass from the table. Setting it in front of Cynthia, Gabby refills it.

"Are you trying to get me drunk?" Cynthia asks.

Gabby gives her that warm smile and says, "No, but I am trying to get you to relax a bit. You have to let us do our job. I'll cut you off, don't worry. We need you sharp for sure."

Gabby grabs another glass and pours herself half as much as Cynthia's.

There is a noticeable hum all around them as the agents are talking in the other room, taping up information from Alexander's history on the whiteboard. Another group is in the backyard installing additional security cameras at every corner.

Cynthia is spinning her glass, the liquid sloshing in rhythm with her turns of the stem. Absently, not directed at Gabby or anyone else walking by, she asks, "How?"

"What's that, babe?"

Cynthia looks up, fresh tears in her eyes, and asks Gabby, "How. How did he find us? All these years we've been safe. I've been so careful. I didn't tell anyone. Only you. Now, somehow he shows up and takes Tori? If he was working with this Blue Eyes from the coffee shop and planted him, that means he's been planning this for months."

"We're going to figure out all of that, I promise. We will work through the night while you get some sleep."

Cynthia shakes her head.

"You need to sleep. You will be useless to me if you don't. We can get by on less because we aren't as emotionally drained as you are. You need to trust that we'll find her."

The wine is hitting Cynthia. She realizes she hasn't eaten all day. "And he had the audacity to call me. And taunt me."

As if reading her mind, Gabby asks, "Have you eaten anything?"

Cynthia just shrugs.

Getting up, Gabby goes to the fridge, pulls out some cheeses and meats, and places them on a tray. She rummages through a few of the tall cabinets and finds a box of crackers between various snack foods and cereals. She pushes it in front of Cynthia and says, “Eat. Nibble, at least.”

Cynthia obeys and places a couple of slices of salami with cheddar on a cracker. She takes a bite and Gabby says, “I was thinking, if he is bringing up the last time, maybe he’s keeping her somewhere that in his mind connects to that period.”

Cynthia has always been able to tell when Gabby is holding something back. She does this thing with her face where the right corner of her lips pulls back, like she’s chewing on the inside of her cheek, and she taps her index finger.

Cynthia notices her doing both things and says to her, “Tell me.”

Gabby locks eyes with her. “There is no good time to share this. We dug into that finsta account you told me about. It wasn’t hard for our techs to break in once we knew which account we were looking for. We tagged a handful of the kids and I sent some agents out earlier to talk with them. It’s not good.”

“And?” Cynthia asks.

Gabby hesitates and says, “I’m not going to give you every detail. It is something that we will investigate properly. But the high level is, a lot of those parties could be defined as hazing on a massive scale. I don’t know how involved Tori was or if she was just there, but there was a lot of alcohol and other substances at these events. Regularly, pictures would be taken and then sent to the individuals as blackmail to get them to do what others wanted.”

Before Cynthia can ask anything further, Gabby’s phone rings. “Agent Hayes.”

There is quiet for a moment, then Gabby says, “Sure, hold on.”

She puts her phone on speaker and says in a more official voice, "You're on speaker, Detective Harrison. Cynthia is right here."

"Hello. Hi Mrs. Burrows. Has your daughter made contact yet?"

Cynthia ignores this and asks, "What can I do for you, detective?"

"Well, I'm glad you're both together. I wanted to follow up with you and let you know we were able to ID that couple from earlier. I was hoping the names may ring a bell for you, since you seemed to find your way to the crime scene."

Cynthia puts her hands up and mouths to Gabby, "What do I do?"

Gabby encourages her to respond, so Cynthia says, "Okay. What were their names?"

Detective Harrison says, "According to their fingerprints, they are Mr. and Mrs. Daniel and Cheri Matthews."

Cynthia shakes her head and says, "Sorry, those names don't ring any bells."

Gabby's face is scrunched up, her eyebrows knitted together.

"What?" Cynthia mouths to her.

Gabby puts up a finger and asks the detective, "Were their IDs not with them? Why the need for fingerprint verification?"

There is silence on the other end for a moment and Detective Harrison replies, "Well, that's the strange thing. The IDs on the bodies don't match the fingerprints we pulled."

"What were the names on the IDs?" Gabby asks as a follow-up.

He ignores the question and says, "My main reason for calling was to ask if you can come down to the station tomorrow first thing. I'd like to revisit how you ended up there and what you may know. We can talk about the IDs then as well. I really need to understand what Agent Hayes meant by there being more at stake here than I may know. I have been instructed by my captain to play nice with the FBI, but I just want to make sure you all won't push your way into my investigation. There has to be a way we can work together."

Gabby and Cynthia exchange looks, and Gabby raises her eyebrows at Cynthia. Cynthia nods to her and Gabby replies, "Yes, of course. We'll be there. Does 9:00 work?"

"9:00 would be great. Thank you. See you in the morning."

CHAPTER 32

THEN

I CAN'T BELIEVE they're taking her mom's side, Samantha thought, kicking a stone as she walked home from school. Her anger got the better of her and she kicked the rock hard. It ricocheted off the bumper of a car, and she could tell it left a small dent. She didn't care to wait around and figure out whose car it was. There were more important things happening in her life right now.

She refused dinner last night because she didn't want to have to talk to her parents. When she came down for breakfast, her mom tried to be sweet and act like she cared about Vicky, but Samantha wouldn't talk. She ate her cereal, grabbed her backpack, and left. Everyone at school was asking her about Vicky and where she was.

Samantha didn't know what to say or how to respond, so she just ran to the bathroom and cried. Where was her best friend? What happened to her? Did that boy do something? Samantha thought she knew which boy it was, but she needed to be sure. She'd asked Heather to see if she could find out if it was the one she was thinking of. Heather said she was on it.

Lost in thought, Samantha realized she'd crossed the street as if she was going to Vicky's and almost passed her own street. She turned and looked up. The skies overhead were threatening rain, and that was the last thing Samantha needed, so she picked up her pace. When her house came into view, she noticed that a police car was out front again.

She saw Ms. Sarah in her yard tending to her rose bushes. The woman glanced toward her and gave her a smile. Just as Samantha was passing the large hedge and about to step out into the street, she felt a tug on her backpack. She turned around and Mr. Davies had grabbed her.

"I'm sorry. I didn't mean to startle you. I just wanted to talk real quick."

Samantha was shocked that he had actually grabbed her. He glanced behind her toward the police car and back to her, then lowered his voice, saying, "I feel so bad that your friend is missing. She seems like a lovely girl. I really hope she turns up."

Samantha couldn't take it anymore. The anger was bubbling over. Not necessarily all at him, but a lot of it.

"Did you take her?!" Samantha screamed, spit flying from her mouth. The look of shock on his face as he stumbled backward, falling over, gave Samantha all the ammunition she needed.

"You did, didn't you?! You're always staring at her chest and winking at her. What the hell is wrong with you? Where is she? Give her back!"

Mr. Davies was trying to stand up and lunged for Samantha, grabbing her arm. His grip felt like he might snap her arm in two.

"Listen here, you little bitch. I was just trying to be kind and neighborly. I did nothing to your friend. She probably had it coming, if I'm being honest."

"Ow! Let go of me! You're hurting me!"

"What is going on here?!" Ms. Sarah appeared from the other side of the hedge.

Mr. Davies let go and stepped back. Samantha looked down at her arm and could see the outline of fingers on her forearm. Samantha stepped off the curb, letting Ms. Sarah step between her and Mr. Davies.

"My best friend is missing," Samantha stuttered, trying to hold back the tears. "He always stared at her. Always looking at her chest! He was so creepy about wanting to give her a ride home."

"Is this true?" Ms. Sarah asked, whirling back at him. "Come to think of it, I've seen you several times standing out front just staring at Sam's house. You act like you're working out here, but all you do is stare. Did you do something to that poor girl? Did you take her?"

Ms. Sarah was only inches from his face, which was turning bright red.

"That's enough!" he screamed. "What about you? All your men you parade through your house like it's a fucking turnstile. Any of those horndogs could have scooped up that girl. The way she dressed, she was asking for it, if you ask me."

He didn't let either of them say anything else and turned, stumbling into his house, slamming the door. Across the street, Samantha's parents and Officer Reynolds stepped outside to see what all the commotion was. Mr. Davies' last statement hit Samantha hard. She sprinted across to her house, tears running down her cheeks.

She pivoted around Officer Reynolds and sprinted up the stairs to her bedroom, slamming the door behind her. She flopped down on her bed, breaking down into heaving sobs, begging anyone who was listening up above to bring her best friend back to her.

CHAPTER 33

NOW

CYNTHIA WAKES WITH a start. She has no idea when she fell asleep or for how long. She knows it wasn't restful, filled with horrific dreams of what Alexander was doing to Tori. Sitting up, Cynthia realizes she fell asleep with her clothes on. She pads across the plush carpet of the large bedroom to her ensuite bathroom. The shock of the cold marble underfoot awakens another dream she had last night.

She was swimming in the school pool and had quickly realized she didn't know how to swim. Beginning to sink, she looked up and saw Tori and Sofia both jump in to save her. But just as they were about to reach her, Alexander jumped into the pool and stabbed them both. As Cynthia sank further to the bottom of the pool, the water turned red all around her while the girls' lifeless bodies also sank down next to her.

She'd sat up, gasping for breath.

She realizes that was what had woken her up. Looking at her tired, ragged face in the mirror now, she takes a couple of deep breaths, trying to shake the images from her mind. Cynthia grabs her eye cream, dabbing just a fingertip of the lotion across her lower lids.

She gives herself a quick whiff and realizes she needs to take a shower. Tying up her hair, she takes a quick body shower, and five minutes later, she is out, drying off, pulling on a pair of jeans. Putting on her bra, Cynthia pulls her hair out from the bun she'd tied up and hears her phone ringing. Hurrying out to the bedroom, she can't find it. She fluffs all the sheets, looking for it as it continues to ring.

The sheets snap in the air and Cynthia's phone flies across the bed away from her. She scurries around the bed as quick as she can and picks it up. The screen shows "Blocked Number."

"It's him!" Cynthia yells toward the door, hoping someone downstairs hears her.

She reaches the door of her bedroom and presses accept.

While she is sprinting down the stairs, she says breathlessly, "Hello?!"

Gabby stares at her and makes a rolling motion with her hands. "Keep him on," she mouths.

The same voice that tormented Cynthia yesterday returns. "Just two days left. Are you even trying? Have you found any of my clues yet?"

Cynthia has no idea what he's talking about. "What clues?"

Alexander scoffs and clicks his tongue. "I thought you were better than this. I've been telling Tori how amazing her mom is at solving puzzles. She'll be so disappointed if you can't solve this one."

"What are you talking about?!" Cynthia yells. "What puzzles? What clues?! The finger? It wasn't Tori's!"

Alexander chuckles on the other end. "Well, no shit. It wasn't supposed to be Tori's. Did you even look at it? Christ, you've gotten weak. I thought you were a lawyer. How are you so bad at this? I really thought we'd have a pleasant reunion with Tori, but it looks like all you'll get is the opportunity to find her body."

"Alexander, no! Please just tell me where you are! Take me! Leave Tori out of this. Please!"

"Alexander. Alexander. Why do you keep calling me that?" He says, admonishing her.

"You know why! Give me back my little girl. Please, take me!"

Cynthia hears nothing and realizes her cries are for naught. He'd hung up as soon as he'd finished talking.

"Did you get it? Where is he?" Cynthia begs to know.

"We got it," an agent says with a confident nod.

Gabby comes around and looks at the agent's screen. "It looks like he was calling from an empty field about twenty minutes from here. I'll send some agents to check it out, but I'm fairly certain he's already gone."

Cynthia stands there frozen, rehashing what Alexander had said.

What puzzles?

"Hey," Gabby says, breaking her thought. "Why don't you go put on a shirt? I'll dispatch some agents to that field. We'll eat a little something and then talk to that detective. Maybe he can help us. Maybe there were some clues left behind at the estate. Could that be what Alexander was referring to?"

Cynthia looks down, her face red with embarrassment, realizing she was standing amid all these agents, mostly men, in her bra and jeans.

She ignores Gabby and hurries back up the stairs to finish

getting dressed. Parts of what Alexander said keep bouncing around in her mind.

Two days. Clues, puzzles, reunion with Tori.

He was in an empty field? Why would he do that? Probably because he doesn't want them to know where he's keeping Tori.

Cynthia grabs the first shirt in her closet and throws it on. She glances at herself in the mirror and scoffs at herself. She doesn't care enough to grab another shirt. The white T-shirt with Mickey Mouse's massive head is going to have to do.

She hurries back downstairs and ignores the agents to her right in the great room, going straight ahead into the kitchen. Gabby is standing at her counter, making eggs. The memory of just yesterday morning hits Cynthia, when that was her making the eggs and it was David and Tori coming down the stairs.

"I don't care if you're hungry or not," Gabby says, turning from the stove with the pan of eggs, sliding them onto a plate on the countertop. "You're gonna eat."

Gabby looks up at Cynthia and chuckles. "Well, okay, guess that's the look we're going for."

Cynthia tugs at the shirt.

"I don't care," she says, expressing exhaustion in every syllable.

Gabby shrugs and says, "Fair. Here, come eat at least some eggs and a few bites of toast."

She looks at her watch. "We've got twenty minutes before we have to be at the station and it'll take us about ten to get there."

Cynthia situates herself on a barstool and takes a few bites of the eggs. Her stomach growls in anticipation as the food hits her taste buds. It only takes her only a few minutes to eat everything in front of her.

"Guess you were hungry," Gabby chuckles.

"Guess so. Thanks," Cynthia replies, dabbing her mouth with a napkin. "For everything."

Gabby reaches across the counter and squeezes Cynthia's hand. "Of course. You ready to go?"

Cynthia nods.

The two head out and Gabby says to one of the agents, "Let me know as soon as Billings gets to the field and what you all find. Nothing is more important than this. I'll answer any call. Understand?"

"Yes ma'am," the agent on the couch says.

As the two walk out the front door, Gabby says to Cynthia, "I know the detective wants to talk with you, but let me lead and let me do the talking. The last thing we need is you saying something you're not supposed to in the heat of the moment."

"Yes ma'am," Cynthia replies, mimicking the agent.

CHAPTER 34

JOURNAL

THIS INCESSANT DRUMMING. Why won't it go away? I thought for sure that dream would have done it. The blood, the knife wounds—I was certain killing her would have subsided this pounding. But no.

If anything, it's gotten worse. Let's see if these four ibuprofen will help. If not, I'm going to have to find something stronger. I've been trying to hold it together and act normal, but I'm pretty certain those around me are catching on. I don't know if it's because of what I've been writing, but the paranoia is setting in.

Can you be paranoid if you know you're paranoid? Kind of like a crazy person doesn't actually know they're crazy? Maybe that's my problem. Maybe all of this is just in my head and I'm actually already committed somewhere. Wouldn't that be a twist? I wake up one day and I'm not in my bed, but in some mental hospital.

Yeah, I don't think so either. I'm sure I'm as sane as they come. I may be psychotic and a complete sociopath, but I know what I'm doing.

Maybe if I focus on the dream, take my mind off the pain.

It was so weird to wake up and realize it was only a dream. I could feel the weight of the knife in my hand. I could understand thinking what it would feel like to sink the knife into her gut, only to be surprised by the ease with which it went into her.

When I pulled the knife back, I watched the blood expand across her shirt and studied her expression as she fell to her knees, realizing I had stabbed her. It didn't bother me like I thought it would. We had been so close, but I actually didn't care. It saddened me a bit, but the pleasure and feeling of wholeness that washed over me pushed out any other emotions.

That feeling, that sensation of completeness, now being awake, was gone. I knew I needed to chase it. Find it. Figure out how to have that all the time.

It helped. Reliving the vividness of the dream helped the pain to subside. That or the ibuprofen, I'm not sure which. I'm going to assume it was the dream, though.

The sun is peeking through the slats in my blinds. I know soon enough I'm going to have to put on the smile and the sparkle in my eyes, and pretend like I enjoy the life I'm surrounded by.

The longer I sit here and allow the dream to dissipate from my conscious thought, the stronger the drumming grows once more. The edge I live on grows sharper by the day. I just hope I can hold on long enough that I don't snap in front of others and ruin the life I've envisioned for myself.

I don't know if the drumming will ever subside or cease all together. All I know is I can't continue to live with it.

CHAPTER 35

NOW

GABBY AND CYNTHIA pull into the Safety Center for the Carlsbad Police Department. Gabby parks at the front in a spot that says Reserved for Official Use Only. She shrugs at Cynthia and says, "Seems like an official use to me."

The building gives the impression it hasn't received any updates since the late eighties or early nineties. In a city like Carlsbad, Cynthia thought they'd have the money for a more modern station, but apparently not. They get out of Gabby's car and head across the small pavilion. Directly in front is a group of four doors with an overhang that reads, "Conference Facility."

To their left is another group of four doors, with a circular portion jutting out with the words "Police - Fire" etched on it. They turn left and head inside. There is a large foyer with an officer sitting at a desk to the right. Cynthia doesn't have time to look around and take everything in as the officer asks, "Can I help you?"

He is older and looks like he should be retiring. Maybe he is one of those volunteer officers.

Gabby takes the lead. "Yes, hello. We're here to see Detective Harrison."

He types away on his keyboard for a moment, his head turned to the side, examining his monitor.

"Yes, I see it here. He should be with you in just a moment, if you'd like to have a seat. Help yourself to some refreshments along the back wall while you wait," the officer says, his mustache twitching as he speaks.

Cynthia turns as Gabby is already halfway across the lobby, heading straight to the donuts.

"Really?" Cynthia asks. "A little on the nose, isn't it?"

Gabby shrugs, taking a bite of an old-fashioned. "When in Rome."

Cynthia shakes her head and grabs a cup, pressing down on the top of the coffee carafe. She gives it a couple of additional presses to fill the cup. As she is pouring some creamer into it, she hears behind her, "Agent Hayes. Mrs. Burrows."

Cynthia grabs a stir stick and turns. Detective Harrison is standing there in what looks to be the same outfit as the day before.

Must be his official uniform.

She follows Gabby toward the detective and waits for Gabby to wipe her hand on a napkin before shaking the detective's hand. Cynthia takes a sip and also shakes his hand, nodding at him.

"Thank you for coming in," he says, stepping back. "Please follow me."

Both women step through the door and he makes sure it shuts completely behind them.

"This way," he says, motioning them down the hall.

There is a row of doors at the back end of the room with

about a dozen cubicles interspersed throughout the rest of the room. On the far left-hand corner, there looks to be an office that was constructed after the fact with the word "captain" painted across the door.

Cynthia is in the back of the line of three and slows down as they pass a room on their right. She glimpses a large whiteboard in it, along with a conference table.

She recognizes the address at the top of the board as the one where she thought Blue Eyes lived. Slowing, she allows Gabby and Detective Harrison to pull ahead of her as she takes in as much as she can from the board.

Under the address, she sees both the names "Dennis Matthews" and "Cheri Matthews" written in black dry erase marker. Next to each name is a dash and a piece of paper with a blown-up driver's license. Cynthia can't read any of the information on the licenses from where she is.

Underneath the address, on the left-hand side, are crime scene photographs showing the victims' bodies. Next to that, written in blue, are the words "Possible Motives."

Before she can take in the list, Detective Harrison calls to her, "Excuse me, but please follow me."

Cynthia apologizes and hurries to catch up.

Gabby gives her a look that Cynthia knows is asking what she saw, but she simply shakes her head. Detective Harrison leads them to the back wall and opens a door that has a stencil on it: "Interview 3."

Inside is a simple table with four chairs. Cynthia and Gabby both sit at the end with their backs to the wall and Detective Harrison closes the door, pressing a button on a switch by the door.

"No need to have the cameras recording right now," he says. "We're simply just talking."

Gabby nods and Cynthia looks around, spotting two cameras, one in each corner facing her.

Detective Harrison sits down, dropping a folder with a notepad on the table. He opens it, placing it against his legs while leaning it against the table, and starts taking notes. He asks, "Can you please tell me why you were at the home of the Matthews yesterday?"

Cynthia looks at Gabby, even though she is the lawyer. In this case, she is way out of her depth.

Gabby nods and says, "It's okay. Go ahead. I'll let you know if you're getting yourself into trouble."

Cynthia holds the cup between her hands, the heat welcomed on her icicle fingers. She takes a deep breath and begins, "My daughter is missing. I now know who took her."

Gabby quickly places her hand on Cynthia's arm. Cynthia nods, knowing she is warning her to not reveal too much.

"Yesterday morning, though, I had no idea what had happened to her. Before we left the house, she had told my husband and I that she had a date that night with this kid from The Joe coffee shop. We received an alert from school that she was excused for the day, but neither my husband nor I excused her. So I got worried. When I couldn't get anyone on the phone from the coffee shop to see if this kid was working, I figured I had to go and see. I know it sounds over the top, but I have my reasons."

Cynthia pauses and takes a sip of her coffee. The golden brown liquid warms her all the way down.

"When I got there, the manager said the kid called Blue Eyes wasn't there, but he should have been. So when the manager wasn't looking, I took a quick picture of the employee list. I assumed Tori had ditched school to hang out with him. He's supposedly nineteen, and even though she is eighteen, she is still in high school. When I got to the bottom of the list, the last name startled me. It's a name I know from my past. So I knew I had to check for myself what was going on."

Before she can continue, the detective asks, "What was the name?"

Cynthia looks at Gabby, who nods.

"Alexander Beaufort."

The detective jots down the name and asks, "And how do you know him?"

CHAPTER 36

THEN

THE KNOCK ON Samantha's door was soft, followed by her mother's kind voice. "Sam, can you please come back downstairs?"

"Why? No one cares about Vicky except me!"

"That's not true," her mother said through the door. "That's why the police are here again. We really need to talk to you about Vicky."

At that, Samantha jumped up, wondering if Vicky had showed up somewhere. She threw open the door and asked excitedly, "Where was she?"

Samantha watched as her mom's face went through multiple expressions, none of them happy.

"What? What's wrong?" Samantha asked.

Her mom placed her hand gently on Samantha's back and nudged her towards the stairs. "Come on down and let's talk."

Samantha wasn't sure what was wrong, but her gut was telling her it wasn't good. If she was being honest with herself, she probably knew what was wrong, but somewhere deep down, her soul refused to allow her to make the connection.

She rounded the corner at the bottom of the stairs and saw

the two officers sitting in the same chairs, while her dad sat in the same place he was the day before. Samantha wasn't sure what they were talking about, but as soon as she came in, they all stopped and turned to her. She felt for a moment like she was supposed to say something, but didn't know what.

"Hey, sweetie. Come sit down," her dad said, patting the cushion next to him.

Her mom followed behind her and sandwiched her in on the couch.

Samantha looked at Officer Reynolds and her partner, and blurted out, "Did you find Vicky? Where was she? Was she at Ricky's?"

Officer Reynolds cocked her head to the side. "Who's Ricky?"

Before Samantha could answer, Officer Reynolds followed up with, "Never mind. We'll get there." She took a deep breath and leaned forward, her elbows resting on her knees. "I wanted to come here and tell you myself. We've officially opened a missing person investigation for Vicky."

The words hit Samantha like someone swinging their backpack and not knowing she was behind them. She could see that Officer Reynolds was saying more, but she couldn't focus. *Vicky is missing.* She was right this whole time. If anyone had listened to her, they may have been able to find her already. How long had she been missing now? Was it too late? Where was she? Was it Mr. Davies that took her?

Her mom's hand on her back brought her back to the present.

"Sam? Honey? Did you hear Officer Reynolds?" her mom asked.

Samantha shook her head.

Officer Reynolds smiled and nodded. "I understand. I can only imagine what you're thinking and feeling. What I'd said was you were right. Vicky's mom and boyfriend were out of town, which means you all were the last ones to see Vicky. We will handle her mom separately. Since you all were the last to see her as far as we know, what time did Vicky leave your house?"

"She left probably around eight in the morning on Saturday," Samantha's dad answered.

"I thought you gave her a ride?" Samantha said, looking at her dad, confused. She could have sworn he came in and offered to take Vicky home, since Samantha was so sick.

He smiled at her, patted her knee, and replied, "She said she didn't want one."

Samantha stared at him for a moment. Before she could say anything else, Officer Reynolds followed up with, "What was the situation earlier with your neighbor?"

Samantha looked out the window and across the street. Mr. Davies wasn't there anymore.

"You should look into him. He's creepy. He would stare at Vicky, and the other day, he pulled up next to us and asked us if we wanted a ride home," Samantha said.

"You never told us that!" her mom said, shocked.

Samantha shrugged. "I never thought anything of him, really, but now I don't know."

Officer Reynolds nodded. "Okay, we'll definitely be having a conversation with him. Anything else?"

Samantha shook her head.

Officer Reynolds looked down at her notepad and tapped it with her pen. She looked up and leaned forward again, staring right at Samantha.

"I need you to be as honest as possible with me right now. Can you do that?"

Samantha gulped. She didn't know what she was about to ask, but it felt like it was just the two of them in the room and everyone else had disappeared.

"Do you know who that boy is that you mentioned the other day? The one Vicky said she was going to have come over. Is that Ricky?"

Samantha hesitated for only a moment. She imagined lying and saying no, and the police finding out she lied, coming back to her house and arresting her and putting her in jail for not telling the truth.

She'd already said his name. She couldn't deny that part, so she nodded.

"Okay, good. Now what can you tell me about Ricky?" Officer Reynolds asked, hesitating on the name as she looked down at her paper to make sure she had it right.

"Not much. I don't really know him. All I know is he's a senior that a lot of the girls like. No one actually calls him Ricky. They call him Blue Eyes. You know, 'cause his eyes are really blue."

Officer Reynolds smiled and jotted down a couple of things.

Samantha gulped again, unsure of what else they might want from her.

Weren't they wasting time sitting here asking her questions? Vicky had been missing for several days now. Shouldn't they be out looking for her?

Officer Reynolds said, "Okay, I think we have what we need for now. If there is anything else, please don't hesitate to call."

As she and her partner headed for the door, she turned and looked at Samantha.

"Oh yeah, one more quick question for you. Do you know where this Blue Eyes lives?"

Samantha's eyes flicked to the ground, then back up. "No. Sorry."

Officer Reynolds stared at her for a moment and then nodded. "Okay. We'll let you know as soon as we find out anything."

The two officers walked out, Samantha's dad closing the door behind them. Samantha watched from her spot on the couch as the officers headed down the sidewalk to their police car. They stopped and pointed across the street toward Mr. Davies' house, but got in their car instead of going and talking to him.

Samantha's heart was racing. She'd just lied to the police. But she couldn't have them go to Ricky's before she did. She needed to make sure for herself that Vicky wasn't just hiding out there.

The last thing she wanted was for Vicky to get in more trouble if she was just trying to avoid life right now.

It wouldn't have been the first time.

CHAPTER 37

NOW

"SHE'S NOT ANSWERING that. I'm sorry," Gabby says to the detective with her hand on Cynthia's arm.

"And why won't she?" the detective responds.

Cynthia looks from one to the other, wondering if they realize she is sitting right here. She feels like a small child whose parents are going back and forth about her while she's in the room.

"When we're at liberty to share that with you, we will," Gabby says with a tone indicating for him to move on.

"Let me ask a different question," Detective Harrison says, smiling like an alley cat playing with a mouse. He leans forward, slowly interlacing his fingers, and says, "So you saw a name on a sheet and it sent you directly to this address, where you were compelled to climb over a locked gate, and opened a door to a double homicide. I could hold you for trespassing."

"I don't hear a question," Gabby states.

"Are you in witness protection?" the detective asks, narrowing his eyes.

"And we're done," Gabby says with finality, half standing.

"Wait, hang on." Detective Harrison extends his arm towards Gabby. "I had to ask it. But I'll leave it alone—for the moment. Please sit down. I do need to tie up a couple of items."

Gabby stares at him and eventually lowers herself back into the chair. Cynthia takes the moment and asks a question that has been haunting her since she saw the board.

"I saw the whiteboard back there and noticed the victims' names on the board. You said there were other names that came up with them?"

Detective Harrison nods. "That's the strange thing. We know their names are Dennis and Cheri because that was what had returned with their fingerprints. But their driver's licenses in their wallets had different names. The correct address, just different names. We aren't sure why or if they were trying to hide their identities. It's something we're still digging into. Maybe the reason they had different names is the same reason someone killed them."

While he stops for a moment to take a breath, Gabby asks, "So what were the names?"

"Dennis' ID had his name listed as Graham Davies, and Cheri's as Sarah Barlow."

He looks at Cynthia and asks, "Do either of those names ring a bell?"

Cynthia stiffens, hoping it isn't obvious to the detective. The chill at those names washes over her. Her hands and feet sweat. She shakes her head back and forth and tries with everything she has to be confident in her response.

"No, they don't ring a bell."

It must have worked, because Detective Harrison leans back and blows out a breath toward the ceiling. He looks back at the two and says, "Well, okay. I was hoping you'd have something for me. I think I've been forthright with you so far and I just hope I'm getting the same from you."

Cynthia bristles at his comment. She can spot a passive aggressive comment a mile away. "I'm sorry, but my daughter is missing. I don't know why these two people were killed or how it relates to my daughter, but finding her is my main priority, not solving your crime. Isn't that your job?"

The detective puts his hands in the air, trying to lower the tension. "Hey, I'm sorry. I meant nothing by it. I truly hope she comes home to you and your husband."

Gabby steps in and asks, "Is there anything else, Detective Harrison?"

He looks from one to the other and says, "No, that's all. You're free to go."

Cynthia glares at him. She doesn't trust him. He says one thing, but everything else about him screams another.

The two of them stand to leave and head toward the door. Detective Harrison turns in his chair and asks, "Oh, one more question. Did Alexander ever have a partner?"

The question stops Cynthia dead in her tracks. She turns, not believing he's trying this tactic. Who does he think they are?

Cynthia shakes her head and Gabby asks, "Why?"

Detective Harrison shrugs and says, "Well, there is security camera footage from the home and there are two people entering. Unfortunately, both have hoods up and no discerning marks."

Both Gabby and Cynthia stand at the open door, and Gabby asks, "Can we see the tape?"

He turns away from them, scratching something out on his pad of paper, and says, facing the table, "Sorry, but I have to draw the line somewhere."

Cynthia fumes as the two walk back the way they'd come. She starts to slow at the conference room with the whiteboard, but Gabby grabs her wrist and pulls her away from it.

"Let's get out of here," Gabby says under her breath.

They push through the door and walk back through the lobby toward the main doors.

"Have a good day," the desk officer calls after them.

They ignore him and walk out into the sunshine.

The fresh air hits Cynthia, and all of her anger and frustration bubble over as she paces in the courtyard. She wants to yell and scream at the building, at that detective and his passive aggressive attitude, at his fake desire to help.

"Hey, hey," Gabby says. "Calm down. I know he's a dick. But what's going on?"

Cynthia slows her pacing and turns to Gabby.

"We need to go back to that crime scene. Now."

Gabby nods and the two head toward her car. "Do you want to tell me why?"

"On the way," Cynthia says.

Alexander's statement about clues had been ringing in Cynthia's head ever since the detective mentioned the driver's licenses. But the thing that concerned Cynthia more than anything was Alexander had never had a partner. Until now.

CHAPTER 38
NOW

PULLING UP TO the crime scene, Cynthia can't believe it was just yesterday she was here. Staring at it from Gabby's car at the gate, it actually looks smaller than she remembers it. It still reminds her a bit of The White House, but the black porte-cochère gives it a more modern feel.

Gabby is speaking with the officer at the gate and he hands over a clipboard.

"We'll need you both to sign in. There is another officer at the front door who will hand you gloves and coverings for your shoes, and escort you around. Please keep them on at all times inside."

Cynthia leans down to see the officer out Gabby's window and asks, "Can we explore the grounds first?"

"Yes ma'am," the officer says, all business.

Gabby passes the clipboard back to him, then he takes a quick look at their names and enters a code. The gate opens and Gabby maneuvers her car down the cobblestone driveway. They get out and Cynthia takes a quick look around.

"What are you looking for?" Gabby asks.

Cynthia shrugs and walks around the front perimeter of the house.

"Alexander said he was surprised I hadn't found any of his clues yet. The names of the victims, and the name of Blue Eyes for that matter, could have been the clues and nothing else, but I'm just making sure there aren't any others. I don't think he would have made them difficult to find, but still."

Gabby points at the edge of the porte-cochère where the camera points towards the gate. "That's probably the footage the detective was talking about."

Cynthia nods and walks back down to the gate, glancing at the bushes by the fountain where she lost her breakfast the day before. She gets to the same spot she had climbed over and looks back toward the house.

She starts back toward Gabby and calls out to her, "It would have been very easy for him to see the camera from the street and avoid being seen. It still isn't like Alexander to work with someone else. Are we sure it was him?"

Gabby looks at her as Cynthia rejoins her under the porte-cochère. "You tell me. You said only Alexander would know those names."

Cynthia nods as they take the gloves and booties from the officer at the front door and says, "You're right. It has to be him. It must be this Blue Eyes he's working with. Did he plant him at the coffee shop to lure Tori? How did he even know Tori was mine? Ugh, there are so many questions still."

Gabby wraps the bootie over her heel, assuring her, "We'll get them answered. And quick. We know the urgency."

While they are putting them on, the overweight bald officer stationed at the door says in a deep voice, "I'll be inside with you. Please be sure and mind the markers." He steps up to the door and pushes it open. Cynthia asks, "How do we know what happened?"

"I have access to the crime scene report," Gabby says, pulling up the information on her phone.

The two step inside while the officer positions himself near the ornate Spanish-inspired staircase a few feet away. Cynthia glances down at several yellow markers on the dark floral print area rug covering the entryway terrazzo tile. In the middle of the markers, there is a noticeable deep red stain spread across it.

Cynthia can hear Gabby's tone shift into what she calls her "work mode" as she reads from the report, "The female deceased, Cheri Matthews, was found just inside the doorway."

They pivot around the area rug, their heel clicks dampened only slightly by the booties. Cynthia pauses a moment, taking in the scene as Gabby explains what Detective Harrison believes to have happened.

"It looks like Mrs. Matthews answered the door and the assailants pushed their way in. When she turned to run, the perpetrator hit her over the head with some kind of blunt object. She fell right here and bled out."

Gabby walks down the hall toward the kitchen, the muffled echo of her heels bouncing against the walls. Cynthia stares at the bloodstain as she moves around it, as if it is a serpent coiled and ready to strike.

Gabby waits for her to catch up in the kitchen. Cynthia slows and takes it all in. There are several yellow markers with numbers on them along the floor in the hallway. There are what look like drops of blood near each marker.

The entire home has a Mediterranean and Spanish flair to it, and the kitchen is no different. A massive marble slab island sits in the middle of the stainless steel appliances. It looks more like something you'd find in a commercial kitchen, not a home. The floor is a deep red Spanish tile, with little black diamonds interspersed throughout.

There is another blood stain between the island and the built-in refrigerator. Gabby continues the tour. "Detective Harrison believes the assailant or assailants, as it were, moved this way down the hall and surprised Mr. Matthews as he came around the corner to see what the commotion was at the front of the house. According to the Medical Examiner's initial findings, it looks like both victims were killed at the same angle."

Cynthia asks, "What does that mean?"

"It means the same person killed both husband and wife. We can assume, because of the height of Mr. Matthews, that it was Alexander who did the killing, and the other person was here to learn."

Cynthia stares at the slight difference in color between the bloodstain and the tile.

"What are you thinking?" Gabby asks.

"I'm thinking Alexander never had help before. It feels really off to me."

"I agree," Gabby says. "But there are a lot of unknowns at the moment. I think we have to go on the assumption that he has changed his methods, and maybe he is trying to keep his legacy alive. He wouldn't be the first."

Cynthia, lost in her thoughts, mumbles, "Yeah, that's true."

Gabby's phone rings, the sound echoing around the large kitchen. "Agent Hayes."

Gabby moves back toward the entrance. Cynthia takes a moment to look around, seeing if Alexander could have left any other clues. She sweeps her eyes across the horseshoe kitchen. The refrigerator and sink next to her, the commercial oven and stove, with its brass accents, along the far wall. There is a door at the corner, which she assumes leads to a butler's pantry.

There is another sink along the other side of the horseshoe, with an oversized window leading out to the backyard. Cynthia gravitates toward the sink and looks out the window. The whole yard is an oasis of trees and shrubs, with a kidney-shaped pool in the middle. Cynthia's eyes rest at the far end of the yard where a small wooden gate sits with a canopy of trees over it. Whatever is beyond the gate, she can't make out, but it brings her back to a core memory she wishes she could forget.

Gabby disrupts her thoughts, coming back into the kitchen. "Hey, we gotta go. My agents are in the field that Alexander called from. They don't see anything, but they want me out there to take a look. They said there seems to be some odd rock formation and they've called in some excavators to help, just to be sure."

Hearing those three words sends chills down Cynthia's spine, especially with the memory at the forefront of her mind. "Odd rock formations?"

"Yeah, they aren't sure if it's just some kids messing around, or if it's more of a memorial set up. But knowing Alexander and his comment around clues, we can't be too safe."

Cynthia nods and says, "I want to go."

Gabby shakes her head. "I don't think that's a good idea."

"I don't care. No one knows him better than me. If this has to do with Tori or that finger, I need to be there. I saw the map too on the computer earlier. So you can either take me with you, or take me home and I'll drive myself there."

The two women stand in the kitchen staring at one another.

Gabby breaks first and sighs. "You know, it makes sense you became a lawyer."

Cynthia purses her lips and nods. "I know. And thank you. I really didn't know exactly where the field was, but I'd figure it out."

Gabby shakes her head and the two head back out to Gabby's car, removing their gloves and booties, handing them to the officer.

Getting into Gabby's car, Cynthia allows herself to head back down memory lane. She is confident of the formation she is going to see there, and she knows there is certainly someone's body buried underneath it.

CHAPTER 39

NOW

THE FIELD COMES into view as Gabby and Cynthia crest the hill. Half a dozen unmarked cars, four police cars with their lights flashing, and a white van are lined up against the street. Traffic crawls as everyone tries to glimpse what is happening. A white tent stands in the middle of the field with police tape roped off around it.

Cynthia and Gabby pull up behind one of the police cruisers and park.

Gabby looks at Cynthia and says, "Stay here while I see where they're at."

Cynthia shakes her head. "Not a chance. If there is any possibility of a clue from him, I need to see it immediately."

The two stare at each other for a moment, then Gabby sighs. "Fine, but stay back just in case."

They make their way along the police tape line and stop at an officer deciding who gets to come in. She can't be over twenty-two or twenty-three and is probably fresh out of the academy. Her sunglasses reflect Cynthia and Gabby as they approach, and her dark brown hair is pulled back into a bun.

Gabby pulls out her FBI identification and shows it to the officer. The officer nods, pulls up the police tape, and says, "Ma'am."

She holds it for the two of them and they duck under. Gabby glances back at Cynthia and instructs her, "Walk directly behind me. The last thing we need is any hint of crime scene contamination."

Cynthia is careful to follow directly in Gabby's steps. The field is a perfect square between two major thoroughfares, El Camino Real and Palomar Airport Road. It would not have been difficult for Alexander to make the call from here and vanish just as quickly in any direction he chose.

Gabby slows as they approach another roped-off area in the middle of the field. Cynthia takes a moment to look around.

How did Alexander get the body out here? Did he drag it here? Drive a car over here? How did no one see him do this?

If he did it in the dead of night, there would be no light out here, but would he take that risk?

Cynthia notices police tape angled from the white tent across the field and ending at Palomar Airport Road. There are several yellow markers on that path, as well.

"Agent Hayes," one of the other agents says, holding up the police tape. The two step under this interior tape, and another agent opens one side of the white tent for them. They both step in and Cynthia's world slows down. She was almost sure of the rock formation she would see, but seeing it again in person brings everything back. Just as if she was that child once more.

The tent is fifteen by fifteen and big enough for the central area of focus, even with two forensic excavator specialists and three agents inside.

Cynthia knows the rock formation. When she saw it as a

child, she thought it was a one-time occurrence, but evidently, it had been his calling card all this time. How Alexander had ever thought it up, she didn't know and probably never would. A dozen small stones form an arc toward the far end of the tent, and a larger, jagged rock is pointed straight up in the middle.

Another rectangle of police tape surrounds the mound of dirt. The two excavators in white gear are using brushes to remove dirt and debris, ensuring they are not disturbing what they assume is the body.

"Do we know if there's a body yet?" Gabby asks one of her agents.

"No, ma'am. They only just started. It took some time getting them out here and getting everything set up. We also noted tire tracks coming off the main road."

Gabby nods.

Cynthia stands and stares, waiting. She knows that the finger didn't belong to Tori, but it doesn't necessarily mean that the body is not hers. Even though no one is saying it, Cynthia knows there is a body buried here. She pushes the thought out of her mind and thinks of David.

Should she have called him? She assumed this whole time that the body wasn't Tori's, but now, standing here, she wonders.

"Should I call David?" she asks quietly.

Gabby purses her lips. "Let's wait."

The two stand there and watch, and Cynthia's mind drifts back to when Tori was little and how happy their lives were. She remembers how grateful she was to have escaped Alexander. But she has always carried a pang of guilt for not telling her family about her past.

"We've got a body!" one excavator calls out.

Both excavators are now focused at the top of the arc, brushing away dirt and debris to reveal the face of whoever was unfortunate enough to come in contact with Alexander.

Cynthia is confident it will be a young girl, but who?

The excavator says, "Female, looks about sixteen, seventeen."

Cynthia's heart drops. *Please, not blond*, she thinks. She hates herself for the thought, but she cannot help it: *Not blond hair, not blond hair.*

"Brown hair. Looks to be Hispanic."

"No!" Cynthia shouts, her hand shooting up to her mouth. She lunges toward the tape, but Gabby grabs her and pulls her back. Cynthia gets a look and rushes out of the tent, collapsing to the ground.

Gabby follows her out. "You know her?"

The image of the sweet young girl's face, caked in dirt and blood, her cloudy white eyes staring up at her, embeds itself into Cynthia's mind.

"It's—it's Tori's best friend, Sofia," Cynthia ekes out.

Cynthia digs her hands into the ground, her anger, fear, and anguish pulsing through every inch of her. "Oh my god! No, no, no!"

Gabby squats down beside her and places her hand on Cynthia's back.

"How?" Cynthia asks, her thoughts coming in fragments. "How did Alexander get a hold of Sofia? I should have figured it out! She wasn't there. She was supposed to be."

"What are you talking about?" Gabby asks.

"Oh my god! Her father! He's going to—how am I going to tell him?"

"You won't, sweetheart. We will." Gabby tries to reassure her. "That is not your job. It's ours."

Cynthia pulls her hands from the dirt, brushes them off on her pants, and runs her fingers through her hair.

"Why her?" Cynthia shouts. "What does he want?"

Two officers look in their direction, but Gabby waves them off.

"We'll figure that out. I promise."

"Agent Hayes!" one agent shouts.

Gabby gets up and hurries back to the tent.

Sofia and Tori as little girls fill Cynthia's mind, pushing away the fear and anger and submerging her in anguish and sadness.

Images of the girls crowd Cynthia's vision: playing dress-up, running around their backyard, jumping into the pool. Cutting through the homemade movies in her mind is Gabby walking towards her.

She now has white gloves and is holding a phone in one hand.

"They found Sofia's phone in her jacket pocket," Gabby says softly.

She hands Cynthia a pair of gloves and Cynthia puts them on. Everything feels like a fever dream right now. How can this be happening?

Gabby hands her the phone and Cynthia opens it. She is surprised there is no passcode on it.

"We think Alexander turned it off—"

Gabby pauses and Cynthia catches it.

"What?" Cynthia asks. Even in her haze, she knows Gabby was going to say something else.

Gabby answers her, her voice soft. "The finger. It's Sofia's."

Cynthia bursts into new tears and heartache. She can only hope Alexander removed it after he killed her, but she is too afraid to ask. Cynthia looks down at the phone through her tear-filled eyes and can't even comprehend what she should be doing.

She glances down at the bottom of the screen and notices only one app—the messages app. Clicking on it brings up what would normally be a list of people Sofia has texted. But there is only one name on the list: Tori.

CHAPTER 40

NOW

CYNTHIA STARES AT the screen. She wants to press on her daughter's name and see what the text message string looks like, but also, she doesn't.

What if it's nothing? What if it's just Tori saying good morning, and that's it? What then? They will be no closer to finding Tori or figuring out Alexander's clues.

What even was the point of those names on those driver's licenses? Telling her it was him? She knows that. What kind of sick game is he playing?

"Hey," Gabby says, startling Cynthia out of her thoughts. "Do you want me to look at it?"

Cynthia shakes her head. "No. I have to do it."

Cynthia presses Tori's name and the text string opens up. It looks like their entire text history. She does a quick scroll and sees it goes on and on.

Cynthia swipes back to the bottom of the text string, the most recent one where Tori texted Sophia yesterday morning and said: *hey. coffee?*

Sofia responded with: *pls!*

Cynthia scrolls back and scans different segments of the text string.

Tori: *hey, wyd?*

Sofia: *pretending to study* (INSERT laughing emoji) *u?*

Tori: *planning hookup* (INSERT Devil horns emoji)

Sofia: *spill!*

Tori: *haha. i will. tomorrow. ugh my mom is yelling for me. ttyl*

The conversation is dated a week ago. Was this supposed to be Blue Eyes that Tori would tell Sofia about?

Cynthia continues to scroll backward through the messages, scanning various conversations about how mean their parents are and how Mr. Reynolds is so hot; they swear that Mr. Reynolds and Ms. Samuels are hooking up. Cynthia pauses there and reads for a second.

Tori: *can you imagine how much they'd make on OF?*

Sofia: *right? I might even pay to see that* (INSERT laughing emoji)

Tori: *shit, we should start one! become billionaires! we're hot enough* (INSERT hot face emoji)

Sofia: *u for sure. i'll stick with feet pics* (INSERT laughing emoji)

Tori: (INSERT laughing emoji)

Cynthia shakes her head, unsure how she should feel reading these texts.

Does any parent know their child? Was I like this when I was her age?

Cynthia doesn't want to keep scrolling, afraid of what else she might discover, but she has to. There is a reason Tori's text string was the only one on Sofia's phone. Alexander did this on purpose.

Cynthia scrolls back further, barely scanning messages as

she goes. Nothing looks important, but then she sees something that stops her.

A text from Tori that says: *kk, i'll pick my phone up when we're done. just leave it in the same place. i'll be quiet so ur dad doesn't wake up.*

Cynthia scrolls farther, trying to find the start of this conversation, and stops when she thinks she has it.

Tori: *hey. Need to drop my phone off like last time. worked perfect.*

Sofia: *kk. same guy, same place?*

Tori: *same guy, new place.*

Sofia: *where?*

Tori: *old vista. J found it. says its been abandoned for a while. city took the last one.*

Sofia: *kk. good to know.*

Tori: *here's the address, jic. hes a decent lay, but still creepy. 378 Lone Oak Ln.*

Sofia: *haha, for sure. what time u dropping it off? need to make sure my dad isn't here.*

Tori: *like 7?*

Sofia: (INSERT thumbs up emoji)

Cynthia scrolls down a bit and only sees Tori saying the word *dropped*, and then at midnight, there's one more text from Tori: *got it. see ya in the am,* with a kissing face emoji.

Cynthia is still on the ground and pushes herself to stand. Gabby is staring at her and the other agents are moving around, coming in and out of the tent. Traffic is still crawling on both roads and drivers are trying to see what is happening.

"Anything?" Gabby asks.

Cynthia looks down at the phone again, trying to figure out what to say or where to start. "Yes? No? I'm not sure."

Why would Tori drop her phone off at Sofia's before meeting someone named J? Who was J? Why wouldn't Tori keep her phone with her?

Cynthia's phone rings and she freezes for a moment, unsure of what to do. Sofia's phone is in one hand; she has latex gloves on and is afraid of touching anything else. Gabby holds out her hand and Cynthia gives her Sofia's phone. She removes one glove and pulls her phone out of her back pocket.

It's David.

She answers it on the third ring. "Hello?"

"Hey, where are you?"

"What?" Cynthia responds.

"I came home to talk, but you're not here. I looked at the Finder app and it shows you're in a field?"

The app! Of course! A flood of thoughts rushes through Cynthia's mind.

"I—I'll explain everything. Please don't leave. I promise I'll answer every question you have. But right now, I have to go. I promise. I love you."

Cynthia hangs up before David can say anything. She quickly brings up the Finder app and goes to the family section. She clicks on Tori's name and clicks on history. She holds out her hand for Gabby to give her back Sofia's phone. With her phone in one hand and Sofia's in the other, Cynthia scrolls back through the text string to around two months ago. Thankfully, the app keeps the last ninety days of data.

Cynthia scrolls back to the same day, two months ago, and sees a message from Tori to her:

i won't be home for dinner. studying at Sof's.

Cynthia had responded: *Okay, sounds good, sweetie. Do you know what time you'll be home?*

Tori: *late. prolly like 11 or 12.*

Cynthia: *Okay. Text us when you're on your way home.*

Tori: *kk*

The following text is from the next day and continues their everyday conversations.

She had never been at Sofia's that night. She dropped her phone off at Sofia's so that if she or David checked, it would look like she was there studying. Instead, she went to some abandoned house to do God knows what with some boy whose name starts with a J.

Who is this girl? What happened to our sweet little Tori?

"Cynth, what is it?" Gabby asks.

Just then, as if the distraction helped her brain connect, she knows who J is. Jacob fucking Harris.

Cynthia looks up at Gabby. "I know where we have to go."

CHAPTER 41

THEN

EVERYONE WAS ACTING too normal. *Don't they know she's missing? Why hasn't the world stopped to look for her?*

Those thoughts and more were ravaging Samantha's mind. She sat at the dining room table while her parents worked on dinner on the other side of the counter in the kitchen. Samantha's dad's favorite band was playing over the speaker. She didn't know who would name a band The Rat Pack, but the music didn't sound like anything she or her friends would listen to.

Her mom stood at the counter facing her, cutting vegetables. Her dad had his back to her and was stirring what she thought was spaghetti in a pot on the stove. They hadn't said a single word about Vicky since the police left. Didn't they care?

Samantha watched a local news station on mute on the small TV that sat on the counter. Any other time, she wouldn't even think about watching the news, but she was eager to see if they had any information about Vicky. She wasn't sure they'd even talk about her. No one else seemed to care.

Samantha focused on the TV, ignoring her parents' humming music and doing gross stuff like kissing. The news had a segment at a park, then they cut back to the news person at the studio. Samantha sat as close as she could to hear what the newscaster was saying. The words "MISSING CHILD ALERT" flashed on the screen.

Samantha sat up with alarm. The news showed a picture of Vicky!

An emergency hotline number popped up on the screen under Vicky's picture.

Samantha looked at her parents, who were laughing while the music was crescendoing throughout the kitchen. Her anger was building toward them and the police, who weren't acting concerned at all.

Looking back at the TV, Ms. Barnard was now on the screen. Samantha leaned very close to the small TV and turned it up just enough to make out the words.

"We caught up earlier today with the principal of Lincoln Middle to get an idea of who Vicky was," the newscaster said.

"Vicky is just the kindest student," Ms. Barnard said. "We have been concerned about her whereabouts and hope she is safe and unharmed."

The news next cut to a clip from Vicky's neighborhood, where her mom and her boyfriend were standing on the sidewalk with the camera facing away from Vicky's home. Samantha rolled her eyes, as she had never seen Vicky's mom so clean and put together.

"We are here with Mrs. Smith and her boyfriend, Victor Bruce," the newscaster said. "They are worried sick about Vicky and hope she comes home soon."

"Vicky, if you can hear me, I miss you, sweetheart," said Vicky's mom. "I need you to come home. Wherever you are, please just come home. You aren't in trouble. I want you back. You are the most important thing in my life."

Samantha slammed her hands on the counter.

"Are you kidding me?! None of you care! Where were you days ago when I was worried about her?!"

Samantha's parents stopped what they were doing and rushed around the counter, glancing at the television. Samantha's mom saw Vicky's picture and turned to her. "Oh, sweetie. We care. There is only so much we can do at the moment."

Samantha pointed to the TV. "They don't care. Not really. Vicky's mom has never looked like that. It's just an act. Why isn't there a search party? Why aren't we combing every inch of the woods? The lakes? We need to do something!"

Samantha's dad hugged her. "Hey, we'll do whatever we can. But we can't get a lot done if it's just us. There needs to be lots of people, and they're starting to put the word out. Let's see if something comes of this, and if not, then we can look to organize something bigger. Okay?"

Samantha wriggled out of the hug and marched out of the kitchen. She turned and stared at them, her arms crossed over her chest. "What did you mean when you said Vicky was rough around the edges?"

"Well, you see, sweetie," her mom started. "Not everyone has a good home life. Look at you. You have parents who love you and love one another. That makes you well-rounded. Others don't have it quite so great."

Samantha stared at her with a look of confusion on her face.

"What does that even mean?" She grabbed her shoes at the entryway and put them on. She took her coat and jammed each arm in.

"Where are you going?" her dad asked, his tone firm.

"If no one else will look for her, I will. I have to do something!"

Samantha yanked open the door and slammed it shut. She marched down the street thinking, *If you need to do something right, do it yourself.*

CHAPTER 42

NOW

"TURN RIGHT UP here," Cynthia says, looking at the map on her phone. The navigation is playing, but Cynthia needs something to do. She doesn't know where her mind will head if she doesn't distract herself.

"Are you sure this is it?" Gabby asks.

They park at the end of a cul-de-sac, staring at the most dilapidated house they've ever seen. Cynthia can recall some run-down homes, but this is next level. The roof is missing in some areas. The weeds have to be at least three to four feet tall. Roots and other greenery are growing up through the shattered concrete. Someone has boarded up every window with spray paint and obscene gestures.

Staring at the home, Cynthia realizes that if she looks at it just right, it looks like the house is leaning.

"I'm sure. Meaning I'm sure it's the address. But I can't believe Tori would come here."

"Let me go in and look around first," Gabby offers.

Cynthia shakes her head. "No way. I need to see everything

as it is. I don't need you sugarcoating anything. I'm almost certain Tori isn't here, but she was at some point."

She pauses momentarily, taking in her surroundings, realizing how history repeats itself. "My daughter isn't who I thought she was, but Alexander has her. For some reason, he wanted me to come here. I know that much."

Gabby sighs. "Okay, but let me clear the house first. As an FBI agent, I cannot in good conscience allow you to enter an unknown premises."

Cynthia stares straight ahead, weighing if it makes sense to argue that point. She agrees and says, "Fine. But I'm giving you five minutes, then I'm coming in either way, and you better not hide anything."

"Understood," Gabby says and gets out of the car.

She moves slowly toward the entrance, her gun drawn. Gabby disappears inside and Cynthia glances at the clock in the car, setting a mental timer for five minutes. While she waits, she thinks about the last day and a half, and about Tori.

Cynthia knows Alexander will keep his promise and wonders how many poor girls have died since he escaped all those years ago. She had assumed the Marshals were doing all they could to find him, but now she isn't so sure. She believes someone high up has helped him escape and wonders if the same person has been helping him all these years.

If so, they should get what's coming to them.

Cynthia wonders where life is going to go once they get Tori back. Now that she knows she isn't as innocent as she assumed, how will it change? Are she and David going to let Tori stay at home? Will it be time for her to go out on her own? Will therapy be an option?

Before she can overthink the questions, Gabby walks out

the front door and waves Cynthia over. She gets out and maneuvers around the mounds of dirt, roots, and concrete blocks.

"It's all clear, but—" Gabby starts to warn her.

Cynthia shakes her head and waves her off. "No. Don't tell me anything. Let me see everything fresh."

Gabby hesitates, a look of concern in her eye. "Okay. But—"

"I said no," Cynthia says firmly, pushing past Gabby and walking inside.

She pulls out her phone's flashlight and uses it to look around. From the weak light, Cynthia can tell right away that there are several mattresses strewn about the living room floor. Directly ahead is a hallway with a staircase on the left.

Gabby comes up behind with a high-powered flashlight and hands it to Cynthia. A layer of dirt and dust is on the floor, leaving footprints behind with every step they take. Cynthia assumes she knows why the mattresses are there, but she is shocked that teens would even do that kind of thing here.

Next to each mattress is a box of condoms. Some boxes are empty and smashed, while others remain sealed shut. Taped to the wall by each mattress are Polaroids. Cynthia moves closer to one mattress, shining the light directly at the Polaroids. As a mother and a respectable woman, she can't believe what she's looking at. She might expect something like this in a crack house or some human trafficking place, but seeing it somewhere a bunch of teens come shocks her.

A third party took some Polaroids, and others were selfies. All of them show at least two teens, sometimes three, engaging in all kinds of explicit acts on the mattresses. She only looks at them long enough to realize they are all like this. Each picture has the teens' names in the image with a month on it.

The text from Tori to Sofia returns to her, and she moves quicker around the room, trying to only look at faces. She hopes she won't see Tori's face, but deep down, she knows it's here somewhere.

Finishing the living room, Cynthia moves up the stairs. There are three bedrooms up here. She goes through one of them and is soon on to the next, which has three mattresses in it. Stopping at the second, her heart drops. It only takes her a moment to recognize the bright blond hair and piercing blue eyes of her not-so-little girl. The names are Tori & Blue Eyes—March.

March? How is that possible? Tori only told her and David yesterday that she was going out with him. How was this image taken over a month ago? Were there even more things Tori had hidden from them? Why would she just now tell them about this boy?

Cynthia looks away as quickly as possible but sees another Polaroid with Tori's face. She glances down at the names, trying to avoid looking at the other body parts in the Polaroid.

Tori & Jacob—February.

Cynthia's stomach knots as she reads the name. She hurries out of the room, not wanting to see any more images and needing fresh air. She was sure the *J* stood for Jacob, but seeing it in print and the picture now seared into her mind makes her want to hurl.

She fumbles down the stairs and outside, bending at the waist, trying to get fresh air and expunge those images from her mind.

Gabby comes up behind her. "I'm sorry."

Before Cynthia can say anything, her phone rings. She assumes it's Alexander, and he somehow knows where she is.

"I swear to God, I'll fucking kill you!"

"Cynth?"

Cynthia pulls the phone away and sees David's name on the caller ID.

"Cynth? What's happened? Where are you?"

"I'm coming home and telling you everything."

CHAPTER 43
THEN

SAMANTHA STOOD ON the curb, staring at Vicky's house. Was it yesterday or the day before when she and the police had been there? She was confused because she had seen the news people interviewing Vicky's mom, so she figured there would be news cameras and police all over. But Vicky's house was quiet. Nothing was going on. If Samantha hadn't known Vicky was missing, she would have thought nothing was different.

Samantha walked closer to the house and looked around at the neighbors' homes. She thought they would be out front trying to find out what was going on, but no one was out. It was almost as if no one even knew Vicky was missing.

Samantha took a deep breath, stood up as tall as she could, and marched toward Vicky's house. Everything looked the same: the tarp over the garage and the yard's weeds. Didn't Vicky's mom care about how her house looked?

She stepped up to the front door and knocked politely. She waited a moment, glancing around, still confused and angry that no one was there looking for Vicky. No one came to the door. Samantha tried again, knocking louder this time. Everything was still quiet.

Was Vicky's mom home? Maybe she was out looking for her?

Samantha doubted that but had to hope.

She thought about leaving for a moment but thought she heard a bottle knock over inside. Samantha pounded on the door this time. She would not be so polite. She needed to know for sure that Vicky's mom wasn't at home.

Samantha continued to pound, letting her anger and frustration get the better of her. Once she stopped, she glanced at her hand and saw the redness on the side. She could hear movement inside and what sounded like furniture moving.

A smell hit Samantha as the door opened violently and Vicky's mom stood just inside the screen. She wasn't sure what the smell was, but it was sweet and sour at the same time. She assumed it was the smell of alcohol, since Vicky's mom stood there swaying with a bottle in her hand.

"Wha' is it?" Vicky's mom slurred, her head bobbing, squinting at Samantha.

"Why aren't you out looking for Vicky?" Samantha asked, her voice strained.

Vicky's mom scoffed and stumbled backward. "Don't you know she's gone?"

"So? That doesn't matter! I'm going to find her! She's going to come live with me!"

Vicky's mom laughed at Samantha, blowing hot air in her face.

The smell made Samantha want to throw up. She took a step back, stumbling on the top step.

A male voice bellowed from deeper in the house, "Who the hell is it?"

Vicky's mom called back over her shoulder, "That stupid little bitch friend!"

There was a sound of furniture scraping as Vicky's mom's boyfriend appeared from the darkened house. Samantha realized it was the same sound she had heard before—the two of them bumping into furniture, being as drunk as they were.

He pushed open the screen, forcing Samantha down the steps.

"What the hell do you want? Ya know you're the reason she's gone," he said, jamming his finger toward Samantha.

Samantha knew that wasn't true, but when she heard those words, tears formed at the corners of her eyes.

She was shocked someone would say something so hurtful. She couldn't even speak. Vicky's mom's boyfriend continued his verbal assault on Samantha. "If it wasn't for you and your 'I'm too good for you' attitude, she probably wouldn't have run away."

He bobbed his head at Samantha and stumbled back up the steps. Vicky's mom glared at Samantha, now with a cigarette hanging loosely from her mouth.

Samantha stiffened up, finding her resolve. She clenched her hands into fists and stepped back toward them. "Well, I'm going to find her. She knows I don't think I'm too good. She knows she can trust me—we're like sisters. She can come live with me and be *my* sister. And she'll never have to come back to this horrible place."

The boyfriend turned around, now standing back inside behind Vicky's mom. He scoffed and said, "Eh. Good luck. Don't waste your time. She made her choice and left."

He turned and disappeared into the darkened house. Vicky's mom grabbed the screen and pulled it shut. She started to close the main door, but stopped and looked at Samantha before she did.

Samantha thought she saw a glimpse of sadness in Vicky's mom's eyes.

"Go home," Vicky's mom said, the cigarette bouncing on her lips. "Nothing more we can do about it."

The door shut, and Samantha stood there alone once more.

Emotion and pain overwhelmed Samantha, and she stood there and wept.

Samantha felt a hand touch her back and she jumped, spinning around and screaming. Her heart slammed in her chest for only a second as she realized it was her dad standing there.

"What? What are you—" was all Samantha could say.

"I was worried about you. I wanted to make sure you were okay," he said. "You're not. Let's go home. I promise we'll do everything we can to find her. Okay, Sam?"

Samantha nodded and accepted her dad's hug. She followed him back to his car and got into the back seat when he opened the door for her.

She sat there, staring back at Vicky's house as her dad got in and started the car. She stayed fixed on the house as they drove away.

Samantha absently put her hand in the crack between her seat and the middle seat as she watched Vicky's house recede. She felt something in the crevice and with two fingers, wrapped them around the object and pulled it out.

Everything in her world stopped as she stared at the object.

How could this be? What was it doing here? How did it get here?

Sitting in her hand was the butterfly clip she had given

Vicky for her birthday. That was the last time she had seen her. So how did it get in her dad's car?

Samantha thought back to the police at her house and how her parents had said Vicky had walked home. She thought her dad had given Vicky a ride, but he said she was mistaken. How did the clip get in her dad's car if she had walked home?

"I'll help you find her, I promise," her dad said, glancing at her in the rearview mirror and giving her a wink.

CHAPTER 44

NOW

CYNTHIA GETS OUT of the car and slams the door. David has been waiting out front. He runs to her, grabbing her and wrapping his arms around her. Lacing his fingers in her hair, he breathes her in.

"I'm so sorry," he says. "I don't know what came over me. The most important thing is getting Tori back. I know you love me—love us."

Cynthia breaks at these words. She sobs into his shoulder, gripping the back of his shirt. The tears won't stop as she convulses in hysterics in his arms.

"When I called you and you thought I was Alexander, I realized I have no idea what you're going through. I'm here. I'm sorry. Let me know what I can do and we'll find our girl."

Cynthia nods as she's crying, knowing she is leaving tear and snot stains on his shirt.

He brushes his hand down her hair and wraps his other arm around her.

Cynthia doesn't know how long they stay in their embrace, but she realizes she needs this. It's been invaluable having

Gabby here by her side, but having her husband with her, supporting her even without knowing everything, gives her the grit she needs to continue.

She needs to tell David everything. She can't let it go on any longer. Cynthia pulls away from him and wipes at her eyes, knowing it's smearing her mascara everywhere.

"God, I look like such a mess," she says.

"Yeah, well, you're my mess," David coos, leaning in and kissing her head.

He cups her head in his hands and chuckles.

"What?" she asks.

He shakes his head. "Nothing."

"Tell me."

David hesitates, chuckling again, and says, "I say this with all the love in the world, but you kinda remind me of a raccoon right now."

Cynthia smiles at this, knowing exactly what she looks like. She pulls back to look him in the face, but something catches her eye.

Jacob is standing in the middle of the street, staring at the two of them, one arm straight at his side, the other crossed over his body and his hand rubbing at his elbow.

"You!" Cynthia snarls. She breaks away from David and lunges forward.

Even though Jacob is in the middle of the street, her movement startles him and he jumps back a few feet, putting his arms out and stuttering, "I—I—I just want to help."

David grabs her before Cynthia can do anything as Gabby rushes between both Cynthia and Jacob.

"Hey," Gabby says, soothing Cynthia like she's a cornered

tiger. “Let’s not do anything rash. Okay? The focus is Tori, not anything we saw. Right?”

Cynthia is glaring past Gabby at Jacob.

“How dare you touch her like that,” she spits.

Jacob looks confused and mumbles, “I—I didn’t take her. I swear. I want to help find her.”

“Yeah?” Cynthia yells. “What about the house, huh? The abandoned one?”

Jacob’s eyes go wide and he takes a few steps backwards.

“Yeah. That’s what I thought. We know about that. We’ve seen the pictures. Fuck, the pictures!” Cynthia yells, new tears welling up in her eyes.

“I—I—” Jacob starts. “It was her idea. I swear.”

“Here’s an idea,” Cynthia says, jabbing a finger toward his house. “How about you get the fuck out of here!”

Jacob makes a sound like he’s crying, covers his face, and runs back to his house, slamming the door behind him.

Cynthia stands there, slowly lowers her hand, and swallows hard.

“You okay?” Gabby asks.

Cynthia nods.

“Do you want to tell me what that was about?” David asks gently.

“I’ll give you two some privacy,” Gabby says, heading towards the house.

“Agent Hayes,” one of the agents calls from the front door, waving her in.

Cynthia turns around and wipes under her eyes with her index fingers. She looks up at the sky above, the sun shining, and takes a deep breath. She wipes her nose with the back of her hand and says, “God, I don’t even know where to begin. If

I told you where I'd just come from. I don't even know if I can describe it out loud. And the field—"

Thinking about Sofia's body, she starts to tear up again.

"I think I just need to start at the very beginning. We need to sit down for this," Cynthia says. She takes his hand and leads him toward the house.

"Cynthia! David!" Gabby calls from the front door.

They hurry inside, where two agents are sitting on the couch and one is pointing at something on a monitor.

"What is it? Is it Tori?" Cynthia asks, knowing better than to get her hopes up.

"Not necessarily, but it's our best lead yet. Tell them."

One of the agents on the couch explains, "We have a lead on the one you've been calling Blue Eyes. We got into the security system cloud feed from The Joe coffee shop. We had to go back quite a ways to find the right angle, but we found it."

"What are you saying?" Cynthia asks, pressing the agent.

"His car, on the parking lot camera. We got a visual on his plates and ran them. They came back with a hit. We have his address."

"What are we waiting for?" Cynthia asks excitedly.

Gabby responds, "Just to let you know. We're already coordinating with local PD and we have our own team en route. I'm heading there now and assume you'll want to come with me."

"Yes!" Cynthia says, but follows it up by looking at David. "But I owe you an explanation."

David pulls her to the side, just out of the earshot of the agents.

"Go. I'll stay here in case anything else happens. I know you want to tell me everything, and there will be time for that.

But right now, this is the most important thing. Finding Tori and bringing her home safe. Don't worry about me."

Cynthia plows into her husband, wrapping her arms around his neck and kissing him.

"I love you and I'll explain everything as soon as possible. I promise."

He cups a hand on her cheek and stares into her. For the briefest moments, the chaos of their lives falls away as she gets lost in his deep blue eyes.

Everything comes rushing back to her and she smiles, kissing him again. "Thank you. Can you scour Tori's room? I know the agents already went through everything, but they aren't her parents. See if anything looks out of place or missing. Think as if you were Tori wanting to hide something from us."

"Hide what?" David asks.

Cynthia shrugs. "I don't know. I know she wasn't who we thought she was. Put yourself in the shoes of a teenage girl."

David looks at her.

"Do your best."

She squeezes his arm and gives him one more peck on the cheek, feeling his stubble against her lips.

"Thank you. I love you."

"I love you too," he says. "And be safe!"

CHAPTER 45

THEN

SAMANTHA WALKED IN a daze. The world could be on fire for all she knew, and she'd be clueless. Samantha realized she had no idea what any teacher had said during classes. Did she have homework? Was there a test or a quiz?

She had no clue.

Samantha's entire mental energy was focused on Vicky and the small clip she continued to turn over and over in her pocket. Walking down the sidewalk from the school, she pulled it out and looked at it again.

It was definitely the butterfly clip she'd given Vicky, but the *S* and the *V* were already starting to disappear with how much she touched it.

What was it doing in her dad's car?

She hadn't had the courage to ask him about it. When they'd gotten home, he had asked her if she wanted dessert, but she claimed she was tired and had gone straight up to bed. He had come in not long after and she faked being asleep. She knew she couldn't keep avoiding him. It had been almost two days since she found the clip in his car.

Staring at the sidewalk as she made her way home, Samantha tried with all her might to remember that night when she gave Vicky the clip and how much she'd loved it.

She could have sworn her dad had come in, determined she had a fever, and suggested he give Vicky a ride home. Right? Wasn't that what had happened?

He'd said Vicky walked home. She'd even told the police that he had given her a ride, but he told her that wasn't what happened.

So how, then, did the clip get in his car?

She knew she had to pull out the clip and ask him to explain it. Could she even do that?

Samantha looked up, hoping the universe would give her the answer, and then stopped cold.

It was Homeless Harriett.

At least that's what Vicky called her. Samantha was starting to look at everything differently now that Vicky was missing. She realized they hadn't been very nice to this woman. They had no idea if her name was Harriett, and Samantha was fairly certain it wasn't.

It went with Homeless, so that was what they called her.

Whenever she was out, the woman shuffled around, muttering to herself and sometimes trying to pet random birds or people.

She regularly yelled at cars driving by.

Samantha and Vicky would always avoid her, even stepping out into the street or crossing to the other side of the road. But now Samantha was too close. She had no option but to go right past her.

But only a few feet away from her, Samantha realized she wasn't as scary as they had always made her out to be. She could smell her from where she stood, which was unpleasant. But beyond that, if Samantha looked past the ragged clothes, the multiple layers, her greasy hair matted to her face, she could be someone's grandma.

Homeless Harriett looked in Samantha's direction, stopped muttering, and stared at her. She smiled, and the gaps in her yellow teeth caused Samantha to take a step back. That was something she had never seen before.

"It's Samantha, right?" Homeless Harriett said.

Samantha was shocked at how clear her speech was and that she knew her name.

"Uh, um, yeah?" Samantha said.

There was a twinkle in Harriett's eye, and she said, "Are you sure?"

Samantha shook it off and said, "Yes. Yes, I'm Samantha. How, how did you know my name?"

Harriett cocked her head to the side and glanced up. "I just know. I know a lot."

A thought passed through Samantha's mind, and she asked, "Do you know my friend, Vicky?"

Harriett clapped her hands together and said, "Of course! I saw her a few days ago!"

Samantha's heart started to race. "You did? When?"

Harriett rested an elbow on her other crossed arm and tapped her second chin with a gloved finger. "Hmmm, let me see. It was four moons and three pigeons ago."

Samantha's hopes fell. A few *days* ago?! Samantha racked her brain trying to remember a time before Vicky went missing. She did have a dentist appointment about a week ago. Was that what Harriett was talking about?

"I was surprised to see her alone and not with you, but I was even more surprised when she got into the blue car."

"A blue car? Was there anything else about it?"

"Well, I was surprised no one came and asked me about it."

"Why's that?"

"Well, she got in, kissed the driver, and they drove off."

"Did you see what he looked like?"

Harriett shook her head.

"No, but that wasn't the strangest thing. The crazy part was as soon as they drove past, the car lifted into the sky, and they flew away right up to the spacecraft hovering overhead."

Samantha's shoulders dropped. She didn't know if any of this was true or just pieces. She nodded her head and held her breath as she walked past Harriet.

Samantha kept her head down, shuffled by, and said, "Thanks anyway, Harriet."

As she passed her, Harriett said, "It's Carol."

Samantha stopped and turned. She realized as far as Homeless Harriett-Carol was concerned, she was helping out.

Samantha gave her a little smile and said, "Thank you, Carol."

CHAPTER 46
NOW

GABBY AND CYNTHIA step out of the car. Already on the scene are three police cruisers stationed in front of the tiny bungalow. Before Cynthia even notices the other officers, she takes note of a blue car in the driveway. They're three blocks from the coast, and the marine layer is moving in for the late afternoon. The officers are all kneeling behind their open doors, guns drawn toward the house.

"Anything?" Gabby asks, stepping up to one of the officers.

"Officer Baker, ma'am. And no, we were waiting for you."

Gabby taps him on the shoulder and says, "Okay, Baker, let's check it out."

Turning to Cynthia, Gabby says, "Wait here. Let us clear it first."

Cynthia nods, her hand coming to her mouth as she nibbles on her nail.

"Can you wait here with her?" Gabby asks another officer whose uniform looks two sizes too big, like he is fresh out of the academy.

He nods, looking nervous.

"Okay, let's go," Gabby says, drawing her gun.

Officer Baker leads the group with Gabby in the middle and a female officer closing the gap behind her. She is the same height, build, and complexion as Gabby. She has one hand on Gabby's shoulder and the other on her weapon. When they get to the door, Officer Baker stays stationary, while Gabby peels off to the left and the other officer peels off to the right.

Officer Baker pivots towards Gabby, glancing at her, who nods. He quickly raps on the door three times and declares in a booming voice, "Christian Williams. Open up. Carlsbad Police."

He waits a moment, and repeats his quick three raps and his call when there is no answer.

With still no answer, he glances back at Gabby and tries the door. It opens easily, and the three look at each other with heightened senses.

This can't be good. He isn't answering and he hasn't locked his front door. Cynthia doesn't know what they are walking into, but she hopes and prays there won't be any kind of explosion.

She watches as they vanish inside. She can hear calls of "Clear!" coming from inside. It isn't a large place, so she hears soon after, "We have a body!"

Hearing those words, Cynthia rushes up the small walkway and the two wooden steps. The other officer is calling behind her in a squeaky voice, "Ma'am! Wait!"

Cynthia doesn't listen and rushes inside as Officer Baker is heading out. She slams into his muscular frame, then staggers back. Her head rings as if she has run straight into a closed door.

"Cynthia? What are you doing? We didn't give the all-clear!" Gabby is snapping at her.

"I—I heard you say 'a body.' Is it—" Cynthia can't bring herself to finish the statement.

Gabby sighs and shakes her head. "No, it isn't Tori. It's Christian. Or as you know him, Blue Eyes."

Gabby steps aside, and Cynthia can see directly into the small kitchen just behind the smaller living room. There is a round dining room table with a peeling bright green and yellow linoleum floor. Slumped at the table is a boy's body.

Cynthia knows she shouldn't, but she can't help herself and moves towards it. She steps from the carpeted living room onto the linoleum floor. The kitchen has a cupboard and fridge on one side, with a small counter and sink on the other.

There is a sickly sweet scent, reminding Cynthia of the bodies at the other crime scene. It isn't as intense. As if reading her mind, Gabby says, "He hasn't been dead long. The blood is still fresh."

Hearing that, Cynthia focuses on the back of his head. The image of his skull sunk in, like someone took a boot to a pumpkin, makes her gag.

The blood pooled in the space of his skull, dripping down his body and onto the floor, with his brain matter scattered on the dining room table, sends her into upheaval. She rushes past Gabby and out the front door.

"I didn't want you to see that," Gabby says behind her.

Cynthia breathes raggedly and looks around. The officer who had been standing with her is himself now bent over at the curb.

"Jesus," Officer Baker snarls. "Get it together, Williams."

"Sorry, sir," the younger officer forces out.

The sound of a ringing phone in Gabby's gloved hand breaks the tension. Cynthia turns and looks at it, then up to Gabby, who nods.

She hands Cynthia a glove and says, "The phone was on the table. I think it's him. I think he left it for us."

Cynthia quickly puts on the glove and answers it on speaker.

"What?!" Cynthia snaps.

"Now, now," Alexander's calm, measured voice admonishes.

It's the third time she's spoken to him, and she still has difficulty believing it's actually him. She still doesn't know how he found her. She's missing something. Cynthia knows if she can figure that out, she'll be able to find Tori. It's like those times when she can't quite place her finger on a piece of a case, but knows that when she sees the one document, the one email, the one phone call in discovery, everything will fall into place.

"What do you want?" she asks.

"I thought I'd check in," Alexander says. His tone sounds as if he's calling an old friend. "You have been busy. I see you found her friend, Sofia. Did you figure out the other interesting tidbit about our not so sweet Tori? I am impressed you found Christian, or should I say Blue Eyes, when you did. Did you like that little nod to the past? Had I waited around very long, we'd probably have passed each other. I do hope you figure it out in time. It would be a shame for Tori to end up in a shallow grave."

There is a long pause. Cynthia glances at the call to make sure he didn't disconnect. Before she can say anything, he continues.

"You were smart enough to figure it out last time. Can you imagine if you hadn't figured it out before? Wow, where would we be then, huh? Well, let's see if you can do it again. Maybe this time, you'll stop me for good. Because I promise you, I'll never stop if you don't."

The call disconnects and the phone returns to the lock

screen. Before Cynthia can do anything, Gabby takes the phone out of her hand and hands it to the female officer, who drops it in a bag, seals it, and starts writing on the bag.

"Get this to my agents as fast as possible and process it. I want all the data downloaded and cataloged before we get back to Cynthia's."

"Yes, ma'am."

The female agent heads back to her car and is gone.

Cynthia stands up, looks back at the house, and turns, looking around the neighborhood. "Where are you?!"

Looking at Gabby, she asks, "How did he know we were here?!"

Gabby rubs the sides of her arms and says, "Hey, hey, calm down." She points toward the house and says, "Could have been as simple as the Ring doorbell."

Cynthia looks at where she's pointing and nods. She looks back at Gabby and the tears are back, welling up in her eyes. "We only have a day to find Tori before—"

Cynthia can't finish the statement. She can't catch her breath. Her breathing is short and shallow.

"Hey, hey. In through your nose, out through your mouth," Gabby says soothingly.

Cynthia follows the instructions and finishes her thought. "She can't end up in a grave just like her."

Cynthia is pointing back toward the house.

Gabby looks at her, staring deep into her eyes. "There is no girl out back in a grave. That's a boy named Christian. Not a girl named—"

"No!" Cynthia says, shaking her head, walking toward Gabby's car. "How are we going to figure out where he's keeping her? One day!"

Gabby nods, following her toward the car. “We’ll find her. We have the best agents working on this. The Marshals are now doing their part. Let’s go back to your place and be there when they get the data downloaded.”

Cynthia pauses, looking back at the house with her hand on the door of Gabby’s car. With how tightly she is wrapped in anger, hatred, and fury toward Alexander, for the first time in her life, Cynthia can understand how someone could take another person’s life.

If I get the chance, I won’t hesitate, she promises herself.

CHAPTER 47

JOURNAL

IT WOULD SHOCK you if you knew what I now know. I couldn't believe it myself. Thankfully, when I found out, no one was home. I could take the time I needed to go through all the different emotions I felt: betrayal, shock, anger, frustration, denial, and finally—and I think most importantly—acceptance.

The acceptance piece wasn't crucial for me to move on or all that crap that a therapist would say. It was necessary so that I could start figuring out my plan. Once I uncovered the truth, so much of my life made sense. There were so many things I never understood, and now, it's obvious why I never understood them.

It's because they kept my truth, history, and past from me.

Looking back, even in this journal, there were so many times that I struggled with who I felt I was supposed to be. That it wasn't right, that people wouldn't understand. I thought everyone in my life had it all together.

But now that I know the truth and have accepted what is real, the rest of my life looks so easy. I don't have to struggle with trying to be someone I'm not. I don't have to hide my true feelings.

Well, a little of that still.

When I started implementing my plan, I didn't think this would be so much fun.

But if I'm being honest—and that is one thing I have learned, honesty is paramount—she deserves it.

She deserves everything that is coming to her.

Society would dictate that there is something wrong with me. But how can you feel something terrible if you don't feel?

I've never quite understood the construct of feeling bad before; to me, it's just a made-up concept. I tried following the rules for so long, but at a certain point, you have to be honest with yourself and understand that you are the way you are, and you shouldn't have to apologize for it.

I'm through apologizing. Enough people have lied to me and built up this whole world that I now realize is entirely false.

So if they can go through life pretending they're one thing, but being another, then so can I.

This is my true self, though.

The one I will present to the world is my fake life. They'll never know; they'll never suspect. It'll be my little secret.

CHAPTER 48

THEN

SAMANTHA STOOD AT the corner and thought about what Carol had told her, that she had seen Vicky get into a blue car. Whether that was true or when exactly it happened, it was her best lead.

Samantha needed to ask her dad about the hair clip. It could be something simple. Maybe he just forgot that he took Vicky home. Or maybe her mom did.

Why didn't I think of that before? she scolded herself.

Looking straight ahead, Samantha could see the bridge to Vicky's in the distance, but just before that, on the left, was a street that vanished down a small hill. If Samantha wasn't home in the next thirty minutes, her mom was going to get worried. But she knew she could find out if the blue car thing was for real. There was one other person she had not gone to see yet. She hadn't given the police all the details about Ricky and hoped they hadn't been able to find him yet.

Taking a deep breath and tucking her thumbs under her backpack straps, Samantha jogged across the street toward Jefferson Lane. She knew precisely where Ricky lived. He used to babysit her and had lived in the same place his whole life. She turned left and started down the small hill toward Ricky's. The homes here all looked exactly the same. There were three models: two were single-story, and one was a two-story. Single, Single, Two. Single, Single, Two.

Samantha had no idea why they built the homes like this. They were so boring. Most had brown yards and trees with no leaves. It felt like the owners here had given up.

Samantha had to look at the mailbox numbers because all the houses looked the same and used the same three colors of blue. She couldn't remember exactly which one was Ricky's, but she remembered his address: 7034 Jefferson Lane. She was always able to remember it because four plus three was seven.

She looked at the next mailbox, 7032. Looking past the house to the next one, Samantha saw a blue car parked in the driveway. The vehicle's discoloration, rust spots near the wheels, and dusty appearance made her assume it was Ricky's. It would be just like him to have a car like that. She wondered if the police had found him yet. They weren't here, so that had to be a good sign, right?

Standing at the bottom of the driveway, Samantha looked toward the front door, getting up her courage.

Was he the one Carol saw picking up Vicky? That would make sense. One way to find out. Encouraging herself, she said, "Let's do this."

Samantha marched up to the front door and pounded on the metal screen. It only took a minute, then the interior door opened. With the darkness inside, she couldn't see who it was, but she recognized the voice. "What do *you* want?"

Ricky's voice was unmistakable. Some parts were deep, but there were still squeaks in it, giving away the fact he was still a kid. He was a senior, and Samantha heard stories from other girls in her grade about what he would try to get them to do. He was always the one to bring the beer and pot to parties, and some girls would do what he wanted. She knew that as much as she loved Vicky, she was one of those girls.

"Have you seen Vicky?" Samantha asked as firmly as she could.

"Are you serious right now?!" Ricky fired back at her. The screen door unlocked and pushed toward her. She stepped back and Ricky stepped into the light.

Samantha wasn't sure what all the other girls saw. She guessed he was okay-looking. He was tall, at least six feet, with brown hair parted in the middle and an earring in his left ear. His eyes were crystal blue, and if Samantha was being honest, he had really nice lips.

Vicky could never stop talking about how hot he was, especially his lips.

"Yes, I am!" Samantha said with as much force as she could muster. "Have you seen her? Is she here? Vicky!"

Samantha tried looking past him into the house, but there was no response. Turning on him, she asked, "Did you even know she's missing? Did you ever care about her?"

"Of course I did," he yelled, leaning toward her. "Why the hell did you send the cops here? I didn't do anything!"

"Did you see her that weekend? When she went missing. Did you see her?"

Ricky waved her off and said, "Get lost. You don't know what you're talking about. You're just a stupid little girl."

Anger boiled up in Samantha and she couldn't contain herself. She swung, her fist connecting with his body right between his legs. She felt a combination of hitting something soft and what she assumed was bone. She knew she got him right in his man parts as he crumpled to the ground, grabbing at his crotch.

Ricky leaned over and threw up on the brown grass. Tears were in his eyes. He squeaked out, "Why? What the hell?!"

Samantha didn't feel sorry for him. She knew what he did to girls. Instead, with the anger still firing inside her, she grabbed his earring, pulling hard, but not so hard as to yank it out. He squealed like a little pig.

"Did you see her that weekend?!" she screamed in his face.

He shook his head slightly, not wanting her to rip out his earring. "Please, please, let go. I—I'll tell you. Just please let go."

Samantha released his ear and stepped back, ensuring she was out of his reach. She crossed her arms over her chest and stared at him.

He took a couple of deep breaths, slowly releasing the grip on his crotch. The tears in his eyes made them sparkle even more in the sunlight. "I wanted to see her, I did. We had it all planned out. I even went over there. That's how much I liked her. I went to her place. But she wasn't there. She never answered the door. I figured she ditched me for some other guy or *you.*"

The way he said "you" made Samantha want to hit him again, but she didn't. She stared at him and felt he was telling the truth. She had hoped that either Vicky was there or he knew where she was. If one of those were true, then the entire issue with the clip in her dad's car was a minor mystery that Vicky herself could explain.

Samantha glanced at the driveway, his car reminding her of Homeless Harriet-Carol. "Did you ever pick Vicky up in your car?"

Ricky looked at her like she'd grown a third arm and shook his head. "Yeah, but so what? Is that a crime now too?"

"Depends," Samantha said, unsure what else to say.

Everything she had hoped for, the best case scenario being to find Vicky hiding out or discover that Ricky had seen her that weekend, went up in smoke. Samantha reached into her jacket pocket, feeling the clip. She was right back where she started. Only one other person seemed to have seen Vicky that weekend after her. And he had told the police he had not seen Vicky since she left their house.

Samantha turned, leaving Ricky on his knees, dreading what came next. She would have to ask her dad how the clip had ended up in his car.

PART 3

REVELATIONS

CHAPTER 49

NOW

SITTING IN THE passenger seat, Cynthia drums on the door, hardly containing the energy pulsing through her. She feels utterly helpless. If she was driving, she would at least have something to distract her.

Instead, her thoughts gravitate to Tori.

Where is she? Is she tied up? Is she conscious? What is Alexander telling Tori about Cynthia? Has he hurt her yet? How is he going to kill her? Are they going to find her in time?

Gabby pulls the car up to the curb and warns her, "Don't do anything. I'll handle it."

Standing in the middle of the street is Jacob, his hands stuffed in his pockets; he is as still as a statue.

Cynthia opens the door and Jacob takes a couple of steps back, pulling his hands out of his pockets and raising them toward Cynthia. "I don't want any trouble. I know I'm not allowed over here. I need to talk to Mrs. Burrows."

Gabby steps in front of Cynthia and points toward Jacob's house. "She doesn't want to talk to you. Why don't you go home?"

He takes a couple more steps back toward his house and stammers, "But I might be able to—"

Cynthia can't take it. She's already wound so tight. Images of Christian's caved-in head replay over and over in her mind.

"Might be able to what? Take advantage of my daughter again? What do you want to do to her? Might you be able to tell us where she is because you know? Because you helped take her? I will make sure you are prosecuted and convicted as an accessory!"

Jacob turns and runs back to his house. He throws open the door, pivots on the threshold, looks back, and shouts, "It wasn't me. I had nothing to do with it, with any of it."

Gabby turns and looks at Cynthia. "Way to let me handle it."

"I'm sorry, I just can't with him. He *knows* something."

"Then why scare him off?"

Cynthia runs her fingers through her hair. "I don't know. I don't trust anything he says."

Gabby places her hand on Cynthia's back and the lights around the neighborhood begin to kick on. "Let's head inside. Why don't you talk to your husband while we wait for the phone data to be processed?"

Cynthia nods and walks up the stone steps.

David greets her at the door and says quietly, "Maybe he can help."

"I don't know," is all Cynthia can manage.

She maneuvers around the various agents in her great room and goes to the kitchen. She grabs two wine glasses and a bottle of white from the fridge.

When had she eaten last?

Cynthia can't remember if she had eaten anything since

breakfast. Was it just this morning that she and Gabby went to the station?

Not wanting to think too hard about making anything, Cynthia grabs cheese slices and salami from the fridge. Sitting down, she pours the wine into the two glasses and waits for David.

He and Gabby appear, and Gabby smiles. "I'll leave you two alone."

"Sit," Cynthia says, pushing the other glass toward him.

David does as she asks and takes the glass, but waits for her before drinking. Sandwiching a piece of salami between cheese slices, Cynthia pops it into her mouth and follows it with a sip of wine.

She spins the glass, staring at the liquid. The number of thoughts and images running through her mind is overwhelming: the images from the abandoned house of Christian's head, pooled with blood. The bodies from yesterday, along with images of Tori as a little girl running around the backyard. Thinking of her daughter as a little girl, Cynthia's own childhood comes into focus.

The tears flow freely and drop with tiny splashes into her glass. David reaches his hand across and tries to console her. "Hey, hey. It's okay. We'll find her."

Cynthia shakes her head. "I don't know if we will. There is so much to tell you. You have no idea who we're dealing with. Alexander is—"

She breaks off, not even sure what she is going to say.

"Just take a minute and start from the beginning."

Cynthia nods and takes a deep breath. The tears slow and she takes a long sip of her wine, feeling it go down.

She places the glass back down and starts talking. She

knows if she looks up at David, she won't be able to get this all out.

"I told you my parents were dead. That was partially true and partially wishful thinking. I know that sounds terrible, but give me a minute. Growing up, I thought I had a great life. I felt bad for others because they didn't have the parents I did. They loved me, and it was always the three of us. I felt safe. I lived in a community that was like the most wholesome all-American community. Flags on houses, people trimming their flowers in the front yards in springtime. Kids running through sprinklers during summer. It was perfect."

Cynthia pauses and takes another large sip. "That is, until my best friend went missing."

She glances up at David to see his expression. He is completely focused on her, his eyes trained on every word she says.

"That's why I freaked out when we got the text from the school about Tori. It was like my worst nightmare was playing out."

"I'm not sure I understand what this has to do with Alexander," David prods.

"I think you do," Cynthia replies. "Alexander is my father."

"I'm sorry. Can you say that again?" David asks, his jaw slack at the revelation.

Cynthia sighs and spins the glass in front of her. "Alexander Beaufort is my father. My actual name is Samantha Beaufort. I'm in Witness Protection because I was the star witness at his trial. I had just testified and the court had wrapped for the day. That evening, his police escort told us he escaped on the way back to the jail. They quickly whisked my mom and me to a hotel outside the city. Before I knew it, we were across the country with new names, a new school, and no idea if the authorities would apprehend him."

David scratches his head. "I—I don't even know what to ask. I don't know where to begin to process all that. Why were you the star witness? Did you see him kill someone?"

Cynthia gulps hard and takes a deep breath.

Before she can continue, there is commotion in their great room.

"What's going on out there?" Cynthia asks, pushing back from the table. She is thankful for the break from going down a dark path she has avoided for her entire adult life. She knows she will have to bring light to the darkness, but she needs to take it one step at a time.

CHAPTER 50

THEN

SAMANTHA KNEW IF anyone saw her at that moment, they'd think she was crazy. She sat on the edge of the sofa facing her dad's office, turning the clip over and over in her fingers. She stared at the partially open door and saw him typing away on the computer.

What was he working on? Why hadn't he said anything to her yet? Did he even know about the clip?

Samantha knew she had to say something, but what? Was she just supposed to ask him if he'd lied? Was she just supposed to confront him and show him the clip? She didn't know if she could do that.

Her heart beat faster, and she could feel the clip slipping in her fingers as her hands began to sweat. She was trying to work up the courage to say something. She envisioned herself going into his office and saying, "Dad? Can I ask you something?"

He would turn around, smile at her as he did, and probably open his arms wide and say, "Of course, Sammy! What is it?"

She would swallow hard, grip the clip in her palm, hold it

out, and ask him, "I found this in your car. You said you didn't give Vicky a ride home, but did you?"

After that, she had no idea what he would say. The vision of the conversation was clear up to that point. After that, how would he respond? Would he say yes? Had he just forgotten? Would he act confused and have no idea how the clip got in his car? Would he blame Vicky and say she must have snuck into his vehicle?

The phone in her dad's office rang, jarring her back to reality.

"Hello?" she heard him say. His back was to her, and she could only see half of him and half of his screen.

"No! That is not what you were supposed to do. I told you exactly what needed to happen."

He pushed back his chair, half standing.

"Damn it, do what I tell you the first time!"

He ran his fingers through his hair. His sigh was loud enough for her to hear as he grumbled, "Yes, of course. I'll be right there."

He slammed the phone down, angrily clicked his mouse on the computer, and stood. As he opened the office door wide, Samantha turned her body and acted like she was staring out the front window.

He stopped just outside his office door, and she wondered if he'd seen her staring at him.

"Hey, Sammy. You good?"

Without hesitating, she nodded.

Samantha scolded herself as soon as she did it. That was her chance to tell him she wasn't okay, that she wasn't good.

He closed the office door behind him, leaving it open just

a crack. She could see him approaching from the corner of her eye.

He stopped right next to her and turned, staring out the window with her. "Hey, it's okay. We will make sure Mr. Davies doesn't do anything. The police are looking into him. I promise you're safe."

He tousled her hair and she looked toward him, but first glanced at his office. She could see that his computer was still on through the open crack in the door.

She could tell him before he left, or she could not tell him and look at his computer. She didn't know what that would do for her or how exactly it would help her find Vicky. But right now, she just needed to do something.

"Hey, I have to go meet a client. Can you let Mom know I'll be home late?"

He kissed her on the top of the head and turned to leave. "Love ya, Sammy."

Samantha's body didn't budge or move the entire time. She wondered if she'd become a statue and wasn't sure she could move once he left. Fear had a grip on her, unlike anything she had ever felt. She wanted to explore his computer, but she also wanted to pretend none of it was real.

As he reached the front door and opened it, he looked back at her, her attention still focused on the office door.

"Love ya, Sammy," he said again from the door.

His loud voice got her attention. She looked at him, put a smile on her face, and with everything it took, she said, "Love you, too."

She stayed still while the door shut. From where she was, she turned her body to look straight out the front window. She watched as her dad climbed into his blue sedan.

As soon as he backed out of the driveway and drove off, Samantha jumped up and made a beeline to his office. She closed the door quietly. She knew she shouldn't be in there.

Samantha sat in his chair and swiveled it to the desk, staring at the computer monitor. She waited a minute to ensure she couldn't hear her mom coming downstairs. She knew her mom was in her bedroom, doing laundry and making the bed. Samantha wasn't sure how long she had before she came back downstairs.

Her hand hovered over the mouse, nervous about clicking around. What was she going to see? What was she even looking for?

Samantha knew there were maps online to see everything from a bird's-eye view. She opened the internet and waited for the computer's various noises to stop while connecting to the internet.

Once it did and she could open an internet browser, she went to the mapping website they used in school for various projects. Typing in her address as a starting place, Samantha took a deep breath and said to herself, "Let's see if there is anything to find."

CHAPTER 51

NOW

"WHAT IS THIS?" Cynthia asks. The group of agents separates, making space for her and David. Gabby is at the front to the side of the TV.

"This is the location data from Christian's phone. Local PD uploaded it and sent it over. As you can see, he's been busy. We aren't sure what he was doing or where he was going in all of these instances, but we've already sent a copy to our team back in Quantico. They are analyzing any possibilities and looking for patterns, but it could take some time."

Cynthia looks at Gabby, astonished. "We don't have time! We have less than a day to find Tori!"

Gabby nods. "I know. I know the urgency. We just got this ourselves and are trying to devise a game plan. There's this, too."

Gabby hands Cynthia a baggie with the word "EVIDENCE" stenciled across the top. Inside is a photograph. Cynthia flips it over to get a better look, noticing the deceased couple from the other day and Christian, but he looks about five years younger.

"What is this?" Cynthia asks.

Gabby points at the picture. "That is Christian's aunt and uncle. They took him in and raised him for a bit, but he was too much for them, so he ended up in the system. Dad's dead; Mom's in an institution. Seems he was a perfect fit for Alexander to train."

Cynthia has nothing to say and shakes her head. She hands the bag back to Gabby and looks at the map. There are dozens and dozens of dots ranging from down south by the border and Chula Vista up to the Los Angeles and Long Beach area. There are pins everywhere in between, as far east as El Centro. To cover all these locations in the next several hours, they would need at least thirty to forty different teams traveling hours in every direction.

"Everything so far has been a nod to the past," Cynthia says out loud, more to herself than anyone.

"What's that?" Gabby asks.

"Every clue and everything Alexander has said has been related to the past. To before. The names on his aunt and uncle's driver's licenses—the past. Christian being called Blue Eyes—the past. Christian's car being blue—the past. The way he buried Sofia—the past. He's relating everything to when I was a kid."

"Okay," Gabby says, unsure of where Cynthia is going.

Cynthia asks, "Can you get me a list of all the addresses?"

"Of course. We have that," Gabby says, snapping her fingers. One of the agents rushes over to the coffee table, grabs a sheet of paper, and hands it to Cynthia.

"I know one of the street names that would mean something to him. The street I grew up on. Washington Avenue. My school was Lincoln Middle, and all the streets were named after presidents."

Cynthia looks down the list and points to an address on Washington Street. "Here, check this one out."

The agent at the computer highlights it on the map, and the pin grows twice as big as all the others.

Cynthia looks down the list several times and crumples half the sheet in her hand. "I can't believe I can't remember the other street name. All these years later, I never thought I'd forget it, and I can't remember it for the life of me. Even looking at this list."

Everyone is quiet; all eyes are on Cynthia.

Gabby asks, "Would you remember it by the map?"

Cynthia's head shoots up, and she exclaims, "Yes! Of course. I know exactly where it is."

She moves over to the agent at the computer and asks, "Do you mind?"

The agent moves out of her way. Cynthia maneuvers the online map back east, zooming in on her childhood neighborhood. She goes to where she expected the street to be but only sees a freeway.

"I—I don't understand. It was right here." Cynthia looks up at the map on the giant TV.

"Probably urban development," David offers. "Could the street be gone?"

"I don't even know how to find out," Cynthia says, defeated.

"Here, I do," the same agent says.

Cynthia moves out of his way and he pulls up Google Earth. He clicks on a historical time-lapse view beginning fifteen years ago. They can see the freeway construction starting at that point, but all the street names are gone.

"Can we go back any further?" she asks desperately.

The agent shakes his head. "Unfortunately, not in this area."

Tears well up in her eyes as David places his hand on her back. "Hey, let's take a break. Pull away from the moment. It might help spark an idea. Okay?"

David guides her back to the kitchen, nudging the glass in her direction. She takes a sip, knowing what he's doing. He's right—she needs to let her subconscious work for a minute.

"Do you remember when we caught Tori coloring on her wall?" David asks.

Cynthia smiles, envisioning the little blond girl humming a tune, sitting on her floor, coloring a flower she had drawn on her wall. She had yet to learn if what she was doing was wrong or bad—she was just drawing a picture on a big blank canvas.

"We're going to find her, you know that, right?" David asks.

Cynthia doesn't move. It's getting to a point that she isn't sure. She hates herself for that, but if she is being honest, they have what, twelve, sixteen hours? Alexander never gave them an exact time, just three days.

When did he first call? Noon?

They are no closer to figuring out where he is keeping her. Even though the agents are checking as many locations as they can, including the one she pointed out, she knows he's not there.

All of those spots are distractions. She believes the right location is there, but it's a needle in a haystack. She has nothing here as a memory of her old life. That was one of the witness protection rules: take nothing, start fresh.

"Hey, you believe it, right?" David asks again, reaching his hand across the table, his palm face up, expectant. She spins the glass with one hand and places the other in his open, waiting hand. Their fingers intertwine and he squeezes her hand.

"Let me hear you say it," he encourages her.

Cynthia smiles and squeezes his hand back, nodding.

"I need to hear you say it."

Cynthia sighs, looking at the empty glass. She's not even sure when she finished it. Swallowing her doubts, she looks at him and says, "I believe we'll find her."

Before she can say anything else, Gabby comes into the room. "We have agents checking the location on the street you highlighted. It'll take them about an hour to get there. If Tori is there, we'll save her, take him down, and that will be that. If she's not there—"

Gabby stops, realizing she doesn't know what to say next.

"That's my fear, too," Cynthia says, finishing her thought. "I'm almost certain she isn't there. He wouldn't be that obvious. He's been thinking about this for years. He wants me to stress, squirm, and unravel."

Gabby pulls out one of the other dining room chairs.

"Let's think about this," Gabby says, folding her hands before her. "If she isn't there, is there anywhere else you could have that other street written down? Anything you brought with you all those years ago that maybe young Cynthia shouldn't have, but did?"

Gabby glances from Cynthia to David and back again.

Cynthia picks up on her thinking and says, "He knows who Alexander is and what my real name is."

Gabby smiles and nods her head. "Okay, good to know."

"And no, I brought nothing with me," Cynthia says.

Gabby scrunches her lips to the side. It makes Cynthia smile. She used to watch Gabby do this all the time when she was studying.

"What about some old database or map that would have it?"

Cynthia shakes her head, but a stray thought stops her. Thinking of herself as a young girl and the court case gives her an idea.

"I know where it will be! It'd have to be there." Cynthia glances at her watch. "I need to access my work computer system and get into a federal case file. I can't do it from here. I can only do it from the office with my fingerprint reader."

David puts his hand on her arm and squeezes. "I'll drive. Let's head down there and you can fill me in on the rest of your story."

Cynthia nods and Gabby adds, "We'll have as many agents as we can spare, as well as the Marshals, and check out the other spots. As soon as you figure out that other street, let me know and we'll get there. I'll commission a helicopter if needed."

Cynthia smiles and says, "Thank you. For everything."

David and Cynthia are navigating around the agents toward the front door when Cynthia hears one agent on the phone call out to Gabby. "Ma'am, they found three distinct prints at Christian's home. His, Alexander's, and one other—unknown at the moment."

Cynthia stops dead in her tracks and turns, staring at Gabby.

Gabby shakes her head and waves her toward the open door. "As soon as I know, you'll know. Now go."

CHAPTER 52

THEN

THE ONLY SOUND in the office was the clicking of the mouse. Samantha opened the internet, pulled up the map software they used in school, and waited a few minutes while it loaded before entering Vicky's address. She watched as the map smoothed out its pixelation and slowly zoomed in on the neighborhood. She looked around, wondering if Vicky could have gone somewhere else after her dad had dropped her off. There were no woods or hills near Vicky's house for her to wander off and get lost in, nor any spots where she might fall, hurt herself, and be unable to get back. No trails or canyons or rivers or ponds.

Samantha stared at the computer. This wasn't a lead. What was she even doing? What next? What should she look for now?

She minimized the browser, not wanting to wait for the internet to load again. She looked at the home screen on her dad's computer. It was a picture of the three of them standing in the backyard with the woods behind their house as the backdrop. She thought about the secret opening in the fence only she and Vicky knew about, which opened to the forest beyond. The only other way to get back there was to drive around the neighborhood. She focused on the smile on her face and remembered taking the picture. She remembered how happy she was and how simple life had been.

She wondered if she would ever get back to that place. Would life ever be nice again? Or had this event turned into a fork in her life path?

There was a single file folder at the bottom of the screen, and she almost didn't see it because it was the same color as the grass from the backdrop. Samantha clicked on it and a small password window appeared.

That's strange, she thought.

She stared at the input box for a minute, wondering what the password could be. She tried her dad's name, her mom's name, and their street name. But each time, the box jiggled and red text appeared above it: "Incorrect Password."

Samantha paused and jumped up, moving to the door. She could have sworn she heard something and opened the door just a crack. She wanted to call out her mom's name but didn't want to draw attention to herself. After waiting another second and not hearing anything else, she returned to her dad's desk.

She stared at the keyboard and thought about something her computer teacher had said: "Remember, whenever you're using passwords, you want them to be something you can remember, but others can't figure out. For example, instead of a, use the 'at' symbol."

She thought about what her dad always called her: Sammy.

She tried it just like that: "Sammy."

The password box gave the same jiggle and red prompt. She swapped out the *A*, not thinking it would work: "S@mmy."

The box disappeared and the folder opened. Samantha didn't know what she was looking at. There were dozens and dozens of file names. They all had the same setup: a city name, an underscore, a number ranging from ten to fourteen, another underscore, and a color—either blond, brown, or red.

She looked down the list and picked one with a city she recognized. The file was called "pittsburgh_13_red."

Something inside her told her not to click on it—to close the folder, exit the computer, and leave her dad's office. He didn't want her in here, and there was a reason this folder was password protected.

Just get up, push the chair back, leave, and forget you were in here, she told herself.

But in the same thought, Vicky's name coursed through her veins.

Everything she was doing right now was for Vicky. She had to find her. For some reason, her dad had lied to the police. This folder may be the reason.

Samantha took a deep breath and double-clicked on the file. A repulsion wracked Samantha's system as soon as the image appeared on the screen. Her gag reflex consumed her and she grabbed the trash can as fast as she could, shoving her head in it. Her lunch and everything else in her stomach was vomited into the can. She could feel the splatter come back and hit her in the face.

She kept her eyes closed as she continued to vomit into the can. Dry heaving, she wrapped one arm around the can, found the mouse, and glanced up briefly, focusing on the little red *X* in the upper right corner to close the image. She tried to avoid looking at the picture, but the image burned into her mind, and seeing it again brought a fresh wave of upheaval from her system.

Finally finished, she lifted her head and stared at the list of files. She scrolled four times and stopped. The files kept coming. She was terrified to open another, but she had to know. Was that the only one, or were they all like that? And why was this on her dad's computer?

She clicked on one where she didn't recognize the city name, but it had "fourteen" and "blond" in it.

The image that popped up was just like the first, and she closed it out as fast as she could, gagging once again, though there was little left in her stomach.

She assumed now that every image was the same: young girls, ages ten to fourteen, fully clothed, in shallow graves. One of these girls had blood splattered on her face, her eyes closed. The other one's eyes were still open and cloudy. Blood soaked the dirt around both girls.

She found herself moving the mouse, clicking on another image and then another—she could not stop clicking. She knew why but didn't want to admit it.

As she scrolled through the images, she was looking for her city, Wellsboro. She was looking for a specific type of file name: "wellsboro_fourteen_brown." She realized the city names were alphabetical and scrolled to the bottom.

How many files, how many girls?

Toward the bottom, she slowed down as she got to Utica, Vandalia, and Vineland. She stopped at Wellsboro. There were only three, and one of them matched what she was looking for. She moved the mouse toward the file name and felt as if gravity and every force in the world were trying to pull her away from clicking this file.

With everything she had, Samantha took a deep breath and double-clicked the file. She shot out of the chair before the image fully loaded on the screen, causing it to fly back and slam into the door. Her hands flew up to her mouth, trying to muffle her gut-wrenching scream. Samantha fell to her knees, muffling her cries as best she could, but she knew the pain and anguish now coursing through her would be there for the rest of her life.

CHAPTER 53

NOW

CYNTHIA CAN TELL David isn't sure what to do, as he usually does the driving when they are together. But she wants to drive—it will give her something to focus on while she spills her guts about her past. He sits with his hands clasped in his lap the entire time, trying not to fidget or interrupt.

A sleepy attendant glances up briefly when she brandishes her security card to enter the private garage. He gives her a half smile as she passes, and she navigates her BMW into her reserved spot.

"So that's about everything," she says, turning the car off. The two sit silently for a moment, listening to the vehicle settle. The interior lights of the parking garage illuminate most of the spaces, an upgrade the building manager has made after multiple complaints from staffers concerned about working after dark.

David sits there shaking his head. "I can't believe you have spent your entire life with this secret. I wish you would have shared it with me. I can understand not telling Tori, but I would have accepted you and loved you the same."

Cynthia hears what he is saying, but still can't fully convince herself. Even he couldn't know for sure. Now, when their daughter's life is on the line, it's easier for David to accept the horror of who Alexander is and what he does. Before, he may have thought she was blowing the whole thing out of proportion.

Instead of saying all that, Cynthia nods and opens the car door. David follows her lead and gets out, walking around the car, following her to the elevator. The clicking of her heels echoes around the nearly deserted garage.

Once in the elevator, Cynthia pushes the eleven button, whisking them up to her law firm's floor. David leans against the back railing, one hand in his pocket, the other rubbing her lower back.

As they step off, the only lights on are the dimmed security lights and a smattering of soft glow from the cubicles. Without investigating, Cynthia knows it's the first years working longer than anyone else.

"Man, it's been forever since I've been up here. I don't think I've been here since you became a senior partner," David reminisces.

"Really? It's been that long?" Cynthia asks, surprised, as they move toward her office. She doesn't bother to see which first years are still here. Usually, she would take notes and report back to the managing partners, but right now, it's all fruitless.

As they pass the cubicles, a few of them pop their heads up like groundhogs coming out of the ground. They look at her curiously, wondering why a senior partner is here after hours, but she ignores the stares.

They step into Cynthia's office and the motion lights kick on as soon as they enter. Cynthia sits behind her desk and David wanders over to the couch, unsure what to do.

Cynthia opens the laptop and gets it booted up. She navigates to the website for federal case files. The PACER website is available to the public, but she needs the next level of detail.

She logs in and it asks for her to authenticate with her biometric information. Cynthia places her forefinger on the fingerprint reader inset into her desk. It takes only a second, and a screen welcoming Cynthia Burrows pops up.

She immediately searches for *Alexander Beaufort vs. The United States*. The first result is what she is looking for, and she clicks on it.

Cynthia scrolls furiously, knowing what point of the trial she is looking for. It was day two, and she was taking the stand. When she finds it, she slows down and reads the transcript. She swallows hard. The one thing she wasn't expecting was the amount of raw emotions welling up inside her. She had not considered the case or the details for at least twenty years.

Sometimes, she would think about the past, but only in a bit of detail.

"Prosecution: The United States calls Samantha Beaufort to the stand."

Cynthia skips past being sworn in and only skims the first few lines of questioning. She knows what she is looking for and stops when she sees it.

"Prosecution: Ms. Beaufort, do you know Ms. Vicky Smith, who lives at 6178 Orchard Hill Road?"

"Defense: Objection, relevance."

Cynthia doesn't bother reading the rest. She remembers how it had gone and does not care to relive it.

"I found it," she exclaims to David.

He shoots off the couch and the two hurry out of her office, completely ignoring all the first years. Now he needs clarification on what is going on.

As they reach the elevator, Cynthia pulls out her phone and dials Gabby, who answers on the first ring.

"Did you figure it out?"

"Is there an Orchard Hill address on that list?" Cynthia asks.

She waits a moment while there is silence on the other end, sure that Gabby is running her long, slender finger down the list.

"Affirmative. It's about thirty minutes from your place and around forty-five from downtown," Gabby responds.

Cynthia smiles, her other hand reaching for David's arm and squeezing it. "That's where she is."

CHAPTER 54

THEN

SAMANTHA FLUNG THE office door open so hard that the handle left a dent in the wall. She skidded around the staircase, sprinting for the backyard. Somewhere upstairs, her mom called down, "Sammy? Is everything okay?"

She couldn't even register her mom's question. Where was she even supposed to begin with answering that?

She couldn't get her legs to go fast enough. Simultaneously, she was trying to escape everything she had just seen, and also get to the backyard to see that it wasn't true. It couldn't be her best friend buried in the woods behind her backyard.

Samantha had known better than to click on the file, but did it anyway. The first part of the image to load was a group of rocks in an arc at the top of the grave. She recognized them instantly. They were painted—something she and Vicky had done the summer before to a group of rocks in the woods behind her house. She didn't know what she had expected.

It was like any movie Samantha had seen with a person in a coffin.

As soon as the image loaded on the computer screen, it

seared itself in her mind and she couldn't escape it. She would never forget the visual of Vicky's body lying in a shallow grave. Her hair draped nicely on both sides of her shoulders, her eyes closed. Vicky's hands rested by her shoulders with her arms crossed over her chest.

Samantha slammed through the back screen door, jumping over the three steps leading down to the backyard. She had to run twenty yards to their back fence, which butted up against a small forest. Stopping at the back fence, Samantha pushed one of the boards, causing it to swing out and revealing an opening big enough for her. She looked down the small path into the forest and saw the rock formation directly ahead.

She knew she had to go and see, but her body would not allow her to move. Samantha felt like she was having an out-of-body experience. She could see herself from above, looking through the secret opening.

She took slow, deliberate steps toward the marking. She stopped a few feet before the rock arc, realizing if this was a grave and her best friend was under the dirt, she didn't want to walk on Vicky. Samantha circled around the path and stopped at the rocks. Dropping to her knees, she placed her hands on the dirt. Before she could do anything, tears welled up in her eyes, and the dirt below her grew darker with the stains of her tears.

Fear, anger, hatred, anguish, and sickness all revolted inside her, and her hands started digging like a dog after a gopher. She slowed down as she dug deeper, not wanting to disturb Vicky if she was there. She gripped a handful of dirt and pulled it up.

The sight of her best friend's face made her stomach lurch and her hands shake. She took a deep breath and held it. She turned back around slowly and brushed dirt off Vicky's pale, dead face.

Samantha placed a hand on her friend's cold cheek, and the only sound she could squeak out was, "I'm sorry."

A voice behind her caused Samantha to jump.

"Sammy, what are you—"

Samantha turned and saw her father standing a few feet away, his eyes wide with a look of shock and panic. She didn't wait for him to say anything but sprinted past him, shoving him to the side.

He tried to grab her arm but just missed, still causing her to spin and lose her footing. She fell on her backside and scrambled away from him.

"Sammy. I can explain. It was an accident. I didn't know what to do."

Samantha shook her head, trying to get to her feet while simultaneously getting away from him.

"Am I next? Are you going to kill me too?" she cried out.

Her father's face transformed before her eyes. The sweet look of love vanished into a psychotic stare—his true self showing through.

Before he could say anything, Samantha found her footing and took off. Running through the screen door and down the hallway, she found her mom halfway down the stairs, glancing backward at her.

"Sammy? What is it?" her mom asked, oblivious to what was happening.

Samantha got to the front door and tried to yank it open, but it didn't budge. She pulled two more times before realizing the deadbolt was engaged. She fumbled with it, her fingers vibrating with fear. She glanced behind her and saw her dad marching toward her. His face was set, and the fear and horror were now replaced with a look of determination.

She looked back at the lock, disengaged it, and yanked open the door. Then, sprinting out front, she screamed, "Help! Someone, please help!"

Her dad lunged at her from behind and caught her foot. Samantha tripped and fell, smacking her head on the concrete. Just before she blacked out, she saw Mr. Davies run toward her.

He was yelling at her dad, "Hey! Leave her alone!"

She wasn't sure who it was, but she heard a woman yelling, "Call the police!"

As her head fell back onto the ground, she saw Mr. Davies step between her and the looming shape of her father.

CHAPTER 55

NOW

CYNTHIA SLAMS ON the brakes of her BMW and the tires skid to a stop. Lined up on both sides of the street are dozens of police cars, their red and blue flashing lights bouncing off the neighborhood.

Is the entire neighborhood out here? She observes the crowd encircling what Cynthia can only assume is a police barrier.

She gets out of the car and tries to understand what she is looking at. She reaches back and grabs David's hand. The air is crisp, and she can feel the goose pimples forming on her skin but doesn't care. Cynthia pushes through the crowd, using her free hand to create a wedge and get others out of the way.

"Excuse me. We need to get through," she says forcefully.

Cynthia pulls David along, knowing some people are throwing daggers at her with their eyes. She wants to yell at all of them for wanting to catch a glimpse of something horrific, but contains herself. If any of *them* had witnessed or been a part of her last two days, they'd all be comatose on the ground somewhere.

"Please get out of my way!" Cynthia snaps at an older gentleman who intentionally moves in front of her so she can't pass.

This isn't some sporting event, you sick bastard, she thinks to herself.

When the man still doesn't move, she jabs her finger on his shoulder and pushes the side of his arm to get him to move.

"My daughter might be in there, now move the fuck out of the way!" she screams in his ear. This gets his attention, and he stumbles to the side and bumps into others. Cynthia doesn't care if he falls on the ground.

At the front of the police tape, an officer holds up his hands to her. He looks like any typical cop on the street, and she tries to get him to understand. "My daughter might be in there. Agent Gabby Hayes is my friend."

The name drop gives the officer pause, but he doesn't budge. Cynthia sighs and grabs her phone from her back pocket, tapping Gabby's name in her favorites. It only rings once when Gabby answers.

"Hey, are you here?" Gabby asks.

"Yes, but this officer won't let us through."

"Okay, hang on. I'll be right there."

Cynthia can see Gabby emerging onto the small covered porch of the two-story mid-century modern home. It looks like a nice, normal home. Cynthia can only imagine what horrors Alexander has in there for her. If Tori is there, she hopes and prays she is unharmed.

As soon as Gabby gets closer, Cynthia can tell by the look on her face that Tori is not here.

"It's okay, let them through," Gabby tells the officer.

He holds up the police tape, and Cynthia and David duck under. As Cynthia stands back up, she asks, "Is she here?!"

Gabby hesitates and says, "No, Tori isn't here."

Knowing she is not giving her the complete picture, Cynthia demands, "Tell me."

Gabby sighs. "It doesn't look like she was ever here. But Alexander expected you to find this house."

"What does that mean?" David asks.

"It means there is evidence Alexander was in the house at one point."

"Oh God," Cynthia says, her hand reaching her mouth. She can only imagine what horrific things Alexander did to this family.

"No, nothing like that. No one is dead inside," Gabby says.

Cynthia slowly drops her hand, a look of confusion on her face. "Then what?"

Gabby purses her lips, looking from the house to them and back to the house again. She pauses momentarily, her eyes darting from Cynthia to David, and then, with resignation, she says, "Come with me."

They follow Gabby up the small sidewalk to the home. Up close, Cynthia can tell it is a well-kept home and can only assume the family took pride in it. She can envision what the inside had looked like before Alexander got to it—whatever he'd done.

They stop at the entrance and don booties and gloves.

"Even though you have the booties and gloves, try not to touch anything," Gabby instructs.

Gabby walks in first and turns left. "The only thing you need to see is right in here."

Cynthia looks down, following Gabby's every step. As soon as she sees Gabby has stopped, she looks up and tries to comprehend what she sees.

Plastered across the back wall of the living room, where a TV would typically hang with the TV mount in the middle, are pictures cut and torn out to spell the words, "SO CLOSE."

The pictures draw in Cynthia and David, and as soon as Cynthia is close enough, she can tell they're all pictures of Tori. She recognizes some from family vacations she had taken over the years, some that others had taken, and still more, she assumes, are from Tori specifically.

How did he get these? How did he do this? Where is the family who lives here?

As if Gabby is reading her mind, she tells them, "It seems the family who lives here is on vacation and won't be back for several days. We confirmed it was a planned trip; they were all completely unharmed. We're in contact with them and will work to see if there is any connection."

Cynthia is standing close to one picture of Tori from last year's homecoming. She looked like a princess in her aqua teal dress ending just above the knees, with a generous slit on the side. Cynthia remembers their argument over the dress and how it was too provocative, but Tori had bought it with her own money.

Tori's hair in the picture is half up and half down; the platinum blond contrasts with her tanned skin. The dress's color and her tan made her beautiful ice-blue eyes pop.

Cynthia can't help but reach up to touch Tori's picture. With her index finger gently grazing Tori's face, she says, "That won't be quick enough."

"We're working as quickly as possible," Gabby tries to counter.

Cynthia steps away, shaking her head, and turns. "I know, but we both know we only have a little time left."

Rather than continue to argue with her, Gabby says, "I'm going to be here a while processing the scene. Why don't the two of you go home, try to get some rest, and I'll let you know the second we have something."

David's gentle hand on the small of Cynthia's back nudges her toward the front door. Cynthia follows his lead and walks out after him. She stops and turns, looking back at the picture collage, her eyes flitting to Gabby.

"That's why he never gave a specific time."

"What's that, hon?" Gabby asks.

"He never gave a specific time. He said we had till Thursday. Seventy-two hours. Not ten a.m. or noon on Thursday. Just seventy-two hours. He knew we'd never find her in time. He never intended for us to find her in time."

Gabby doesn't hesitate and says as confidently as she can, "We'll find her. I promise."

CHAPTER 56

THEN

THE ONLY THING Samantha heard at first was a steady beeping. She wasn't sure where she was. Every part of her felt heavy. There was a thick fog in her mind. She heard whispers around her. She knew she wasn't at home. The bed felt stiff. She tried opening her eyes, but they would only flutter.

The voices grew louder as her eyes fluttered more.

"I think she's waking up," said a soft female voice.

"Get a nurse," said a deeper male voice.

When Samantha finally opened her eyes, the room was bright and white. She looked around and quickly realized she was in a hospital.

How had she gotten here? She was surprised to see Mr. Davies standing in the room with Ms. Sarah. Where were her parents? Then, like emerging from the depths of a memory ocean, the events before started to come back to her. She remembered Mr. Davies standing between her and her father.

Her father. Vicky. The body. The images.

She squirmed, trying to sit up and get out of bed. Was her father here? Was he going to get her?

"Hey, hey," Ms. Sarah said soothingly.

She rubbed Samantha's arm with one hand, and with the other, she gently pushed her back onto the bed.

"It's okay. You're safe," she said, assuring Samantha.

Samantha looked at Ms. Sarah and couldn't quite put the words together, instead only asking, "Mom?"

Ms. Sarah looked toward the door. Samantha followed her gaze and saw her mom standing inside the room, her arms crossed, leaning against the wall. She had a scowl on her face and was glaring at Samantha.

"You couldn't just leave well enough alone, could you?"

Samantha didn't know what to say. Before she could even process what her mom was talking about, she heard her say, "Whatever happens from here on out, it's your fault."

With those sharp words, her mom yanked open the hospital door and disappeared down the hall.

Ms. Sarah glanced at Mr. Davies and next at Samantha. She stepped in Samantha's line of sight between where her mom had stood and put a smile on her face, asking, "Hey, how are you feeling? Are you hungry? Thirsty? I'm sure we can get you something."

"What's going on?" Samantha asked, hoping for some clarification. She wished everything had been some vivid nightmare. Maybe she fell out of a tree or something. It couldn't be what she was envisioning.

"Well, sweetie," Ms. Sarah started, "Mr. Davies here saved your life. Do you remember running out of your house?"

She didn't need to say anything else. Every detail replaying in Samantha's mind was accurate. It wasn't a dream or a nightmare. It was her reality.

"Hey; I want you to know," Mr. Davies said, rubbing the back of his head, "I need to apologize. I realize how incredibly creepy I must have come across. I would never, I mean never, do anything to hurt you or your friend—or any girl, for that matter. I truly was trying to be neighborly. I've never been great at communicating or interacting with others. I hope you can forgive me."

Samantha could only nod. This was not what was consuming her thoughts right now.

"Sam? The police are here. The FBI, too!" Ms. Sarah said, trying to make it sound exciting. "They'd like to talk with you for a few minutes. Are you okay with that?"

Samantha hesitated, then nodded.

Ms. Sarah gave her a toothy smile and said, "Okay. I'll let them know."

Mr. Davies squeezed Samantha's arm and said, "I'll head out. We don't need so many bodies in here. I'm glad you're okay, though."

He patted her arm and walked out of the room. Was she okay, though?

As Mr. Davies exited, a man and a woman dressed in suits stepped in. The man, who looked like he could be the woman's father, was the first to speak. His voice was much softer than Samantha had expected.

"Hi, Samantha. I'm Agent Saltzer, and this is my partner, Agent Miranda. How are you feeling?"

Samantha shrugged. It felt weird to say fine because she wasn't.

"Can we ask you a few questions?" Agent Miranda asked. Her tone was warm and soft, a voice that Samantha could imagine telling her deepest darkest secrets to.

"My—my mom. Should she be here?" Samantha asked, glancing at Ms. Sarah.

The agents started to trip over themselves. Agent Miranda smiled at Samantha. Her smile somehow lit up the already bright, sterile room. "Yes, well, I think what's most important is to have another adult in the room."

Ms. Sarah piped up, "I'll stay here as an adult for you, so you don't have to answer anything you don't want to. Is that okay?"

Samantha wondered why they weren't getting her mom, but she was too tired to ask for more details.

Ms. Sarah found a spot on the edge of Samantha's bed while the agents looked around for chairs. Only seeing one, they both stood.

Agent Saltzer started, his tone so soft that Samantha had to concentrate on hearing him. "Do you remember the events before you arrived here?"

Samantha nodded.

"Good, that's good. Before, well, before you found the deceased in the woods—"

"Her name was—is—Vicky," Samantha said through gritted teeth.

Agent Saltzer's throat bobbed as he nodded. "Before you found Vicky, were you on the computer?"

Samantha nodded again.

"That's good. That's good," he continued, a forced smile spreading across his face. "Would you remember any of the faces you saw on the computer?"

Ms. Sarah piped in and asked, "I don't understand. You have the computer; why do you need her to remember the faces? Why traumatize her more than she already has been?"

The two agents glanced at each other. Agent Miranda gave a small smile and answered. "Based on the deceased's—um,

Vicky's body, it is reminiscent of a few other cases we have. Because the computer hard drive was fried when the police arrived, we may need Samantha to help identify any faces she can remember against missing person cases."

"How long is that going to take?" Ms. Sarah asked.

Agent Saltzer responded with a stiff tone, "It'll take some time. We'll be careful not to overwhelm her, but it is vital. If he is who we think he is, it'll be the difference between a single homicide and an interstate serial killer."

CHAPTER 57

THEN

THE CONFERENCE ROOM smelled like books. Samantha looked around, wondering what all the different books were for. She assumed they all related to law but had no idea how. She also wondered why the room needed so much wood on the walls. Was that supposed to help the books somehow?

To her, the room felt a little like a classroom, with no windows anywhere and books on all the shelves. The difference, though, was the single large table in the room, the pitcher of water on a tray placed in the middle of the table, and the glasses turned upside down.

The conference room table reflected all aspects of the room. When she stepped in with Ms. Parker, the lawyer helping her prepare, Samantha glided her index finger across the table as she walked the length of the room. She had to keep moving her arm up and over chairs, but she made a game of trying to keep her finger touching the table at all times.

Samantha sat at the far end of the room, swiveling her chair as Ms. Parker sat beside her, making notes on her legal pad.

"Okay, that's good, Samantha. Now we'll get to some tougher questions. Are you ready?"

Samantha took a sip from the glass of water and nodded. It had been four months since she had found the images on her dad's computer. She had sat with the FBI and Ms. Sarah because her mom had done something called waiving her rights. She helped them attach at least six other missing person cases to the trial. Samantha had overheard Ms. Parker tell Ms. Sarah that the location of the missing girls and the set-up of the stones helped them find four of the six victims.

"Okay, Sam. Can I call you Sam?" Ms. Parker asked.

"Of course you can, you know that."

Ms. Parker smiled. "I'm playing that part now. As if you were on the witness stand."

"Oh, right. Sorry. Okay," Samantha said, feeling the heat in her cheeks.

"No problem, you're doing great," Ms. Parker said, reassuring her and patting her arm.

"So, Sam. I know it will be tough, but can you walk us through the events leading up to you going on your dad's computer?"

Samantha spent the next several minutes detailing her relationship with Vicky, the birthday celebration for her that night, and up until she found the butterfly clip in her dad's car. Once she finished, Ms. Parker smiled and said, "That was great! Do it just like that! Do you think you can?"

Samantha liked the praise. It had been some time since someone had encouraged her like that. Life at home had been rough these last few months, with her mom spending all her time in her room or barely cooking for Samantha. She wasn't sure what her mom was drinking, but she was positive it wasn't coffee.

Before Ms. Parker could ask Samantha another question, the door at the end of the room opened, and two more women walked in. The first was Sandy. She had introduced herself to Samantha as a social worker shortly after the conversation with the FBI agents in the hospital. Samantha wasn't sure how she would help her or why she was now in her life, but she reminded Samantha of her grandma and was happy to talk with her. Her clothes always looked like she'd picked them up off her floor, given how wrinkled they were. The other one, though, looked formidable. She glanced around the room, keeping her hands in her pockets, her pitch-black hair falling just to her shoulders. Her black suit fitted her well.

"Excuse us, Ms. Parker, but I wanted to introduce someone to Samantha if that's okay," Sandy said in a soft, raspy voice.

"Of course," Ms. Parker replied. "I'll step out for just a moment. I have a call I need to make."

Sandy came around to the other side of the table, and the new woman took the seat where Ms. Parker had been sitting.

"How is everything going?" Sandy asked.

Samantha shrugged. "It's okay. I'm getting my schoolwork done. Most of the kids have stopped saying anything about the trial and stuff."

"That's good," Sandy said. Turning to the other woman, she pointed to her and said, "I'd like to introduce you to someone. This is Marshal Wright."

Samantha looked at the woman seated on her left and felt an immediate draw to her. Even though she had a stern demeanor, there was a softness to her eyes that Samantha couldn't help but notice. The woman looked like some of the pictures from Samantha's history book, and she wondered if she was a descendant of a Native American tribe.

Marshal Wright reached into the inside of her jacket pocket, and Samantha could see a gun on her hip. Her eyes grew wide seeing it. She'd never seen one that close. The officers who came to her house had guns, but they were on the other side of the room. There was also something different about this woman wearing a suit and the jacket hiding a weapon.

She placed a badge on the table in front of Samantha. It wasn't like a typical police badge. This one was round and had a star with a circle around it. Etched in the circle were the words United States Marshal.

The woman spoke with an accent similar to one of Samantha's uncles who lived in New York.

"It's okay. You can touch it. And you can call me Marianne."

Samantha reached out slowly for the badge, took it in her hand, and turned it over. The black circle was leather, and the metal circle and star felt cool. She looked at the woman and asked, "Is my mom here?"

Marianne smiled at her, and Sandy said, "She asked us to be with you right now. She'll be waiting for you inside. Marshal Wright is here to offer any other help you may need."

"What would I need?" Samantha asked, confused about having this woman with her who carried a gun.

Marianne shrugged, and when she smiled, Samantha noticed how white her teeth were. "It can't hurt to have more than one person looking out for you, right?"

Samantha couldn't help but return the smile and said, "I guess not."

Ms. Parker returned to the room and asked, "Are we ready? Because they'll be ready for you in about ten minutes."

Samantha took a deep breath and looked at the three

women in the room. She wished her mom was here too, but she knew she was safe with these women. They wouldn't let anything happen to her, and if she needed someone to lean on, she could count on any one of them. If she had to pick, though, she'd probably pick Ms. Parker.

Sandy was like a grandma and wouldn't be much help in the protection department. She was great if Sam needed a hug or some sticky candy. Sam was reasonably confident that Marianne, whom she'd just met, would protect her anytime. Samantha could see herself liking her and getting close to her.

But Ms. Parker had been with Sam the entire time, and had made her feel so strong and confident about her testimony. As Samantha pushed out from the chair, she thought about her future and realized she now knew what she wanted to be when she grew up.

She wanted to be a lawyer like Ms. Parker, but with Marianne's strength. That way, she could help and protect those who couldn't help themselves, like Vicky.

CHAPTER 58

NOW

CYNTHIA SQUEEZES TORI'S pillow, inhaling any scent that reminds her of her daughter. The only light is a soft yellow bulb. It gives the whole room a somber tone and fits with Cynthia's mood. Usually, Tori would have her LEDs on, and a variety of greens, reds, and purples would illuminate the space.

Her revelation as she left the last house hit her hard. On the drive back, she realized what she had known all along but had refused to think about. She knew Gabby was trying to be encouraging, telling her they would find Tori, but that was never Alexander's plan. He never intended for them to see Tori.

He wants to string us along for as long as possible and then end Tori's life, just like he had done to Vicky.

Cynthia realized a long time ago that the man who had been her father was nothing more than a complete and utter psychopath. He didn't care about anyone or anything other than himself. He never wanted Cynthia to have the slightest chance of finding Tori.

Being brought to her lowest point, the emotion and ache are there, but the tears escape her. The pain in the base of her skull is growing, and she reaches back to rub her neck. She turns her head from one side to the other and glances at the bedroom door as David walks in.

"Here, take this. It'll help," he says, handing her a few aspirin and a glass of water.

He sits down on the bed next to her, rubbing her leg. Cynthia glances up from his hand to the computer sitting to her left against the window.

"Did you find anything?" she asks him, realizing for the first time she never asked him about looking in Tori's room.

"I'm sorry?" he asks, confused.

"When I asked you if the agents missed anything here, did you find anything?"

He purses his lips to one side and shakes his head. "No, I couldn't get into her computer, and there was nothing else under her bed or hidden in the closet. Not that I could find, at least."

Cynthia hands him the glass and swings her legs over the edge of the bed. She shakes the mouse on the desk, waking up the computer.

"Do we know if the agents could get into her computer?"

David shrugs. "I don't know. I would assume not since it's still locked."

"They probably didn't bother, what with all the other leads we've had. I'll have to ask Gabby," Cynthia mutters, more to herself than David. She wanders over to the bookshelf and wonders what the password could be. There is no point in trying anything from Tori's childhood or what Cynthia thinks she liked, thinking about the hidden detention slips and secrets she'd been keeping.

Cynthia glides her fingers along the various books across

the shelf. There are the more modern books, like *A Court of Thorns and Roses* and *A Good Girl's Guide to Murder*, and classics that Cynthia thought Tori loved, like *The Great Gatsby* and *Great Expectations*.

Cynthia stops on *Great Expectations* and picks it up. She rifles through it, fanning the pages, and stops when the book opens more on a specific page about a third of the way through. Sticking out of the page is a sticky note. Cynthia plucks it out and pivots to David, waving it at him.

"*Great Expectations* has been her favorite book since sophomore year. Every book she's read since, she's compared to this one. We also taught her to ensure her computer is always well-protected with a strong password."

Cynthia sits at the computer and places the sticky note to the side. She glances at it and types in the password: "gR3@+_&xpEcTa!0n$."

David leans over, looking at it. "Damn, we told her to have strong passwords, not impossible ones."

Cynthia shrugs as the laptop comes to life. The background displays Paris at sunset with the Eiffel Tower in the center.

She opens the internet browser and immediately reviews the history, noting the most recent site. Her hands shoot up to her mouth as she exhales, "No!"

Cynthia clicks the link for *dnaforyou.com* and a homepage appears, with verbiage discussing understanding your heritage from the comfort of your own home.

"What is this?" David asks.

"I think it's one of those ancestry websites. For a fee, they'll send you a swab kit, you send it in, and they'll analyze your DNA."

Cynthia is navigating the website and notices a login

option at the top right. She clicks on it, and as she moves her mouse over the email address button, the computer pops up with Tori's email. Cynthia clicks on it and a password auto-generates in the password box.

"Let's see if this works," Cynthia mumbles, clicking the login button.

The screen changes, and a large font at the top says, "Welcome Back, Tori!"

"No, no, no," Cynthia groans. "This must be how she connected with Alexander."

She navigates the user site and finds a spot where you can chat with other family members who use the site. Cynthia clicks on it and a flood of messages between Tori and someone with the username *alex_thefort* appears.

The latest message from Alexander says he wants to meet Tori in person, and that it isn't right she has gone her whole life without knowing her grandfather.

Cynthia covers her face with her hands, mumbling into them, "She shouldn't have found out this way. It should have been me explaining who her grandfather was. This is all my fault. Everything is my fault."

Cynthia is infuriated by Alexander's lies about Tori. If she had just admitted her past to both David and Tori, none of this would be happening.

CHAPTER 59

THEN

SAMANTHA STOOD AT the double doors to the courtroom. She could hear the buzz of voices on the other side. The brass handle was massive in her hand. Sandy stood on one side of her and Marianne on the other. Even though she was almost fourteen, she felt like a three-year-old stepping into a room with people who towered over her. She knew that wasn't true, but it was the sense she got.

"Ready?" Sandy asked.

Samantha didn't know how to answer that. If she was being honest, no, she wasn't ready to testify against her father and possibly send him to prison for the rest of his life. But on the other hand, she was prepared to see justice for Vicky and all the other girls he had killed.

How was that even possible? How could her father be a murderer? Was this right? She still woke up every day wondering if everything had been a dream until the fog of sleep lifted and the daylight of reality shone down on her.

"Well?" Sandy asked again, her voice gentle. Samantha knew if she shook her head violently and yelled, "No, I'm not ready!" Sandy would nod, say okay, and guide her from the courtroom.

But Samantha knew better. She knew that those poor girls deserved better. Taking a deep breath, she said, "Okay, let's do this."

Sandy and Marianne opened the doors, and the room hushed as everyone inside turned to look. Samantha felt a little like a bride from different movies she'd seen, but this was anything but a happy occasion.

People filled the pews, many of whom had notepads and were jotting things down. Four rows of pews lined each side of the aisle, like at a church. Just past the first pew was a half wall with a swivel gate in the middle. A table sat on each side of the room, with a jury box on the right-hand side.

Samantha looked down the middle of the room and up at where the judge would sit like one of those Greek gods she'd learned about, raining down judgment on his people. Marianne guided Samantha to the back row to their right. Samantha gladly slid into the pew, avoiding as much eye contact as possible.

Samantha's mother was the only person who had not turned around to see who was coming in. She sat up in the first row just behind her father. She sat there stone still and didn't turn around once to acknowledge Samantha.

No sooner had she sat down than the bailiff gave the call, "All rise."

Everyone in the room stood, and the jury entered and stood in their spots in the jury box. Shortly after, the judge came in and sat above everyone.

"Take a seat," the judge said in a low voice. "Is the prosecution ready to call its next witness?"

Ms. Parker, who had been helping Samantha, stood up, shuffled a few papers around, and said, "We are, Your Honor."

The judge waved his hand, and she said, loudly and confidently, "The state calls Samantha Beaufort to the stand."

Samantha gulped hard, trying to swallow the fear invading every part of her.

"I don't know if I can do this," she muttered to no one in particular.

Each lady squeezed one of her hands and simultaneously chirped, "You can."

Samantha made eye contact with Ms. Parker, who gave her a warm smile and a slight nod. Samantha knew she couldn't let her down. She'd done too much to help her.

Samantha stood, smoothed out the front of her red and green paisley dress, and kept her eyes focused on Ms. Parker. That had been Ms. Parker's primary instruction that morning. "No matter what, maintain eye contact when walking up to the stand. Don't look left or right. Don't look at your mom and dad. Just stay focused on me. I'll help you every step of the way, okay?"

Ms. Parker swung the gate inward for Samantha, who momentarily glanced down at her hand on the gate, noticing Ms. Parker's nice French tip manicure. Ms. Parker waved a hand toward the witness stand so Samantha knew where to go. Samantha made her way over and climbed into the box.

The bailiff came over, held out a Bible, and asked her to repeat, "I swear the testimony I'm about to give is the truth, the whole truth, and nothing but the truth."

Samantha repeated it and he gave her a warm smile, his teeth shining against his dark skin.

"You may take a seat," the judge said gently.

Samantha sat and Ms. Parker walked up near her, holding a hand on the jury box railing.

Almost under her breath, Ms. Parker asked, "You okay?"

Samantha nodded and Ms. Parker asked her first question. "Is Alexander Beaufort your father?"

Samantha nodded.

Ms. Parker smiled and said sweetly, "I need you to give a vocal answer, please."

"Oh, s—sorry," Samantha stuttered, feeling the heat on her cheeks. "Yes, he is."

"And is he in this courtroom today?"

"Yes, he is sitting over there," Samantha said.

"Let the record show the witness is pointing to the defendant."

The remainder of the questioning went by in a blur. Ms. Parker had prepped her well, and Samantha felt like she was in a play, reciting answers from a script.

Ms. Parker said, "The state has no further questions, Your Honor."

She looked at Samantha and, under her breath, encouraged her, "You did great."

"Defense? Your witness."

The lawyer for Alexander stood briefly and said, "Ms. Beaufort, is it true that this friend of yours, Vicky Smith, had several boyfriends who were much older than her?"

Samantha looked at Ms. Parker.

"The prosecution can't help you, Ms. Beaufort. Please answer the question."

"No, I mean, yes. Well, I mean, I dunno," Samantha stammered.

"And isn't it true that one of those boys lived close to you?"

"Not really, well, kinda."

"So isn't it possible that this boy could have picked her up from your house that night, and maybe she refused him and he got angry and killed her, possibly even before leaving your house, and then he buried her in the woods behind your house?"

Samantha started to cry. She didn't know what was happening. Ms. Parker didn't prepare her for this. Why was this man defending her father? He was a killer, wasn't he?

"Ms. Beaufort, isn't that possible?"

The defense lawyer was so close to her. She didn't know what to do. She didn't want to get in trouble.

"Ms. Beaufort, isn't it?"

"Objection!" Ms. Parker called out. "Badgering the witness."

Before the judge could say anything, Samantha was already nodding and squeaked, "I—I guess."

"Nothing further, Your Honor."

"The witness may step down," the judge responded, glancing at Samantha.

She sat there frozen, unsure of what to do. The weight of everything she just did crashed around her, and she wasn't sure she could move. She looked over at the defense table and her father, with whom she had been having ice cream just a few months before. She looked behind him at her mom, who didn't glance her way once during the testimony. It made Samantha feel like she'd done something wrong.

Did her mom know this whole time and let it happen? Why wasn't she more encouraging and loving to Samantha now? Did she blame Samantha for all of this? It wasn't her fault.

Samantha couldn't take it, and she started to sob on the

stand. Ms. Parker hurried to her side, as did Marianne, flashing her badge at the judge. She approached the witness stand and held out her hand for Samantha.

Samantha gripped Marianne's hand tightly as she led her down the walkway, past all the pews, and back out into the main hall.

Marianne knelt and took both of Samantha's hands in her own.

"Hey, I can't imagine how difficult that was for you. You did the right thing. Never forget, this isn't your fault. You're a hero. Because of your bravery, you have saved countless young ladies' lives for the future! I want to be like you when I grow up."

Samantha smiled through the tears and blurry vision. She wiped her eyes with the back of her hands. She wasn't sure if she actually believed what Marianne was saying, but right now, she was going to hold on to it.

CHAPTER 60

NOW

CYNTHIA SITS AT the desk, shaking her head. She can't believe all the messages she's reading. She hasn't been able to stop. It reminds her of when she found the file on Alexander's computer and continued to click on the images of those poor girls. She knows all these messages are lies on top of lies, but she can't stop reading them.

alex_thefort: *It's so good to talk to you! I've been hoping for so long that I had a granddaughter!*

torithegreat: *I'm still in shock! She told me you were dead.*

alex_thefort: *That's not a surprise. There is so much to tell you. We've lost so much time!*

torithegreat: *I have to be honest. I looked you up online. Is what I've read true? Did you kill all those girls?*

alex_thefort: *It was all a huge misunderstanding. Before I could explain everything to your mom, she ran from me. She thought I was a monster. But that wasn't how it was at all! I was being thrown under the bus. They needed a scapegoat and used me.*

torithegreat: *That's horrible! I'm not surprised she did something like that. She's been throwing me under the bus my whole life.*

I don't understand why she could have thought you did those horrible things. I mean, even if you did, they probably deserved it, right?

alex_thefort: *I haven't heard someone think like that in such a long time. Not saying I did or didn't do it, but there's always a reason, you know? I'm sorry you've had to live with her like that. She's sneaky. She's always been like that.*

torithegreat: *Is it true you escaped?*

alex_thefort: *Yes. I had to. It was the only way to clear my name. Sometimes in life, you have to take matters into your own hands. The world isn't going to give you anything. You have to take it and sometimes make rules that apply only to you. You know, I've spent so long on the run, at this point, it's going to be hard to share my side of the story.*

torithegreat: *I want to help. Let me help you tell your side.*

alex_thefort: *that would be amazing! But only if you want to.*

torithegreat: *I really do. I really want to get to know you.*

alex_thefort: *I'd be willing to meet you in person if you're up for it.*

torithegreat: *Absolutely!*

"How long?" David asks, shock on his face.

Cynthia scrolls back. She keeps scrolling and looks at the dates. "At least several months. She had to do it for a science class around DNA or something."

"Doesn't sound familiar," David says.

"Of course, it wouldn't to you. You probably weren't even here. I was only half listening myself."

"That's not fair," David says, his tone sharp.

Cynthia stops and reaches up, touches his hand on the chair, and squeezes it. "I'm sorry, you're right, that wasn't. I didn't mean it like that. We both have been so busy lately that we've ignored her."

He takes a deep breath and lets it out.

"He must have used this site," Cynthia goes on, "and probably others that allow you to communicate with people you're related to. And then just waited. It's possible he never would have found me. It just so happened that Tori used this site and found the connection."

Cynthia begins navigating through other parts of the site when her phone vibrates on the desk, startling her. She sees Gabby's name on it and answers quickly on speakerphone.

"Hey, did you find something?" Cynthia asks.

"Not related to Tori specifically, no. I was checking in. We're finishing up processing the scene. We found a couple of sets of prints on the pictures. Alexander's, obviously, and some actually from Marshal Marianne Wright."

"Marshal Wright? Are you sure?" Cynthia asks.

David whispers behind her, "Who's Marshal Wright?"

Cynthia waves him off as Gabby answers, "Yeah, we thought it was odd, too. We're looking into it, and I'll let you know what we find."

"Okay. We found something here. We got into her computer and figured out how Alexander found me. Completely by luck—sort of. I can explain more in person."

"Sounds good. Any insights will help. I'll send a few agents back now and I should be along shortly."

They end the call and Cynthia puts the phone down, resting her hand on it, thinking about Marshal Wright. How did she get caught up in all of this? Did Alexander blame her for taking Cynthia away?

Before she can spend more time on the thought, David asks, "Hey, when did you last eat something substantial? Not cheese and crackers?"

"I honestly have no idea," Cynthia replies, her stomach acknowledging the same.

"Let me make you something. It isn't doing us any good to keep reading these messages. We know they arranged to meet, but it doesn't help us understand where she is," David says, trying to pull Cynthia away.

She nods and pushes back the chair, careful not to roll back too fast and run over his toes.

They head down to the kitchen, and Cynthia parks herself at the end of the bar top while David gets to work boiling water and pulling out ingredients for his famous homemade marinara sauce.

Twenty minutes later, Cynthia is spinning noodles onto a fork while David takes a long sip from his wineglass. They pivot to a Merlot they have on the shelf. The only sounds throughout the house are the clinking of utensils, butter scraping on toasted bread, and slurps of noodles and wine.

"It feels like months since the last time the house was this quiet," David comments, trying to generate some semblance of a normal conversation.

Cynthia only nods.

She picks up her glass to take a sip when her phone vibrates next to her. She picks it up and immediately drops the glass of wine in her other hand. The glass hits the table and falls to the ground, shattering all over the floor, the red wine spreading across the tile like blood.

She ignores the mess, presses answer on the phone, and shouts, "Tori!"

CHAPTER 61

NOW

"TORI?! IS THAT you?!" Cynthia exclaims, looking at the phone in her hand. Somehow, she had put it on speakerphone as she stumbled out of the kitchen. David is right behind her, both ignoring the mess of the shattered glass and spilled wine.

Cynthia trips over a cable in the great room, cursing as one of the agents' laptops tumbles to the ground. Clinging to her phone like a lifeline, she keeps from falling over the edge.

"Mom?" a raspy voice comes back.

Cynthia collapses on the couch and, between sobs, asks, "Sweetheart, are you there? Are you okay?"

David leans in. "Tori, where are you? Did you get away?"

There is silence on the line for a moment, and Cynthia fears Alexander has found out she's gotten away.

"Tori? Are you there? Say something, sweetheart!" Cynthia implores.

"Yeah, yeah, I'm here," Tori responds, sounding like she's whispering.

"Are you hiding? Are you safe?" David asks, leaning over the arm of the couch toward the phone.

There is quiet again for a moment.

"Tori! Answer us!" Cynthia pleads.

A shuffle and a scraping sound emanate from the speaker, like something is rubbing against fabric. Alexander's voice comes on the phone, scolding, "Now, now. Do you think I would let Tori escape? I wanted her to call you. I wanted you all to get the chance to hear her voice one last time. Tomorrow's it, you know that, right?"

"What are you playing at?" Cynthia yells. "Just give us our daughter back! Take me. Just don't hurt her!"

"I don't know what you're talking about. I've given you almost three full days to find her and so many clues. You haven't figured it out yet?"

"I've been following your clues! But they've led nowhere!" Cynthia snaps.

With a chuckle, Alexander replies, "Well, now, I disagree. I think you've uncovered quite a bit based on my clues. They've led you right where I wanted you to go. I wanted you to know the kind of daughter you were raising. Just like her mother, a liar and a fake. You've had the time and opportunity to find her, but you haven't. That is not my fault."

"It is one hundred percent your fault! You said we had three days! You said you would give me the chance to find her! But you didn't mean any of that, did you?"

Cynthia is up, pacing around the room like a caged lion.

"This whole time, your goal was to play me. You never intended for me to find her. You wanted me to think I would and feel guilty for not finding her in time!"

"Well, well. It looks like you have learned something," Alexander taunts. "Yes, that is all true. And I guess it is my fault for leading you astray. I should have been clearer. I did lead you astray, just like you've led her astray all your life. I guess like father, like daughter, huh? Now, why don't you go ahead and say goodbye—it will be the last time."

There is silence on the other end, and Cynthia looks down at her phone to ensure the call hasn't disconnected.

"Tori?! Are you there? We love you! We'll find you!" Cynthia yells into the phone.

"We do sweetheart! We love you! We're coming for you!" David adds.

Tori's voice sounds farther away, as if Alexander is holding the phone to her from across a room. "Mom? Dad? I love you! Find me, please! Hurry. I'm so sorry!"

Cynthia hears the three beeps telling her the call has ended. She looks down at her phone, the screensaver of the three of them when Tori was thirteen. It has been that long since she last changed it.

Will she ever have the heart to change it now? Will she be able to get an updated picture when Tori turns twenty-one? Will she ever get the opportunity to watch her child have a child? How old was she when she became a mom herself?

Cynthia looks up at David for some hope, but she can see the same look in his eyes. The same thought is ravaging both of them: they've run out of time.

CHAPTER 62

THEN

IT TOOK SAMANTHA a few minutes to regain her composure from her embarrassment in the courtroom. It wasn't just that she froze on the stand and couldn't get off of it, but even more so, the weight of the whole event. She sat there and had to tell the jury that her father, the one she trusted more than anyone in her entire life, wasn't who she thought he was. He was a killer, and not just a killer, but a serial killer of girls her age.

Why hadn't he done it to her? Would he have if she hadn't found out about him? She hated this thought and tried to think about anything else.

Samantha sat on a bench outside of the courtroom, Marianne right next to her, telling her, "Breathe in through your nose and out through your mouth."

It helped her to calm down. She knew she wanted to go back in, but she still had to build up the courage.

The sun shone through the windows, casting four squares of light on the floor. Samantha stared at them and watched as a black shadow passed over. She glanced up, noticing a raven flying by. How simple life must be for a bird. To be able to fly through the air, above so much danger and destruction. The ability to go wherever they please, and make their home where it's safe. They don't murder their own; they have loyalty to their families. Samantha would have given anything to sprout wings, transform into a bird, and fly out of that place. To start over, start somewhere new. That would be amazing.

"You don't have to go back," Marianne said, bringing her back to reality. "We can go down to the cafeteria, get some candy, some soda. What's your favorite TV show? Maybe we can talk about that?"

Samantha thought of Vicky and shook her head. "No, I need to go back."

"Are you sure? No one would blame you if you didn't."

Samantha took a deep breath, held it for a count of three, wiped her eyes with the backs of her hands, and slowly let it out.

"I'm sure. I need to. I'm ready."

Samantha pushed up off the bench, smoothing out her dress again. In any other situation, she would love the way she looked, but now was not the time to think about that.

Marianne stood and walked ahead of Samantha, quietly opening the door, waving an arm for her to enter first.

Samantha gave her a half smile and mouthed, "Thank you."

She sidled in next to Sandy in the back pew and focused on the front of the courtroom, where Ms. Parker was questioning a detective.

"Can you tell us what your officers found once they secured the crime scene?"

"Sure. Once the defendant was in custody, we cleared the home's interior and progressed to the backyard and the woods beyond. Once there, we quickly found the grave on the footpath. It was peculiar that it was out in the open, but as we began to canvas the backwoods, we quickly figured out why. We uncovered several other bodies in the woods, all buried fairly close to the back fence of his home."

"Objection!" the defense attorney shot up, shouting. "Everything he just said is circumstantial at best."

"Sustained," the judge said flatly.

"What makes you confident it was the defendant who buried the bodies in the back?" Ms. Parker asked.

"We were able to recover fragments from the computer in his home, and with that, along with the testimony of his daughter, who spent time on the computer, we deduced he was the one who placed the bodies there."

Ms. Parker paused, turning to the defense, who shook his head and scribbled something on paper.

"What else can you tell us about the other bodies you found?"

"We know from working with Ms. Beaufort, the defendant's daughter, that there were several other cities with images of deceased young women. We are coordinating with other local law enforcement agencies, as well as the FBI, to uncover these bodies and give hope back to families who have reported loved ones missing."

"Of the victims found in the woods behind the Beauforts' home, were you able to identify any of them?" Ms. Parker asked, looking at some sheets she had picked up from the table.

"Unfortunately, many of the bodies were so badly decomposed that our teams are still working on identifications. But the closest one had only been in the ground for about a week or two, and we could identify her as the young girl who had gone missing, Vicky Smith."

Hearing her best friend's name called out on a witness stand as a victim was too much. Samantha pushed past Marianne, stepping on her toes on the way out. Tears flowed from her eyes as she pushed through the back door. She knew she had made a ruckus leaving but didn't care.

She already knew everything the detective had revealed, but hearing it out loud was too much. Samantha dropped to her knees on the cold marble floor of the courthouse, covered her face with her hands, and wept.

She felt a gentle hand on her back and glanced up, seeing Marianne kneeling beside her through bleary, tear-stained eyes.

"It'll get easier, I promise," Marianne whispered. "I know it doesn't seem like it now, but I promise it does. You'll figure out how to cope with this as time goes on. And I'll be there for you as much as you need, okay?"

Samantha nodded, burying her face in Marianne's shoulder.

"How about we go get that soda and candy now? What do you say?"

Samantha could only nod. Marianne helped her up, took a step in front of her, and reached back with her hand. Samantha took it, letting her lead the way. It felt good to have a powerful woman to lean on, and Samantha was certain this would not be the last time she would need Marianne by her side.

CHAPTER 63

JOURNAL

I CAN'T BELIEVE I got to this point! How is it possible that this has happened without anyone finding out? It feels like I began crafting this plan and started putting everything into motion just yesterday. For so long, I've wondered, and now I know. I know everything. I know what I must do—I know who I am, and I've come to accept it.

I've accepted it.

Writing those words gives me a thrill unlike anything before. I've chased the excitement for as long as I can remember. I know people say that, but for me, it's true. I can remember all the way back to when I was little, like five or six, and ever since then, I've been chasing that rush. That thrill to wonder if you'll get in trouble for something or if you'll get away with it.

If everything goes according to plan, the future will be full of possibilities and dead bodies. It has taken me months, and if I'm honest, probably years to plan everything on the horizon. I believe in planning, but also in leaving a bit up to interpretation. I've come to understand that if you try to plan everything, one, it's boring, and two, it never goes exactly the way you want it to. This way, when you leave yourself some room for uncharted territory, it keeps the mind sharp.

I knew I wanted to plan up to this point, but I wanted to leave it open past this. I'm not sure what comes next. I hope that whatever it is takes care of this headache once and for all. I know I'm on the verge of snapping, and if I don't do something that is within my control soon, I may lose it, and who knows what will happen then?

That is not the uncharted territory I'm looking for.

If I had the chance to talk with any of the most notorious serial killers out there, they would probably tell me it's a horrible idea to leave some parts up to chance. But like I said already, in my mind, that keeps me sharp.

In the instances of chaos I have created in my life so far, I allowed room for inspiration, and damn, I'd be lying if I said it didn't feel like an absolute rush to know I might get caught.

It's the only way I've known to work. I plan most of the way, but leaving that extra bit to improvise is a thrill.

If nothing else, it keeps me one step ahead of everyone else. I already know everything I've done, and as long as I cover those tracks, they won't be able to figure out the rest. I know they'll never find me, or should I say, us. They can't. The clues were there to make them feel like they were getting close, but ultimately, she would realize there was no chance.

My only regret is not setting up a camera at each location so I could see her face when she finally knew it. Damn, the look must have been something.

Will it be tragic and sad that they'll never find their little girl? I guess that depends on who you ask. Of course, if you ask them or any of their friends, then yes, it is one hundred percent tragic and sad. If you ask me, no. It is not tragic and not sad.

If anything, it's justice. It's payback. It's—what is the word I'm looking for? Retribution.

For everything she has put me through over the years, this is the least I could do to get back at her. If I feel bad, it's a slight tinge of remorse for him, but that is the tragic result of collateral damage.

She is going to get what is coming. She has no idea what is in store for her.

CHAPTER 64

THEN

SAMANTHA SAT AT the end of the long conference room table, her math book open on her left. She was working on an assignment for her algebra class while several adults stood at the far end, talking in hushed tones. She knew she wouldn't get any homework done with everyone around, but she had to at least make an effort.

Samantha's grades had dropped precipitously throughout the ordeal, so the school had called her mom to discuss them. Samantha knew it was the school because Sandy had been at the house when they called and answered the phone.

"Mrs. Beaufort? It's the school," Sandy called out.

Samantha's mom dragged herself to the kitchen and took the phone from Sandy.

"What?" her mom snapped.

Sandy returned to the couch with Samantha, sitting beside her, and picked up the cards she had placed down. They had been playing a game of Go Fish.

"What are you talking about? Her grades are fine," her mom snarled, glaring at her. "No, you don't know what you're talking about. And honestly, I don't care. That is the least of my worries right now."

Samantha's mom slammed the phone back on the wall and shuffled past them. The smell coming off her reminded Samantha of going to Vicky's house.

She had expected her mom to say something about her grades, but she'd said nothing. She just strolled past them and back up the stairs to her room.

Samantha decided then that she wouldn't let anything affect her grades. She would need good grades to get out of there someday and become a lawyer like Ms. Parker. After that, she started bringing her backpack to the courthouse.

She got the most done when there were lulls in the trial, or when they left her alone in the conference room. Samantha knew she wouldn't get a whole lot done with everyone in the room. She closed the book, purposely a little louder than she needed to. Ms. Parker glanced her way and smiled. It was the same smile she'd given Samantha when she was on the stand.

It was a drastically different look than the one her father had given her as she'd passed him after her testimony. Even through her bleary vision, she had never seen him scowl like that. He hated her. She didn't understand how this could be the same man who had called her Sammy a couple of months before and told her he loved her. She wondered if she would ever see him again.

Would she visit him in prison? Would she try to have a relationship with him after this? If she was being honest with herself, she knew she wouldn't. But that still hurt too much.

Marshal Wright pulled up a chair and sat beside her. She said, "When the trial continues today, you don't have to sit there. They will be going over some pretty gruesome aspects of the case. I'd recommend you don't. You're welcome to stay here and get your schoolwork done."

Before Samantha could respond or reject the request, the door at the far end slammed open, and three officers and another person in a suit burst into the room. Marshal Wright jumped to her feet and hurried over, asking, "What is it?"

The new person in a suit waved her outside when they saw Samantha sitting there. Everyone entered the hall, but the door caught and didn't shut. Samantha got up and tiptoed as close as she could to the door without them seeing her.

She couldn't hear everything, but she caught certain words: "Escaped," "Had help," "They're looking everywhere," and "Keep her safe." As she heard those last words, Marshal Wright glanced back, saw the door ajar, and quickly closed it, but Samantha's anger bubbled as soon as she did.

She had a right to know if something had happened with her father. Their entire case was because of her. Yanking open the door, she asked, "What's happened?"

Marshal Wright ushered her back in and said, "I'm not sure. We're figuring that out right now. As soon as I know something, I promise I'll come in and tell you. Okay? Please wait here."

Samantha hesitated, but knew Marshal Wright was looking out for her. So she returned to her seat and stared at her math book. There was no way she was going to get any homework done right now.

Were those the words she'd heard? Had her father escaped? If so, what would that mean for her? Would he come after her? Would she be his next victim?

Samantha wondered if anyone was even outside the door anymore. It felt like it'd been hours. She glanced at the clock and groaned, realizing it'd only been ten minutes. As she watched the seconds tick by, the door at the end of the room opened. Marshal Wright returned with the same man who had rushed in a few minutes ago. They both came over to Samantha and sat down. He pulled out a badge just like Marshal Wright's and introduced himself. "Hey, Samantha. I'm Marshal Samuels. I'm going to be helping Marshal Wright here. Is that okay?"

Samantha squinted at him and flicked her eyes toward the woman she'd come to know and trust. "What's going on?"

Marshal Wright put her hands out and Samantha instinctively put hers on top. She squeezed Samantha's hands and said, "I'm just going to be straight with you. It seems your father has escaped. They aren't sure how yet, but everyone is looking for him, and we'll find him. I promise."

Samantha swallowed hard at the words.

"But until then, we'll need to protect you and your mom, okay?"

Samantha nodded, not understanding what that meant. She didn't know what else to say, but she trusted Marshal Wright, who took a deep breath and patted Samantha's hand.

Marshal Wright stood and said, "Okay, okay. Marshal Samuels here and I will escort you and your mom to a hotel where we'll have agents and other Marshals to watch over you. I'm sure it'll only be for a few days at most. Okay? You ready?"

She collected her school things and shoved them into her backpack.

Samantha hoped it would only be for a few days. She had a test coming up that she needed to be at school for and a dance that she was hoping to attend.

A few days at a hotel wouldn't be too bad. Would it?

CHAPTER 65

NOW

CYNTHIA SMASHES HER finger on Tori's number in her favorite contacts list, putting it on speakerphone. It immediately picks up with her voicemail. She presses the end button forcefully and redials the number. It's still voicemail. She repeats this process several more times, all with the same result.

Pacing around her great room, Cynthia is trying to comprehend what happened. Alexander did everything simply to taunt her, to make her feel like she was in control, and to take it away from her.

"Cynth," David says, trying to be assuring. "She's not going to pick up."

Cynthia stops and glares at him. Doesn't he care? Doesn't he realize they were so close but so far?

Cynthia ignores him and presses another favorite in her contacts. Gabby answers on the first ring.

"Hey, I was just about to call you. What's up? I'm on my way to your place," Gabby says.

Hearing Gabby's voice, Cynthia breaks down into sobs.

Between trying to catch her breath and tears running down her cheeks, Cynthia explains what just happened.

"We talked to her. We heard her voice," Cynthia squeezes out between sobs. "He said what I'd feared. He never meant for us to find her. How are we going to find her?"

David comes up next to her, putting his arm around her and rubbing her shoulder. He gently guides her towards the couch and gets her to sit down.

"Hang on," Gabby says. It sounds like she is muffling the phone with her hand. "We could pick up the ping from a couple of cell towers. We've got it narrowed down to a mile radius. This is huge, Cynth! We're going to get her back. I promise!"

"What? Are you serious?!"

"Yes. I told you we would get her back. We are working right now on getting a smaller target, and we'll have agents in the area in the next fifteen to twenty minutes."

"I—I don't know what to say."

"We were just getting in the car as you called. Agent Milo here had just opened the laptop. When you talked to Tori, he noticed the ping."

"Thanks, Gabby," David adds. "We would be an absolute wreck, even more than we already are, if it weren't for you and your team."

Cynthia can only nod between her tears.

"Of course, that's what we do. I'll let you know when we have something more concrete and tell you where to meet us."

Cynthia can only manage, "Thank you. Love you."

"Love you too, Cynth. Talk soon."

Gabby hangs up the call and Cynthia stares at the phone.

"We spoke with her," Cynthia breathes. For the first time

in the last couple of days, she has hope, but she is also trying to temper her hope, because she knows Alexander.

"What if we can't hug her again?" Cynthia asks. "When was the last time I hugged her? I'm a horrible mom—I can't even remember the last time I hugged my daughter!"

"What are you talking about? You're an amazing mom. Of course you'll hug her again. Didn't you hear Gabby?"

"Yeah, a mile. How many homes is that? What will they do, knock on every door in that mile? That's a lot of houses. We only have hours left, if he even sticks to his timeline."

David comes around, squats down in front of Cynthia, takes both of her hands in his, and says, "Look at me."

She looks into his piercing blue eyes and sees the reflection of tears in them. "We're going to find her, and we're going to get her back. You will be able to hug her all you want. Gabby and her team are going to figure it out."

"But what if—"

Before Cynthia can finish her thought, there is a knock at the front door. David pushes up, padding his way across the great room and up the tile steps to the door. He opens it, but she can't see who it is.

She can hear him whisper, "Right now is probably not the best time."

Cynthia pushes off the couch and curves around enough to see past him and see Jacob standing there, his hands shoved in his sagging pants, his shoulders rounded.

Before she can say anything, he pulls his hands out and pushes his way in. "I'm sorry, but this can't wait."

Focusing on Cynthia, he stammers, "I—I know you probably hate me. And that's fine, but I don't want to see anything bad happen to Tori. I know I'm not a great guy, but I had nothing to do with her disappearance."

He pauses for a minute and the three stare at each other. In a softer tone, putting his hands back in his pockets, realizing his boldness is fading, he asks, "Did she just call you?"

Cynthia steps towards him and asks breathlessly, "How did you know that?"

He pulls his hands out again. One reaches into his back pocket, pulling out his phone, and the other scratches at the back of his head. He holds the phone out toward them so they can see a map. There is a glowing red pin on the map.

Cynthia rushes forward and grabs him, asking, "What is this?"

"I—ugh, I hate myself, but I installed a hidden AirTag in her shoe. I knew she was seeing someone else and I couldn't handle it. I had to know where she was at all times. I know I'm horrible—"

"What does this mean?" Cynthia asks, grabbing the phone and staring at the map.

"It means I know where she is."

CHAPTER 66

THEN

"ALRIGHT, HERE WE are," Marshal Wright said. Samantha could tell she was forcing excitement. The house was as basic as it could get. She caught herself wondering if it would be big enough. She then remembered it was only her and her mom now.

Her backpack dug into her shoulders, full of as much of the stuff from her room as she could pack. Her suitcase, which she rolled behind her, felt like it was dragging her arm down. It was an odd sensation, having to pack up her entire life into a suitcase and a backpack. Marshal Wright had told her multiple times that she couldn't take this or that because it was too close to her old life.

She had told Samantha that part of witness protection was starting over. Clothes and hair stuff were okay, but sentimental items or anything referencing her life before were not. Any pictures of her and Vicky or other friends had to stay behind. She would have given anything to leave all her clothes and find new ones if she could take one or two pictures.

Marshal Wright stepped inside and waited for Samantha and her mom to enter. When her mom walked across the threshold, she scoffed and cried. Samantha wondered why she was crying, but she understood when she looked around. She set her suitcase inside the door and looked to her right. A small kitchen had enough space for the stove, fridge, and sink, but nothing else. A folding table and two folding chairs made up the tiny space just outside the kitchen. Samantha assumed this would be considered the dining room. Two other agents with a few Chinese food cartons sat around the table. As soon as they saw Samantha and her mom, both stood up, using napkins to wipe their hands and mouths.

Looking to her left as Marshal Wright closed the door, Samantha noticed a living room that looked smaller than her old bedroom. There were two other folding chairs and a television that looked like it was from the mid-seventies. Samantha took a deep breath and let it out.

It's better than the hotel room. At least I'll have my own room.

As if reading her mind, Marshal Wright commented, "Look at the bright side. At least you both will have your privacy now and have your own rooms."

Marshal Wright waved toward the other two agents and introduced them as they exchanged handshakes.

"This is Marshal Williamson and Marshal Delago. They will be here to help you get settled in. If you need anything, you can reach out to any of us," Marshal Wright said.

"Welcome," Marshal Williamson answered gruffly. He looked like he could be Samantha's grandpa, even though she'd never met her grandfather. Samantha smiled at him and hoped she wouldn't have to interact with him too often.

"How are you doing, sweetie?" Marshal Delago said. Her tone was the exact opposite of Marshal Williamson's. She looked like she could be Marshal Wright's younger sister, but looked more Hispanic and had a strong accent.

All three were dressed in similar attire: black pants, black suit jackets, which were open, and white shirts with no ties.

"If you both can come over here, we can go over some basics," Marshal Williamson said. He laid out a folder and flipped it open.

"We have new socials for you both and a new birth certificate for Samantha." He held up a couple of cards that looked like credit cards. "Here is a new credit and debit card in your new name. Your checks will arrive in the next three to five business days. We'll handle all utilities for the first six months while we help you get a job and settle in."

Samantha's thoughts trailed off during his instructions, as she assumed most of it was for her mom, anyway. She heard him say something about school and refocused.

"The school is only about three blocks away and is very easy to walk to. Classes have already started back after the holiday break, but we have spoken with the school and told them you just moved from back east. They don't know the details. That is probably the most important piece of information. No one, I repeat, no one knows your past."

He paused, glancing from Samantha to her mom and back again. "No one will know. Do not, under any circumstances, tell people about your past. Do not let on about your actual name or history. This is of the utmost importance. If we determine you break any of these rules, we will have to move you again. That is not a pleasant experience. Do not try to contact your past family or friends. Any witness who has followed these rules has lived."

Samantha thought that was a weird statement and asked, "What happens to witnesses who don't follow the rules?"

"Samantha!" her mom scolded.

"No, it's fine," Marshal Delago said. "If you contact old

friends and family, you risk Alexander getting wind of where you are and coming to find you. We understand it may happen completely unintentionally. If that happens, let us know as soon as it happens. That gives us a chance to keep you protected."

"How long do we have to be these new people?" Samantha asked.

Marshal Wright answered, "Until we find your dad."

"I thought that was only going to take a couple of days or weeks. Why do we need new lives if it isn't that long?"

Marshal Wright nodded. "Another great question. At this point, unfortunately, we don't know where he is. We've checked everywhere, and if we get to this point, the odds of finding him will have slimmed dramatically."

Samantha's mom muttered, "What's the point?"

"What's that?" Marshal Delago asked.

"I said, what's the point? If I can't be with the man I fell in love with, what's even the point of living?" her mom snapped.

Marshal Wright pulled Samantha's mom down the hall, and Samantha couldn't hear what they were saying except for Marshal Wright saying something like, "You need to do this for Samantha."

Samantha didn't know what else to say. She gravitated to the table and looked at her new Social Security card.

The enormity of what was happening began to hit her. This was now her life. She would have to make up a story about her past and make new friends. No one in her new life would ever know about her history, and she needed to make sure of that. The last thing she needed was for her father to find her. She couldn't fathom building a new life and having it destroyed again because he was able to find her.

She ran her finger over her new name, getting used to the sound of it: Cynthia Davidson.

CHAPTER 67

NOW

CYNTHIA RIPS THE phone out of Jacob's hand, studying the screen.

"What am I looking at?" she asks desperately.

Jacob sighs, scratching the back of his head. "I'm not proud of this. You're looking at where she is. The AirTag works when a working iPhone is in the vicinity and turned on. It pinged a few minutes ago. That's how I figured you talked to her."

"So you're saying this blinking red spot is where she is now?" Cynthia asks, confirming.

Jacob nods his head.

"I'm going to need this," she says, holding up his phone, turning on the spot and heading to her bedroom.

Jacob protests as Cynthia jogs up the stairs to her room. She doesn't care if Jacob or David are following her. She knows what she has to do now, and nothing will stop her. Alexander is going to die for this.

She steps into her master suite and pads across to her oversized walk-in closet. Moving a group of dresses out of the way, Cynthia punches in a code on the wall safe and one green light blinks on. As she places her index finger on a biometric fingerprint reader, a second green light appears. There is an audible click as the safe door opens a crack.

Cynthia yanks on the handle, pulling the door fully open, revealing a Ruger 9mm handgun in the middle. In the back is a group of folders, and next to the handgun is a complete magazine of bullets. On the other side is a box of more bullets. She pulls out the gun, loads the magazine, pulls back the slide, and sees the bullet in the chamber.

She has never used the gun, but has taken classes and knows her way around the weapon. Making sure the safety is on, Cynthia places the gun in the back waistband of her jeans. Turning to leave the closet, David is standing in her way. He glances at her waist; she assumes he saw her put the gun there.

"Are you going to tell Gabby?" he asks.

The initial question surprises her. She was confident it would be about the gun, and how she should let the police handle the weapons because that was what they trained for.

Before she can respond, he follows up with, "I think you should. You don't know what we'll be walking into."

The two stand there as if in a face-off. The last thing Cynthia wants is for Alexander to be tipped off and disappear. Of course, she trusts Gabby, but someone still has helped Alexander, and Cynthia can't afford an officer screwing up this situation.

"Cynth, please, think about this," David pleads, holding Cynthia's phone out to her. For half a second, she wonders how he has her phone when she's holding one, but then remembers it's Jacob's phone in her hand.

She takes a deep breath, and against her better judgment, she takes the phone from him and dials Gabby's number.

She answers on the first ring. "Hey, we're on the way. What's up?"

Cynthia stares at David, still afraid something is going to get screwed up if she does this.

"Cynth? You there? You okay?"

"I know where she is," Cynthia says flatly.

"What?! What do you mean? Did she call again?"

Cynthia shakes her head. "No, nothing like that. Jacob, the kid across the street, hid an AirTag in her shoe, and it pinged when they turned her phone on to call."

"Well, shit. Kudos to the creepy kid. Send it over and we'll get there quickly."

"Sending it now," Cynthia replies.

"Okay, got it. Looks like it's a bit closer to you. Do not, I repeat, *do not* do anything until we get there. Do you understand?"

"I understand," Cynthia says reluctantly. She hangs up and pushes past David, still annoyed at him for making her call Gabby.

Jacob is still standing in her entryway as she comes down the stairs. She grabs her purse and opens the front door. Jacob yells, "You can't just take my phone!"

Cynthia pulls the gun out from the back of her waistband and drops it in her purse.

Seeing the weapon, Jacob puts his hands in the air and says, "That's fine. You can take it."

"Are you coming?" she asks David.

He comes right up to her, looking down at her, his additional height in full effect. He puts his hand on her arm and urges, "Yes, but I want to make sure you heard Gabby. You don't need the gun."

Cynthia rolls her eyes. "We're not having this conversation right now. They're the ones who let him escape in the first place. I love Gabby, but I'm not waiting to get my girl back. And I'm certainly not giving him any chance to get away again. He's hurt enough young girls. He might be my biological father, but he stopped being my dad the day he killed my best friend."

"Who?" Jacob interjects.

Cynthia and David ignore him, and David sighs, letting go of her arm.

"Thank you," Cynthia whispers.

Turning her attention to Jacob, she points at him and then at the front door. "You. Out."

Jacob wastes no time exiting their home and jogging across the street. He stops at the curb before his house.

Once in her car, Cynthia places Jacob's phone on the holder and taps the red dot. She sets the directions from their house and says, "He has no idea we're coming."

"How can you know this isn't part of it?" David asks.

Cynthia shrugs. "Because I do. You heard him. Tori didn't know he was tracking her. And Alexander is not a tech genius. I'd be surprised if he even knows what AirTags are. He knew enough to disable the app we used, but that was easy to find. An AirTag hidden in a shoe? That's a whole other level."

Cynthia backs out and starts heading up the hill away from their house, glancing at the directions for which exit she needs after getting on the freeway.

"What are you going to do when you see him?" David asks as Cynthia merges onto the 5-South freeway.

"I'm going to kill him."

CHAPTER 68

THEN

WHILE WALKING HOME from school, Cynthia had a realization: tomorrow will be three years.

She never thought she'd still be walking home from school as a senior, but here she was. Just because she got her license a year ago didn't mean there was a car for her to use regularly. She had to practice with the neighbor's car to get enough behind the wheel time to take her driver's test.

The car the Marshals had commissioned for her and her mom to use died about eighteen months ago, and her mom had not been able to hold down a steady enough job to get a new car. They were lucky they could even make rent every month. Cynthia had to step up and contribute her part-time job money to help pay for the groceries and keep the lights on.

She had gotten used to the other kids making fun of her for walking to and from school. Her high school was on the wealthier side of town, and almost every sixteen and seventeen-year-old not only had a car, but usually a new one. The irony of now being at the bottom of the teenage food chain wasn't lost on Cynthia. Vicky had held a similar status, and it was her death that caused Cynthia to end up where she once was.

Her current mood did not match the central California heat. Hers was one of gloom and sadness, as tomorrow marked the third anniversary of when Vicky had gone missing.

Now, three years later, she was getting ready to graduate high school. Would her mom even be at the graduation? She had no idea. Did she care? As her younger self, as Samantha, of course she did.

But as the new young woman she had transformed into, Cynthia Davidson, no, she did not much care if her mom was there. All she wanted to do was focus on graduating, finishing up her summer job, and starting at Stanford in the fall.

With the help of the US Marshals, her impeccable grades, and her work ethic, she had scored enough scholarships and grants to go to Stanford at no cost. And then, hopefully, on to law school. Ever since Ms. Parker had spent all that time with her, she had never lost her desire to earn a degree in law.

Cynthia trudged up the pebble-laced stone steps of the dilapidated apartment building, holding onto the hot metal railing. After those first six months of the Marshals covering their bills, Cynthia and her mom couldn't even afford to stay in that tiny house. They'd found a small apartment on the even worse side of town.

When she opened the door, it was a pleasant surprise not to find her mom slumped over in the living room chair, as usual.

"Mom?" Cynthia called out. She was hopeful that maybe, for some reason, her mom had finally left. She knew it'd be challenging, but she could make it work by herself. She wouldn't even bother telling the Marshals. She would finish up the year herself and get out.

Cynthia made her way down the small corridor to her mom's room, with her own room directly across the hall. She had spent countless nights trying to drown out the sobs and wails from her mother's room.

Cynthia started to call her mom's name again as she rounded the corner, but the word caught in her throat. She rushed to her mom, who was slumped over on the bed, a pill bottle still lightly clutched in her hand.

Several pills had spilled out on the carpet. Her mom's body was cold, and spittle had bubbled up on her lips, creating a white residue in her mouth. Her eyes were still open, long gone and vacant.

Tears welled up in Cynthia's eyes. She knew it was from sadness, relief, and, therefore, guilt. She grabbed the phone on the nightstand and dialed 911.

"911, what is your emergency?" the operator asked.

"My mom. She—she's dead. She killed herself."

CHAPTER 69

NOW

CYNTHIA AND DAVID pull up as close as they can, but there are police barricades starting several houses down.

"We're gonna get her back, Cynth!" David says excitedly.

Cynthia reaches into the back seat and grabs her purse. She pulls the gun out, checks the chamber and the safety, and shoves it into the back of her pants.

"You don't need that. The police, the FBI are already here; they will provide all the protection we'll need."

Cynthia stares at him, nightfall cresting around them. "You never know. Especially with Alexander."

David sighs and the two get out of the car. Cynthia doesn't wait for David to meet her around the car and starts toward the police line. She glances back briefly to ensure he is following her. There are a handful of curious onlookers. Cynthia stops behind an older couple who were ready for a nice quiet evening at home, by the looks of it. Both are dressed in robes and are wearing matching Disney Crocs.

Cynthia needs to get past the officers, who aren't going to take the time to get a hold of Gabby. She could call her, but most likely, Gabby would not answer her phone right now. She hangs back behind the couple, watching the officers to find a time when none of them are looking her way. Inside the barricade, officers are stationed every hundred feet or so, and two houses down, there is an ambulance and a fire truck. She understands why the ambulance is there, but isn't sure why the fire truck is also at the scene.

Various questions hover in the air while Cynthia stands there waiting. "What's going on?" "What are they looking for?" "I heard it was a meth lab situation," and "What is becoming of this country?"

Cynthia waits for her moment and then sees her chance. The officer to her right turns to answer a question from a young woman in business attire. The officer to her left turns around to glance down the street where all the action is. Cynthia pushes to the side of the older couple and ducks under the tape. She hears David call out from several paces behind her, "Cynth! Let them do their job!"

The street is empty except for a SWAT vehicle parked diagonally one house away from the target home. Several officers are gearing up behind the vehicle, and Cynthia hears the patrol officer behind her say, "Hey! Ma'am. You can't be here!"

Cynthia makes eye contact with Gabby, who shakes her head and points back toward the police line. Cynthia looks behind her at the patrol officer marching toward her. Gabby turns her attention back to the agents and SWAT officers. She steps toward the agents and SWAT as the patrol officer grabs her arm. She looks at him, anger and fury spreading through her. Yanking her arm away, she moves towards the SWAT team encircling the house.

She glances across the street and stares at another house.

What was that sound? Was it someone slapping on a window? The curtains weren't moving. The house reminds her of the run-down one that the kids were using as a hookup spot. But there is something else about the house eating at Cynthia. She isn't sure if it's her mother's intuition, or if its run-down nature reminds her of the hookup house, but something isn't sitting right in her gut.

The patrol officer grabs her arm again and squeezes. "Ma'am, you need to come with me now or I'll place you under arrest."

Cynthia glances from the patrol officer's hand as he pulls her toward the police line, then to the dilapidated house. It hits her. Everything slows down in her mind's eye. The lead SWAT officer puts up his fingers: three, two, one. She rips her arm away from the patrol officer and sprints toward the other agents. She glances back at the run-down house, and something in her gut tells her this scene is wrong. She's about to yell for Gabby when she hears one of them shout, "Breach! Breach!"

Cynthia tries to yell for them to stop, but there isn't time. She opens her mouth to yell, only three houses away, as one of the agents breaks down the door. As soon as the door hits the ground, a fireball explodes out the front of the house. Cynthia has made up ground and is only a house away.

The blast sends her backward. As she flies through the air, she knows Tori was never in that house.

She lands on her backside, the gun skittering away from her. Her head hits the ground, and it reminds her so much of her father trying to grab her foot as she escaped out the front door of her childhood home.

Cynthia quickly sits up, taking a few seconds to collect herself. There is shouting and screaming coming from the house and the police line. Firemen and paramedics are running to the house, along with hoses. She hears David behind her, "Cynthia! Are you okay?!"

His hands are under her arms, pulling her up. His voice sounds far off, even though he is standing beside her. She can see Gabby sitting in the grass, waving off the paramedics to help a couple of the officers at the front of the blast. The fire-fighters are quickly working the blaze.

Cynthia's ears are ringing, and full sound is coming in and out. It's like someone is turning the volume up and down. The sensation is as if she is bobbing up and down in the water, breaking to the surface to hear everything clearly for a moment, then back down under the water.

"Cynthia. Are you okay?" David asks again, now standing directly in front of her, his hands on each side of her face.

She nods at him and doesn't realize it, but yells at him, "Yes! I'm fine. Move!"

She pushes him to the side and takes a few steps toward the charred house. Two firefighters hand off their spots on the hoses and move inside the home. Just as quickly as one of them enters, they rush back out and yell, "We have a body!"

CHAPTER 70

NOW

THE PHRASE "WE have a body" slams through Cynthia's mind. It propels her forward toward the house.

Her instinct told her Tori wasn't there, but hearing those words now fills her with doubt. Could she be wrong? Could Tori be dead?

Before she can get any closer to the house, Gabby wraps her arms around her, tackling her to the ground.

"No," Gabby yells. "Let them do their job!"

Gabby's grip is firm on Cynthia.

"But Tori!" Cynthia cries out, not wanting to believe this is how it ends for her little girl. She will do so many things differently moving forward—she needs another chance.

The words aren't coming coherently for Cynthia. Her cries and anguish are consuming her. She has tried so hard for what feels like a lifetime—even though it's been three days—to hold it together, to believe she'll get her daughter back. To have hope that it won't end like it did for Vicky. But now, collapsed on the grass, being held at bay, everything is telling her it's over.

This has been her worst fear ever since she became Cynthia.

That Alexander would find her and ruin her life once more. It has been her quiet anguish all those nights when she couldn't sleep and was left alone with her thoughts.

David sits on the grass next to her and wraps his arms around her on the other side. She is completely surrounded by those who love her; now, she just needs her girl. It has been her job to protect her, and she has failed.

All of a sudden, it is quiet around Cynthia. She looks back toward the house and realizes the water has stopped. The spray from the hose had created a white noise effect, and now that it is off, there is only silence, as if everyone is holding their breath and waiting to hear about the body inside.

One of the firemen comes out and Gabby stands up. "Hang on to her," she says to David.

The firefighter walks over to Gabby, who is still only a few steps away from Cynthia.

"What is it?"

His gruff voice matches his overall stature and look. "We'll need to wait on fingerprints or dentals for an ID. Family pictures are of a white family. It looks like a woman, mid to late sixties, African American or Native American. She's badly burned, but the fire didn't consume her."

Cynthia pushes up, even though David tries to keep her seated. She stands up and is about to ask about the body when Gabby and the fireman walk toward the house.

Woman, mid to late sixties. African American. Native American.

Not Tori.

It's not Tori!

Cynthia turns away from the house and focuses on the neglected one she'd noticed moments ago. What had that sound been? Had it been Tori locked away in a room, slapping her hands on a window? Was it Tori's cry for help?

Looking at the house again, Cynthia sees what had been eating at her when she glanced at it before. From this side, she can see the other part of the garage and a blue tarp covering what is most likely a hole in the garage roof.

The house looks almost exactly like Vicky's did.

That is where Tori is. She was never in this other house.

Cynthia has no idea how Alexander made it seem like Tori was here, but that must have been his plan all along: to watch the explosion. He probably assumed it would burn up more, and they'd think it was Tori.

Tori!

Cynthia realizes she is wasting time thinking about what Alexander had planned. She is confident she knows where Tori is.

"I'm coming!" Cynthia yells.

David turns from the commotion at the charred house to see what Cynthia is yelling at. She takes off running, dodging agents, firefighters, and other patrol officers. She reaches into her back waistband for the gun, but it isn't there. Glancing down at the ground, she sees it lying next to her sweatshirt.

She isn't sure when she pulled that off but doesn't care. She reaches down and scoops up the gun as she runs.

As soon as she brings it level with her body, there are shouts all around her of, "Gun!" and, "She has a gun!"

Ignoring all of them, Cynthia ducks under the police line as the crowd separates for her like Moses parting the Red Sea.

Pushing harder, she sprints and leaps over the curb, across the overgrown weeds in the front lawn, and stops at the front door. She reaches for the door handle, her hand shaking violently as she grips the knob and turns.

The door is unlocked and opens with ease. Cynthia flicks off the safety on the Ruger and steps inside.

CHAPTER 71

NOW

THE HOUSE IS bathed in darkness, except for the blue and red lights of the police cars and fire trucks. Cynthia immediately wonders if this whole thing is happening in her imagination. She has to be careful now and not accidentally shoot some unsuspecting homeowner.

No, this is the place.

She can feel it. She knows Tori is here.

The living room is directly on her right, with a couch separating it from the walkway leading to what she assumes is the kitchen. The couch faces a fireplace with a large TV above it. Another armchair is angled toward the TV, the back of it butted up against the outside window. There are no curtains or blinds on the windows downstairs, and just past the living room is a small dining room table and a half wall separating the space from the kitchen.

Cynthia raises her gun and lightly steps across the linoleum walkway as quietly as she can. She pauses at the entrance to the stairs, which are protected on both sides by walls. She needs to peek around and check the stairs, but she has no idea if Alexander has some booby trap prepared for her.

She flattens her back to the wall, the staircase directly to her left, and takes a deep breath. She is about to swivel her head around the corner and glance up the stairs when a light flicks on, illuminating the staircase. She raises the Ruger with both hands and swallows hard, pivoting quickly and swinging her arms upward, and looks to the top of the stairs.

Alexander is at the top of the landing with his back to her. She knows it's him. Just past him, Tori stands there wide-eyed. Alexander has his arm raised, a hammer glinting in the light.

Without hesitation, Cynthia yells, "Alexander, no!"

He spins around, and before even thinking about making sure Tori is safe and out of the way, Cynthia pulls the trigger.

She knows she hit him center mass as he drops the hammer with a grunt and doubles over, grabbing at his stomach.

Before Cynthia can step onto the first stair, Tori scoops up the dropped hammer and raises it over her head. Cynthia opens her mouth to get Tori to stop, but isn't quick enough. Tori swings the hammer down on Alexander's head, hard and fast.

There is a crunching sound, like someone smashing an egg on the ground. Alexander's arms and legs flail with gravity as he tumbles down the stairs, slamming into each wall. Cynthia leaps backward, her body hitting the back of the couch, causing her to tumble over it, her grip loosening on the gun. Alexander's body lands with a thud on the floor.

Cynthia rights herself, grabs the gun from the carpet, and comes around the couch, the gun aimed squarely at Alexander. She is ready to unload the clip into him, but sees the blood seeping from his stomach and the back of his head, forming a pool of blood around his body. Keeping the weapon aimed at him, she glances up at Tori, who is standing at the top of the stairs, the hammer hanging loosely in her hand, blood dripping from the end of it.

Cynthia glances again at Alexander, making sure he isn't breathing, and starts up the stairs. As she hits the first step, Alexander's hand shoots out and grabs her ankle. She slips on the stairs, her arm slamming on the crest of the second step. She kicks at him with her free foot and he immediately lets go. Scrambling to her feet, Cynthia stands on the second step and aims the gun back at him.

She pauses for just a moment and hears him growl, "Bitch, liar."

Before he can utter another sound, Cynthia unloads the remainder of the clip into his chest. She continues pressing the trigger a few more times before her brain catches up and realizes the gun is empty. She drops it to the ground, sprinting up the stairs to her little girl, wrapping Tori in her arms. A thud reverberates around them as Tori drops the hammer and falls into her mother's grasp.

Cynthia can't even form words. All she can do is weep and stroke the back of Tori's head. "I'm sorry. I'm so sorry," are the only words Cynthia can form.

Commotion and voices are shouting at the front of the house. Cynthia turns her head toward the stairwell and shouts, "David! Gabby! Up here!"

CHAPTER 72

NOW

NO MATTER HOW many people are coming up the stairs, the last thing Cynthia will do is let go of Tori. A flurry of activity swarms around them. Every memory and emotion of motherhood runs through her mind.

She remembers the pain of childbirth, of wanting the epidural, but it being too late and having to push naturally. Images flash in her mind of Tori taking her first steps, the struggle of returning to work as a successful lawyer, and feeling like she was failing as a mother.

Memories of princess and Barbie birthdays. Then there was the one year Tori was really into dinosaurs, and all the other little girls made fun of her while she ran around the backyard pretending to be a T-Rex, trying to eat all the other children.

The school pictures showing Tori grow into a young woman. The time when she entered Cynthia and David's room, crying because she didn't know what was wrong with her. Cynthia went to her room, saw the small bloodstain, and knew her little girl was no longer little.

Flashes of Tori entering high school and Cynthia praying

to whatever God was up there that her little girl wouldn't get eaten alive, as she looked so small compared to all the seniors.

"Tori! Oh my God! I'm so glad to see you!" David cries, smashing into Cynthia and Tori, still huddled at the top of the stairs.

The landing is getting crowded. Between the three of them, Gabby, two other agents, and two paramedics, there isn't room to move. They are trying to get Cynthia and Tori to stand up, but Cynthia won't let go. She has a death grip on her daughter and she refuses to release it.

Gabby's soft touch grazes Cynthia's shoulder. "Hey. It's okay. We're here. We're all here. Nothing bad is going to happen. We need to get her looked at. As well as you."

For the first time, Cynthia realizes she is trembling. Her brain tells her body to calm down, but it isn't working. Every part of her is vibrating.

Gabby puts a hand under Cynthia's elbow and gets her to stand up. Cynthia's legs won't hold her and she crumbles back. A paramedic comes over, but Cynthia shakes him off.

"I'm fine. I'll be fine," she says, getting up to her knees. She takes it one leg at a time and gets herself to stand up fully. She reaches down, takes Tori's hand, and helps her up with two paramedics beside her.

"We've got it from here, ma'am," one of them says to Gabby. She nods and goes downstairs first, creating a blockade so they have to go around Alexander and through the living room.

One paramedic focuses on Cynthia and the other focuses on Tori. They hold them by the elbows, guiding them down the stairs, taking it one slow step at a time. Once outside, the paramedics try to split up and head to different ambulances, but Cynthia yells, "No! I won't leave her!"

Gabby rushes outside and directs the paramedics, "Just take her to the same ambulance. It's fine."

One paramedic helps Tori into the ambulance while Cynthia sits on the vehicle's bumper. The other one shines a light in Cynthia's eyes and asks, "Do you know your name?"

Cynthia's attention is on Gabby, standing at the house's entrance, pointing at various agents and officers, directing some into the home and others back outside.

"Ma'am? Do you know your name?" the paramedic asks again.

Cynthia brushes the penlight away from her face and answers, "Yes. Saman—I mean, Cynthia. Cynthia Burrows."

The paramedic looks at her, concerned. She stares back at him and says, "I'm fine. I know who I am; I know where I am. I didn't hit my head or anything."

Cynthia glances back at Tori, looking like a young woman, not a child. Her platinum blond hair is matted to her head; her eyes, usually sparkled with mischief, are half shut; her cheeks are flushed from the heat in the ambulance. Cynthia is struck by this thought, as she's always thought of Tori as her little girl, but she isn't now, especially with what she's just been through. Cynthia steps up into the ambulance and squeezes Tori's foot. She wants to be next to her, but the paramedic attending to her is in the way.

"How is she?" Cynthia asks.

"We're going to get her checked out, but on the surface, she looks to be okay," the paramedic says, his words measured.

Focusing on Tori, in a hushed tone, Cynthia says, "You're safe now."

Tori gives her a weak smile, an oxygen mask covering her nose and mouth.

From behind her, Cynthia hears Gabby's voice. "How is she?"

Cynthia turns and throws off the blanket that had been placed on her. "I think she's going to be okay. Probably a lot of therapy in her future, in all of our futures, but I think she's okay. It could've been much worse."

Cynthia looks back at Tori, who is staring up at the ceiling. She grabs Gabby's elbow and pulls her a few feet away. She calls back to the ambulance and Tori, "I'm right here, sweetheart. Just talking to Aunt Gabby."

Cynthia looks past her to the house, "Is he—is he dead?"

Gabby squints at her and cocks her head to the side. "Are you sure you're okay? You don't seem okay. I want you to go to the hospital and get checked out."

"I'm fine. I'm going to the hospital with Tori, but I'm fine."

"Yes, he's dead," Gabby replies. "What happened? Is that your gun on the stairs?"

Cynthia looks to the house again, reimagining the entire sequence of events. The sounds—and the smell of gunpowder—stick with her the most.

"Hey, I need you to tell me, friend to friend, what happened," Gabby implores.

Cynthia looks back at her and her voice catches in her throat, the emotion overwhelming her. "I—I killed him. I went in and saw him at the top of the stairs; I yelled his name because he had the hammer above his head like he was about to kill Tori. He turned and I shot him."

Cynthia pauses. Gabby looks to the house and back at Cynthia. "What else? Because the clip in the gun is empty, and there are several more bullets in him than just the one."

Cynthia swallows hard. "He dropped the hammer when I

shot him. He fell down the stairs and I thought he was dead, but when I stepped over him, he grabbed my ankle. I turned and I guess I continued shooting him. I—I don't remember."

She avoids telling Gabby about Tori smashing Alexander's skull.

"And how did he get the head wound?"

"Must have been from when he fell," Cynthia lies.

Gabby glares at her. "There is no way that much blood is from falling down the stairs."

Cynthia breaks into sobs. "I won't let them take her. She was protecting us. We both were!"

Gabby grabs her and hugs Cynthia tight. "Hey, it's okay. I know. No one will think twice about it, I promise. Just don't lie to me or anyone else. Okay? Just tell the truth. They'll find out very soon exactly what happened to his head. You shouldn't try and hide it."

Gabby breaks their embrace, holding Cynthia's shoulders so she can look her in the eyes. "Tell me you understand."

Cynthia nods.

"I need to hear you say it."

"I understand."

Gabby hugs her again, squeezing her. "Good. Okay. Go. Be with your family. Get yourself checked out. I'll be in touch soon."

She nudges Cynthia toward the ambulance, where David is already waiting.

"Can I come with her?" Cynthia asks the paramedic.

"Of course, but only one of you can."

David nods. "No problem. You go with her. I'll take the car and meet you there."

He hugs Cynthia, kissing her on the head. She climbs

into the ambulance and sits across from Tori, an IV already connected to her and a blanket wrapped around her. Cynthia reaches out, takes her daughter's hand, and gently squeezes it. The doors to the ambulance shut, the paramedic taps on the back of the door, and the vehicle lurches forward.

As they pull away, Cynthia can only watch as Gabby continues to direct people where to go. Lights flash across the houses, illuminating the night while the neighborhood looks on, wondering what chaos took place in that house.

Cynthia turns back to her daughter and looks into her sharp blue eyes. Despite everything she has gone through, she still looks put together, beautiful as ever.

"Are you okay?" Cynthia asks.

Tori's full, soft pink lips curl up, a tear forming at the corner of her eye. She nods and says softly, "I am now."

CHAPTER 73

ONE MONTH LATER

CYNTHIA IS USED to the view from the therapist's office. It is a view of La Costa in a small business center, where if Cynthia looks just right, she can watch the ocean while they all talk.

They've been coming here weekly with and without Tori since she got out of the hospital. Partly, it was what Cynthia and David wanted to do as a family, but it was also ordered by the court due to the circumstances. The DA still had some unknowns about the future, but part of the case was for a therapist to examine Tori.

The therapist, Dr. Sandra Katz, also wanted to meet with Cynthia and David due to Cynthia's unique past. She felt there were extenuating circumstances she would like to understand before giving her recommendations to the courts.

Her office is simple enough. A leather sofa is situated against a wall, with bookshelves directly above it. A chair sits across from the couch at an angle, with the window Cynthia likes to look out. Beyond the chair is Dr. Katz's desk, with her diplomas and various certificates hanging on the wall.

"So how are we feeling today?" Dr. Katz asks. Her maroon

skirt and white blouse with a blue bauble necklace give the impression that she's going for a patriotic look as they approach summer.

Cynthia takes a deep breath and nods. "Good. We sat down as a family, and I answered every question both of them had until there were none left. I probably answered some things Tori wishes she didn't know about me, but nothing was off the table. Not just about Alexander, but life overall, college experiences, etc."

Cynthia gives a shy smile, feeling the heat on her cheeks. Dr. Katz returns the smirk as if she has some embarrassing college stories she would rather keep hidden herself.

"And what about you?" she asks David.

He nods and reaches over, grabbing Cynthia's hand and giving it a squeeze. Cynthia always loves it when he dresses down and gets out of a suit and tie. She loves how he looks in a casual pair of jeans and a Travis Matthews t-shirt.

His Nike shoe bounces on his crossed leg as he chuckles. "Really good. I learned things about my wife I had no idea about."

Dr. Katz gives him a warm smile. "I think we've all learned that honesty is always best. No matter how much you think the truth can hurt, keeping the truth from those we love can have lasting consequences beyond anything we can imagine."

Cynthia swallows hard. They've done a lot of work to help her understand that she shouldn't blame herself, but she is still struggling with it.

"Our session today will be short, unless you all have specific things to discuss. I wanted to connect again, as I believe this will be our last time together."

Both Cynthia and David smile and nod.

"I probably shouldn't let you all know, but I've already submitted my report to the court and wanted to inform you of my recommendation."

Cynthia finds herself holding her breath. She forces it out through her nose and waits.

"I am recommending the courts clear Tori of any potential wrongdoing in the death of Alexander. I believe her actions were justified given the circumstances, and I believe her when she says she was protecting herself and you as well."

She nods toward Cynthia.

Hearing this, Cynthia recalls the image of Tori swinging the hammer at Alexander's head and shudders.

"Also, I do believe Tori has remorse for the type of person she was prior to these events. This circumstance has helped Tori see the bigger picture and given her a new lease on life. I am encouraging her to make amends with those she hurt at school and outside the classroom. Even though the three of us are concluding our sessions, I would still like to see Tori once a week for the next few months."

Cynthia is a bit surprised to hear this, but also thankful for Tori staying on track with her thoughts and feelings. If having regular sessions with a therapist will help her in the long run, Cynthia will gladly pay for it.

"I've given Tori homework in these categories, and we'll keep working on them. Moving forward, though, what Tori and I talk about will be privileged, as she is over eighteen. I felt okay sharing all this with you as you were involved in the same situation."

Dr. Katz stops and looks at each of them.

"Do either of you have any last questions for me?"

David uncrosses his legs and rubs his palms against his knees. "I don't. Do you, Cynth?"

Cynthia shakes her head.

Dr. Katz nods and places her notepad on the small table beside the chair. She pushes up, smoothing out the back of her skirt. She holds out her hand to Cynthia as she stands. Dr. Katz says, shaking both of their hands, "It's been my pleasure working with you both. I look forward to hearing, through Tori, about how life is going."

"Thanks again, doc," David says.

The two head out and are walking down the carpeted hallway when Cynthia's phone rings. She sees it's Gabby and answers.

"Hey you," she says.

"Hey, glad I caught you. Do you have a few?" Gabby asks.

Wherever she is, there is quite a bit of noise in the background.

"Where are you?" Cynthia asks.

"Getting ready to jump on a plane back east. Got a new case."

"I see. So what's up?"

"Well, I have some good news," Gabby says.

Cynthia's stomach knots, as they've been waiting to hear what the DA will decide to do with the case against herself and Tori.

"I heard back from the DA. He is choosing not to press any charges against you in the death of Alexander. Also, Tori's testimony and interview about what transpired all check out, and the DA has no reason not to believe her. He found it all credible—the account of Alexander keeping her at that first house and moving her after they made that call to you, and how he'd taken her upstairs to watch all of us and then was going to take her to the backyard and bury her, which is when you saw him and stopped him."

"So it's over," Cynthia says, more as a statement than a question.

"It's over."

"Is there anything else?" Cynthia asks.

There is a pause on the other end of the line. Cynthia feels her stomach tighten again. "What is it?"

Gabby sighs. "I don't have all the information, so I hesitate to even share this with you."

"Out with it, no matter what."

"We were able to identify the woman at the house explosion. The prints and dentals matched with Marianne Wright."

"Oh God!" Cynthia says breathlessly, her hand covering her mouth. Her knees feel weak and she leans against the wall, sliding down.

"I've had a team digging to understand how she got wrapped up in this. It looks like she was the one who helped Alexander all those years ago. That's what I was hesitating to tell you. I don't have answers as to why or how yet, but we'll get to the bottom of it and I'll let you know."

A tear rolls down Cynthia's cheek. She doesn't know what to feel. Marshal Wright was so instrumental in getting her set up for success—she can't believe what she's hearing is true. But also, Alexander is gone. He can't hurt anyone else ever again.

David squats down next to her. "Hey, you okay?"

Cynthia gives him a little smile and nods. She pushes herself up and stands.

"Cynth? You there?"

"Yeah, yes, I am. Thank you for telling me. Honestly, I don't know what to do with that. I guess I'm not done with therapy yet. Is there anything else?"

"Only for you to take care of yourself and your family. Heal. Move on."

"I will. We will. Thank you, Gabby. I love you."

"I love you too. Next time I'm in town, you better be sure to invite me over for dinner."

Cynthia chuckles, forcing herself to smile. "Deal. Let me know when and we'll do that."

Cynthia hangs up, pockets her phone, and slides her hand into her husband's. She leans her head on his shoulder and squeezes her hand intertwined with his.

She thinks about Gabby's words and decides it is time to move on.

CHAPTER 74

NOW

THE KNOCK ON the door is sharp but gentle. Dressed in a casual, conservative summer sundress, Tori hopes it will quell Mrs. Harris's concerns. She waits a moment and the door opens.

"Hi, Mrs. Harris," Tori says in her sweetest voice. "It's so good to see you! I'm so happy to be home!"

"Oh my goodness! I heard about everything that happened. I can't imagine what you went through, sweetheart!" Mrs. Harris gushes over her.

"Thank you for that. I hope I can have more of your amazing homemade banana bread again soon," Tori continues, laying it on.

Mrs. Harris tears up, bringing her clasped hands to her mouth. "For you, sweetheart, anything! Just don't share any with those parents of yours."

Tori chuckles. "Of course. I promise I'll keep it all to myself."

Tori brings her hands down in front of her body and swishes her dress from side to side. She knows what Mrs. Harris thinks girls should be. "I was hoping to see if Jacob is home.

One thing my therapist is encouraging me to do is to make amends where I may need to. I'm sorry to say I owe him a big apology."

"Of course, of course. I'm sure it's just been a big misunderstanding. He's in his room. Go on up, dear."

Mrs. Harris steps to the side, and Tori gives her a big smile and leans in for a quick hug. Tori hurries up the stairs and glances over the railing to see if Mrs. Harris is watching. She has already made her way into the kitchen, and Tori is certain she's working on the banana bread.

Without knocking, Tori barges into Jacob's room.

He is sitting on the edge of the bed and quickly looks up when his door opens violently. He closes the book he had in his lap, drops it to the side of his bed, and stands up. Tori closes the door quietly behind her, not breaking eye contact with Jacob.

"Uh, hey—hey, Tori," he stammers.

Tori moves purposefully toward Jacob and stands directly in front of him, not losing eye contact once. She cocks her head to the left and gives him a slight little smirk.

In her sweetest tone, dripping with even more kindness than when speaking with his mother, she asks, "Where is it?"

"Uh—uh, I—I don't know what you're talking about. It's good to see you!" he says, trying to change the subject.

Before he can react or say anything else, her hand strikes out, quick as a cobra latching onto its prey. She grabs him by the balls and squeezes, her tone shifting from kindness to spewing venom, "Where—is—it?"

Before he can say anything, Tori gives her hand a torque, and a half squeal, half squeak ekes out of Jacob's mouth as he tries to drop to the ground. But the grip she has on him won't allow it, and he's now half kneeling, half standing, his head leaning against her arm. His hands are clawing at hers to get her to release her grip.

He glances behind him toward the side of the bed and nudges his head. She releases her grip as he falls to the ground, grabbing at his crotch with one hand and groping around the side of the bed with the other. While kneeling, he lifts the book to her like a peasant offering a sacrifice to its god.

Tori takes the book from him and flips through the pages. "Enjoying yourself, were you?"

She puts a hand gently under his chin, forcing him to look up at her. She takes her palm and runs it down the side of his face, and before he can say anything, she smacks him hard on the cheek. The sound of the smack echoes in his room. His whole face is red from her grip on him, but one side is turning a brighter shade, with small lines from her fingers.

She bends over and whispers in his ear, "Thanks, sweetheart. I'll see you soon."

She turns and leaves his bedroom, half skipping down the stairs. She leans over the railing almost at the bottom and calls into the kitchen, "Bye, Mrs. Harris! Can't wait for that banana bread!"

Tori leaves the Harrises' and walks nonchalantly across the street to her house. She makes her way up to her bedroom, knowing she has the house to herself for at least the next hour. Her parents were at the therapist, and then they were grabbing lunch.

She makes herself comfortable on her bed, grabs her favorite pen from her nightstand, and flips the book open.

"I'm sorry I've been away so long. I needed to get some things out of the way," she says to the journal, flipping to the next empty page.

CHAPTER 75

JOURNAL

I CAN'T BELIEVE it's been a month since Alexander—or as he wanted me to call him, Grandpa—died. It certainly was not how it was supposed to end, but I guess it would have gotten to this point eventually. Don't get me wrong, I was planning on killing him at some point, but I was hoping to learn the ropes from him more than I did.

We had planned everything together. From the moment I found out about what my mother had been keeping from me, I needed to know who I indeed was in terms of my heritage. I knew the feelings and desires I had were not just from me. So imagine my surprise when I found him and then discovered his history. It was like a gift from above. It was that killer mentor I was seeking. And he fell right into my lap.

Once I understood my heritage, I knew I needed a plan. She had lied to me and kept his granddaughter from him. It wasn't her place to decide whether or not I got to know him, so we set a plan in motion.

Christian was the easiest part. He would do anything I wanted. I had him by the balls quickly, so he didn't think twice when I suggested he get a job at the coffee shop. It was Alexander's idea to give him the nickname Blue Eyes. I wasn't sure why, but he told me to trust him, and that it would throw my mother into a spiral.

Sure, why not? I was down for the ride.

It was my idea to have him use the name Alexander Beaufort. When Grandpa heard that idea, he laughed so hard. He called me his little instigating genius. I left a lot of the clues up to Grandpa since he and my mother had the history. If I'm being honest, I didn't know we were going to kill Christian's aunt and uncle, but watching Grandpa work was something else.

When it came time for the pictures, I had to source all those. That took a while; thankfully, we could print them without being watched. If anyone had seen all those pictures printed from my childhood, they would undoubtedly have wondered what was going on.

The one thing I wasn't expecting, though, was Christian's murder. Grandpa said we needed to talk to him about the next steps. It surprised me. I thought I would have been more affected, but I wasn't. Watching him swing that hammer down on Christian's head, and the crunching sound it made against his skull, I thought for sure the dull drum would disappear, but unfortunately, if anything, it grew even louder.

I was thinking nothing would take care of the pounding in my head. He was going to show me what to do, teach me how to get away with murder. My shoe was feeling funny, and that was when I found the fucking AirTag from creepy stalker freak. I knew instantly what it was, and thankfully, Grandpa had been using an Android phone the whole time.

We probably flew too close to the sun, though, wanting to taunt my parents one last time. We let them get too close. We could've just destroyed the AirTag and moved on, but I truly didn't know she'd put it together. I wasn't sure what it was about the house that Alexander loved or what drew her to it.

Nonetheless, she found us. I had just asked him to show me again how to hold the hammer and the downward trajectory to ensure it only took one swing. That's what he was doing when she yelled his name. He was showing me the ropes.

I knew that was my chance. I could commit my first murder, and I could get away with it.

The most surprising thing happened afterward, though. The drumming had finally stopped. There was peace in my head. My mother thought my tears were from the relief of being "rescued," but actually, it was relief from the constant drumming ache that had been plaguing me for what felt like years.

The next several days, when I woke up, it was amazing to have no pain, no noises, no drumming inside my skull. I had forgotten what mornings were supposed to be like. I found myself waking up each day, though, reliving the feeling of taking Grandpa's life. I know it's how he would have wanted to go, murdered by his own.

All my wonders and thoughts of what it would feel like to have someone's life in your hands and complete control over their future livelihood were just as glorious as I thought. Each morning was like a breath of fresh air, anticipating who would be my next.

After that first week, though, I knew it was back. It was small and quiet, but there was the slightest buzz at the very base of my neck. I knew what it was as soon as I opened my eyes. I'm unsure how long I'll have before I have to do something about it.

It's still manageable right now, so I have time to plan and do it right. With Grandpa, it'd gotten so bad that I was lucky I could cover up committing murder with self-defense. I know I won't be that lucky again.

At least now I know what I'll have to do to quiet it when it starts to get bad.

This time, though, I have no doubt about who my next victim will be. It isn't like before, when there was theory, conjecture, and wonder. Now, as I look out my window and across the street, I know exactly who will be my next.

He should have left it alone. He had no right to sneak into my room and take what belonged to me. He had no right to stick that AirTag in my shoe. Yes, Jacob, I found it. I'm not that dumb. I know you. You've been my plaything for years now. Ever since I had you take the blame for breaking that girl's arm, you've been wrapped around my little finger.

But I'm done with you. I have no more use for you.

I know that sooner or later, I'll plan it out, I'll have it organized, and you, Jacob Harris, will be next.